PRAISE FOR THE CAIT MORGAN MYSTERIES

"In the finest tradition of Agatha Christie . . . Ace brings us the closed-room drama, with a dollop of romantic suspense and historical intrigue." —*Library Journal*

"Touches of Christie or Marsh but with a bouquet of Kinsey Millhone." —*Globe and Mail*

"A sparkling, well-plotted, and quite devious mystery in the cozy tradition." —*Hamilton Spectator*

"Perfect comfort reading. You could call it Agatha Christie set in the modern world, with great dollops of lovingly described food and drink." —CrimeFictionLover.com

THE Corpse WITH THE Diamond Hand

CATHY ACE

TouchWood
Editions

TouchWood Editions
touchwoodeditions.com

LIBRARY AND ARCHIVES CANADA CATALOGUING IN PUBLICATION
Ace, Cathy, 1960–, author
The corpse with the diamond hand / Cathy Ace.
(A Cait Morgan mystery)

Issued in print and electronic formats.
ISBN 978-1-77151-144-5

I. Title. II. Series: Ace, Cathy, 1960– . Cait Morgan mystery.

PS8601.C41C647 2015   C813'.6   C2015-904115-5   C2015-904116-3

Editor: Frances Thorsen
Copy editor: Renée Layberry
Proofreader: Claire Philipson
Designer: Pete Kohut
Cover image: *Tropical Hawaiian Cruise Ship*, digital94086, istockphoto.com
Author photo: Nick Beaulieu Photography

We gratefully acknowledge the financial support for our publishing activities
from the Government of Canada through the Canada Book Fund and the Canada
Council for the Arts, and from the Province of British Columbia through the
British Columbia Arts Council and the Book Publishing Tax Credit.

The interior pages of this book have been printed on 100% post-consumer
recycled paper, processed chlorine free, and printed with vegetable-based inks.

This book is a work of fiction. Names, characters, places, and incidents are either
products of the author's imagination or are used fictitiously. Any resemblance to
actual events or locales or persons, living or dead, is entirely coincidental.

1 2 3 4 5   18 17 16 15

PRINTED IN CANADA

For Edna and Nolan

Star Code, Star Code, Star Code

THE LUXURY CRUISE SHIP *Stellar Sol* was about halfway between Hilo, Hawai'i, and Vancouver, BC. For the past two days the crew had been doing a great job of maintaining the Aloha Spirit: lei-making classes, hula lessons, demonstrations of how to prepare food using pineapples or SPAM, and lectures about the flora and fauna of the Hawaiian Islands were taking place in venues all over the vessel. Snuggled into a massive wing-backed chair in the Games Room on Deck 5, I hummed "Ke Kali Nei Au" as the ukuleles strummed the now-familiar tune over the background music system; the Hawaiian Wedding Song was something Bud and I had heard many times during our belated honeymoon. *Lovely.*

I laid the book I'd been reading in my lap and peered over my reading cheats at my husband. *My husband.* I couldn't help but smile as I mused that every experience, big or small, good or bad, has the potential to shape us. What the last one hundred and twenty-four days had taught me was that even the best of experiences need time to percolate their way through, and show us how they will affect our lives. When Bud Anderson and I married, I knew I was going to be happy. What I hadn't expected, because I'd never experienced it before, was the complete sense of contentment I would begin to feel. Every day of our marriage had felt like a honeymoon, but the last ten of them, spent first in Honolulu, then on this wonderful ship sailing between the Hawaiian Islands, had been the best so far.

I could see Bud's foot tapping on the thick, luxurious carpet in time to the subtle music, though his brow was furrowed. Indeed, the only reason he didn't return my smile was because Tommy Trussler, the onboard card-game tutor, was schooling him in gin rummy at one of the green baize-covered tables. Bud's expression informed me that he was concentrating. Hard. Tommy had his back to me so I could see the cards he was holding. I'd watched as he'd thrown away an ace, then an eight; now he held a run of seven diamonds, from the five to the jack, and a set of three threes. Bud didn't stand a chance. I wondered why the coach hadn't already called gin. It would have been a merciful release for my husband.

"Oh look, dolphins! Derek, quick, bring that camera o' yours," squealed Laurie Cropper, a delightfully polite—and almost irritatingly petite—woman from Nashville, Tennessee, who was unabashedly enthusiastic about pretty much everything. All I had to do was turn my head to see the thrilling display; hundreds of Pacific white-sided dolphins were leaping, bounding, pirouetting, and, yes, even grinning at us as we lumbered past them in the almost unnaturally navy blue Pacific waters at a stately eighteen knots. *Fabulous!* As people crowded toward the window to get a better view of the spectacle, I relinquished my seat and joined them.

Enjoying the odd glimpse of the show between the backs of folks pointing flashing phones and cameras at the ocean, I called over my shoulder to Tommy, "You should try to get a quick look. This might be it for the rest of the trip." I wasn't looking at him as I spoke, because he was still sitting at the card table behind me. When he didn't reply, I turned to see why he hadn't rushed forward with everyone else. *Maybe he's seen it all before?*

As soon as I saw him, the smile froze on my face. Although I could see only his back, I could tell Tommy Trussler was convulsing, his entire body gripped by a terrible force. It was as though he was being shaken from the inside. I raced around to be in front of him, hoping I could somehow help by making eye contact. *What an idiot I am!*

The poor man's teeth were clenched in a grimace. Blood from his tongue oozed from the corners of his mouth. His eyeballs bulged. His head hit the table with a deadly thud. I called for Bud as I darted toward the house telephone, which sat at the end of the linen-draped buffet table.

Bud was at Tommy's side almost immediately. He checked for a pulse. As the expression on my husband's face confirmed my worst fears, I punched the emergency button on the rather clunky phone. I heard no ringing, but a woman answered immediately.

"What is the nature of your emergency, please?"

"A man has collapsed in the Games Room on Deck 5. It's very serious. Critical, I'd say. We need urgent medical assistance." I spoke rapidly, and tried not to sound panicked, but I was.

"Hold, please," said the disembodied voice. A couple of seconds later, a piercing claxon cut through the excited chatter beside the window of the Games Room, and, I suspected, throughout the entire ship.

The voice of the woman I'd been speaking to on the phone rang out clearly. "Your attention, please. The following is an announcement for the ship's crew, and the ship's crew only. Star code, Star code, Star code. Games Room, Deck 5, amidships, Fire Zone 3. I repeat, this is an announcement for the ship's crew only. Star code, Star code, Star code. Games Room, Deck 5, amidships, Fire Zone 3. Thank you."

"Are you there, madam?" The woman was speaking to me on the phone again.

"Yes."

"Are you traveling with the guest who has become unwell?"

"No. And he's not unwell, he's—" I stopped myself before I said the word. "No, I'm not," I said with finality.

"Does he have a traveling companion nearby?"

I looked around the room. The emotions I saw expressed on the faces there ranged from confusion to horror as people spotted Tommy's collapsed body. I used a professorial tone as I asked, "Does anybody know if Tommy Trussler has a traveling companion?" Heads shook. Shoulders shrugged.

"He's traveling alone," said Derek Cropper, the large, balding husband of the perfectly coiffed Laurie. "Had a stateroom to himself."

I nodded, and returned my attention to the telephone. "The man who has collapsed is named Tommy Trussler. He is onboard as a tutor for card games, on behalf of your cruise line. He is traveling alone."

"Oh, I see," the woman at the other end of the line replied. She sounded disconcerted. At that moment the glass door set into one of the glass walls was pushed open by a gaggle of the ship's crew, drawing the attention of the people sitting in the coffee lounge beyond our aquarium-like Games Room.

"Your crew members have arrived," I told the woman on the phone.

"Good," she said, sounding relieved. "They will do what is needed now. Thank you for raising the alarm. May I have your name and stateroom number, please?"

"Certainly," I replied. "Professor Cait Morgan, 8221." *I wonder why I used my professional title?*

"Thank you, Professor. You have been most helpful. Goodbye." The line went dead.

As dead as Tommy Trussler. As dead as the chance of two more romantic days at sea for me and Bud.

Operation Rising Star

A SHORT, DARK-SKINNED MAN WITH an English accent took charge of the room and the crew members. He announced, "Could everyone please stand back, but remain in the room. Thank you." He was polite, professional, and sounded as though he'd left the East End of London about five minutes ago. He got to work on Tommy's body.

I moved to stand with the rest of our group beside the window, and watched the man whose badge proclaimed him to be BARTHOLOMEW, NURSE PRACTITIONER. He checked for vital signs; first at Tommy's pulse points, then with his stethoscope.

"Officer Ocampo, curtains, please," said Nurse Bartholomew, his voice now tinged with a harder edge.

A short woman with hair that shone like black patent leather, and enveloped in a uniform that pretty much de-gendered her, appeared. She manipulated discreet pulleys that allowed multilayered aquamarine voile curtains to swoosh around all three glass walls of the Games Room. The tension in the room ratcheted up as the drapery concealed us from the interested gaze of our fellow passengers; until the kerfuffle, they had been sipping specialty coffees and nibbling handmade biscotti in the comfort of the Italian-themed coffee lounge.

Nurse Bartholomew spoke quietly into a small cellphone. He appeared to make two phone calls. Each of us strained to hear what he said, but not even my sharp ears could catch any discernible words.

Almost immediately, the claxon sounded again. This time a male voice rang out.

"Your attention please. This announcement is for the ship's crew, and the ship's crew only. Operation Rising Star, Games Room, Deck 5, amidships, Fire Zone 3. Once again, this announcement is for the ship's crew only. Operation Rising Star, Games Room, Deck 5, amidships, Fire Zone 3. Thank you." The disembodied voice sounded almost jolly.

"So, he's really dead," said Kai Pukui, our stately on-board Hawaiian cultural interpreter. He spoke quietly, and looked toward the ceiling as he whispered, "*Mahalo.*"

"How d'you know he's dead?" asked Derek. His Tennessee drawl conveyed more curiosity than accusation.

Kai bowed his head. He managed to endow the slight gesture with as much grace as his on-stage performances of traditional Hawaiian dances. "It is the code used to prevent guests from becoming concerned about the fate of a fellow shipmate, while informing the crew that someone has died."

A moment later, a woman flapped open the curtaining and entered the room. Despite her casual clothes, she had a professional air. She dropped her wide-brimmed hat and sunglasses onto an empty chair, and accepted a pair of surgical gloves from the nurse practitioner.

Snapping the latex onto her hands, her gaze swept the room. I noted intelligent eyes that matched the light blue gloves, a pale, freckled oval face framed by a practical bobbed cut of what appeared to be naturally copper-red hair, and a nasty bruise on her bare left forearm.

Nurse Bartholomew stood beside Tommy Trussler's corpse. "Thank you for coming so quickly, Dr. White," he said. "You'll need to pronounce."

"Will I?" she said enigmatically. It didn't sound like a put-down, but it wasn't far off.

Repeating the processes already undertaken by the nurse, Dr. Rachel White, as her badge announced, took her time. Finally she nodded and looked at her watch. "Note pronouncement at 11:37 AM, please," she said curtly. Pulling the curtains back, she told the waiting crew members they could enter.

None of our group had spoken. Bud and I clung to each other, as did Laurie and Derek Cropper. Another married couple—Nigel and Janet

Knicely—stood stock-still, agape. Kai Pukui stood next to, but apart from, Frannie Lang—a lone cruiser we'd come to know a little—and close to the young waiter who'd been allocated to the Games Room as our buffet and refreshment server and runner. His badge told me his name was Afrim, and that he was from Albania. A little star on his badge further informed me he was one of the highest-rated staff members of the month.

By this time, we guests were outnumbered by crew members. The glossy-haired female security officer named Ocampo was attending to the door access, and the first group who'd arrived had departed, with the exception of Bartholomew the nurse, who remained hovering over the body, marshalling its installation into a wheelchair.

Dr. White approached our somewhat tense group, pulling off her latex gloves. "I'm terribly sorry you all had to witness this," she began. "A death, especially a sudden one, is always terribly distressing. Did any of you see what happened, exactly?"

Her tone was light, but I detected an edge in it, which suggested a high level of anxiety. *Not surprising for someone who's just pronounced a person dead, maybe?*

I could see that Bud was about to answer, but he was interrupted by the arrival of a man whose presence distracted the doctor. Tall, lean, fit, and tanned, with a shock of lustrous black hair, the new arrival's short-sleeved white shirt strained to contain his well-developed upper body. He ignored all of us, and gave his attention to the doctor. He whispered close to her ear. She nodded in response to his question. He sighed, and shook his head angrily. Although he was holding only a cellphone, he wielded it as though it were a weapon. He trained it on our group. His dark eyes glittered as he regarded us each in turn.

"Allow me to introduce myself, ladies and gentlemen. I am Ezra Eisen, head of security. I am pleased to meet you all, despite these unfortunate conditions."

A few of our group muttered a muted response to his terse, yet professional, greeting.

"You are all clearly aware that this gentleman, Mr. Tommy Trussler, has died unexpectedly, and every member of the Stellar Cruise Line family is terribly sorry that you had to witness such a sad and upsetting event." The expression of sympathy on his face was unconvincing. "As you can imagine, a sudden passing at sea needs to be reported upon fully. I would like to begin by ascertaining who everybody is, and your relationship to the deceased. I would ask that you do not share your experiences with your fellow guests. I would welcome the chance to have a few moments with each of you over the next few hours so I can gather the information needed to complete the necessary paperwork. But first, we must respect this man's remains."

A general hubbub ensued as Tommy's corpse was wheeled out, over which I heard Eisen instructing Officer Ocampo to accompany the body.

Derek Cropper raised a hand with slight hesitation. "My wife and I met him at the USS *Arizona* Memorial at Pearl Harbor a couple of days before we sailed out of Honolulu," he said. "Didn't know the guy before that. We've hung out in this place a fair bit in the past few days, though I wouldn't say we knew him well."

Officer Eisen smiled. "And you are?"

Derek flashed a sincere, warm smile in response. "Derek Cropper, and my good lady-wife, Laurie, from Nashville, Tennessee. At your service, sir." He mock-bowed while his wife smiled and tilted her head like a cute little girl.

"Stateroom number, please?" added Eisen.

"We're in the Star Signature Salon Suite, Deck 12," replied Derek.

Eisen scribbled in a little notepad. When he'd finished, he looked up, thanked the man, and turned his thoughtful gaze toward the next couple in line. "And you? Names and stateroom, please."

We all followed Eisen's gaze. Looking at the British couple, Nigel and Janet, I noted that the small, neat woman's outfit—completely free of style and consisting of various shades of beige—seemed to match her skin tone. I realized how pale the couple was, especially considering they'd spent the better part of two weeks in the Hawaiian sun. Nigel had been cleaning his wire-rimmed spectacles with a cloth while Officer Eisen had been conversing with the Croppers, and I watched as he purposefully replaced them. In stark contrast to his wife, Nigel was wearing a vivid, clashing get-up, as usual. Today it was red shorts with a yellow shirt and green deck shoes.

At the security officer's question, Nigel became animated, grabbing his wife's hand and gesticulating with it as though it were his own. It was strange to see, and oddly, his wife didn't react in a way that indicated anything outlandish was happening.

"Hullo. Pleased to make your acquaintance—though not under . . ." His sentence trailed off to nothing, though he flapped his wife's hand about. "Quite right, quite right," he added, apropos of nothing. "Nigel Knicely, with a K. The K is silent." It was exactly what he'd said when he'd introduced himself to me back in Honolulu.

Eisen scribbled, then held up his hand. "Where is this silent K?"

"At the beginning."

"You spell Nigel with a K?" Eisen sounded baffled.

"Of course not," snapped Nigel. "You spell Knicely with a K, at the beginning of the name. As I said, it's silent."

I noticed Laurie Cropper stifling a smile as Eisen crossed through something he'd written and glared at Nigel.

Nigel continued in a louder voice, speaking slowly. "Wife Janet. From Bristol. England, of course. On holiday. Well, what else, really? Room 3749. Deck 3."

"And your relationship to the deceased?"

"None. Met the man when we were taking a day trip organized by the ship around Maui. He was on the bus as the sort of guide. You took to him, didn't you Janet?" He looked at his wife, realized he was waggling her hand about, and dropped it as though it was on fire. He blushed.

"Yes, Nigel," she said, though without a smile. "As you say, a very nice man. Poor thing. His heart, was it?" She sounded both sympathetic and hopeful, though her manner of speech was such that everything she said sounded like a whining apology. I noted that Janet's weird and unsettling habit of closing her eyes when she spoke to someone made Eisen give her a stern look, which, of course, she couldn't see.

I also realized, as she mentioned Tommy's heart, that of the guests in the room, Bud and I were the only ones who'd seen the dying man's contorted face; everyone else was still hovering near the window at the time.

Eisen didn't respond to Janet Knicely's question; instead he directed his gaze toward Bud and myself. "And you?" he said. I opened my mouth to respond, but Bud was just a little quicker than me. *Unusual.*

"Bud Anderson, and wife Cait Morgan. C-A-I-T. Maple Ridge, British Columbia, Canada. Cait was introduced to the deceased for the first time here, about an hour ago, though she's seen him about the place, from a distance, during the cruise. I happened upon him in the ship's gymnasium on the first morning of our time onboard. We've encountered each other on several occasions since, and engaged in general chit-chat. I know almost nothing about the man, other than that he was here to teach card games to those who might wish to learn, and that he lived on O'ahu. My wife and I are in stateroom 8221."

Good job, Bud.

Eisen scribbled as he said, "And you?" He looked at the woman who'd been playing cards with the Croppers and Kai Pukui.

"I'm Frannie. Frannie Lang, room 8739," said the woman brightly. "Another Canadian," she beamed at Bud and me. "I'm from Alberta. Born and raised in the boonies, but now I live in Edmonton. My lovely sons have sent me off on this cruise for a special birthday, though it's not until November. They're both in Calgary now, when they're home.

Oil sands, you know." She looked at me as she spoke, seeming to seek a sympathetic response. I smiled politely.

The head of security prompted her. "Did you know the deceased at all?"

Frannie laughed. "Me? Oh good heavens, no. I also met him on the cruise. Well, ashore during the cruise."

"Thank you," Eisen said, a little exasperated. He made eye contact with Kai Pukui. "Maybe we can talk later?"

Kai nodded graciously. *They're friends.*

"And I'll speak to you later too," he said to the server, who looked terrified.

Eisen smiled at our group with a professional air. "Thank you, everybody. You've been helpful."

"It *was* his heart, wasn't it?" whined Janet Knicely.

The pause before the head of security responded allowed the nervous energy in the room to increase.

"Did anyone see him suffering his attack?" he asked—choosing his words carefully, I noted.

"I did," I replied.

All eyes turned toward me. I decided that it was best to say less, rather than more. "It was sudden. I'm pretty sure he was dead by the time his head hit the table."

I pressed myself even closer to Bud. He squeezed my hand, then backed me up.

"My wife is correct. He had no pulse. I'd been sitting opposite him less than five minutes earlier, and he'd shown no signs of medical distress at that time."

Dr. White, who'd been silent while Eisen addressed us, looked Bud up and down with some suspicion. "Do you have experience in finding a pulse, Mr. Anderson?" she asked. Her clipped English accent made her sound like a schoolmarm. *A copper-topped English rose—with thorns?*

11

"Yes, Doctor, I have established signs of life, or the lack thereof, on many previous occasions."

"And you'd have done that because . . . ?" The doctor's cornflower-blue eyes glinted with the challenge.

Bud was about to answer, but Eisen held up his hand.

"This is best discussed in private," he said. "I suggest, therefore, that everyone return to their own stateroom for a little while, until I can visit each of you there, and where we will speak further about this matter."

Our fellow guests were then escorted to their respective staterooms by members of the security team, and a guard was posted discreetly outside the Games Room when it was locked after our departure.

Eisen himself escorted Bud and me. I was glad, because it gave me a chance to speak up as we walked. "Officer Eisen, I must mention that I saw the face of the deceased as he was in his death throes; I don't think he died of natural causes."

Eisen stopped in his tracks; his almost-black eyes regarded me with disdain. I noticed that he stood rigid as if a rod ran from the top of his head to his ankles.

"Really?" was all he uttered. His tone said the rest.

I looked at my husband. "Bud, backup, please?"

Bud nodded and extended a hand toward Eisen. "Bud Anderson, retired law enforcement officer. My wife, Cait Morgan, professor of criminal psychology at the University of Vancouver, and sometime consultant to the integrated homicide squad I used to head up. I realize you'll want to check us out, but might I suggest that you consider my wife's opinions to be worth listening to? She's no amateur when it comes to dealing with sudden death."

We'd all paused as we rounded the bottom of the staircase, which opened onto the long corridor to our stateroom. Veneered walls and subtly patterned blue and green carpet stretched ahead of us. I thought of the Overlook Hotel in the movie *The Shining*—odd, because there wasn't anything remotely menacing about the ship.

The two men regarded each other, and I took the chance to look at them both. Bud was tanned from our time in the sun, and his hair had bleached to an even white, the silver in his eyebrows and the color of his skin making his eyes look even more piercingly blue than usual, an effect heightened by his choice of an aqua-colored, casual linen shirt. Eisen was a little taller than Bud, and possibly twenty years his junior—so that would put him in his late thirties. He glowed with health, and I was convinced he could have broken a person's arm with his little finger; he gave off no aura of being threatening, but it was clear he'd be a man you'd want on your side in a fight.

They both started walking again. I followed suit.

"I think it would be more appropriate if we had any such conversation in the privacy of your stateroom," said Eisen. With a military bearing, he strolled effortlessly, smiling broadly at a few passing guests as he did so. He seemed to be cool and calm; I felt less so, and almost had to canter to keep up with him. I was desperate to tell him what I'd seen.

Arriving at our room, Bud opened the door. Eisen gestured that we should enter, which we did. "I must see the captain now," he said, hovering at the door, "but I will return presently. Please do not leave your stateroom until then, and do not discuss your theory of an unnatural death with anyone at all. Understood?"

We both nodded, and he left. I felt as though I'd been scolded by an obnoxious schoolteacher; even Bud looked deflated.

"Well, that was rude," I said. "And shortsighted too. Tommy Trussler didn't look like a man having a heart attack; he looked like a man who'd been poisoned by something particularly aggressive and swift acting. I wish he'd let me tell him what I'd seen."

Bud sighed and placed his hand on my shoulder. "If I were him, I'd check us out before I took any sort of statement, and I bet that's what he's doing right now."

"What are we supposed to do while we wait for him to come back?"

"What everyone else who was in the Games Room has to do: hang about until he's ready to talk to us. There'll be procedures he has to follow."

I plopped myself on the edge of our bed in a huff. *Procedures? I hate being on the wrong end of procedures.* "Wonderful," I grumped. "What a waste of time! And I don't mean because we could be sitting in the sun—I *mean* because I could be helping that Eisen chap with his investigation."

Bud sat beside me on the bed. "We've done pretty well, haven't we, Wife?"

"How d'you mean, Husband?"

"You know, ten days away together without encountering a dead body." He half smiled; I shrugged. "I don't think it was natural, either." Bud paced about as best he could, given the size of the room; it was similar to a good-sized hotel room, delightfully appointed with light wood furnishings upholstered in shades of sea blues and greens, which toned well with the carpeting and curtains. It had been cleaned and made up by our stateroom attendant since we'd left a couple of hours earlier.

I scooted up onto the freshly made bed and propped myself up against the comfy pillows. "Even if he doesn't want our help, we have to offer it, right?" Bud gave me a look that spoke volumes. "Why don't I do my recollection thing for the time we were in the Games Room? It might help us both to understand how Tommy Trussler died, and give me some facts I can share with Mr. Grumpy Security Man."

"Good idea, though I wouldn't say he was especially grumpy. Do you want to stay there? I'll sit over here on the sofa out of your way."

I nodded and got going. I screwed up my eyes to the point where everything goes fuzzy and begins to hum—it's the best way for me to recollect that which I can pull from my eidetic memory bank. "I'll talk it through, but I might not make much sense, so bear with me," I said.

"I'm listening," said Bud, picking up a pad from the desk. "I'm going to take notes."

"I'm rushing along the corridor from our room. I'm feeling a bit hungover and sorry for myself. I'm cross that I feel this way. You've gone ahead to the Games Room, and I am also cross with myself that I am late. When I open the door to enter, Tommy Trussler is sitting at his little desk in the corner, arranging notepads and pencils that he's still pulling out of a small cupboard behind him. You are standing at the buffet, pouring coffee. The server is hovering, but allowing you to help yourself. I read his badge: Afrim. Nice name. He looks nervous. Why?

"We three are alone in the room with the server. I smell warm chocolate. It's delicious. It's coming from a tray of *pain au chocolat* that's sitting on the table at the buffet. I join you, and you pour me a coffee. I pick up a pastry and we agree it'll help settle my tummy. Derek and Laurie Cropper arrive. I haven't seen them since the first formal dinner. You greet them, and Laurie kisses my cheek. I smell her expensive perfume. She gives you a big hug, then laughs and pats your tummy. She seems to act more warmly toward you than me, as does her husband. I wonder why this is. It's clear to me they have a connection with you they don't have with me. I remind myself to ask you about this."

I paused and opened my eyes. "What sort of secret life have you been living on this ship, Husband? What's going on between you and the Croppers that I don't know about?"

Bud smiled and looked up from his notepad. "It's the gym, Cait, that's my secret world. You know very well I get in there for at least half an hour every morning, leaving you to besport yourself in the bathroom, or whatever. Laurie Cropper is always there, too, and sometimes Derek accompanies her. Laurie and I sweat together every day—me more than her, because I slog it out on the elliptical machine, while she walks on the treadmill overlooking the sea. Derek pretends to lift weights, though it's obvious he's just there for show, but at least he joins his spouse sometimes." Bud winked.

I chose to ignore his barbed remarks, and continued with my recollection.

"Laurie is the epitome of cruise-chic in a lemon ensemble; her high-lighted hair is perfect, as is her makeup. Derek looks a little disheveled. He's well tanned, but looks tired, drawn. I wonder if he has a hangover, like me. Their attitude seems bright and jovial, which is the only way I've ever seen them act. They leave us and go talk to Tommy who is still at his little desk. They crowd him. They are both close to him. I leave you so I can settle in a chair with my book. Do I hear what they say from my seat? Yes. Derek asks if Tommy will have time to play poker with them, and refers to something about Laurie wanting to practice with someone other than her husband. Their voices drop. I notice that Derek's neck is getting red. Tommy is shaking his head and saying, 'No, no.' They are still at Tommy's desk when Kai Pukui rushes in. Laurie turns and beams at him. He apologizes to her for being late; she says it's fine because they have just arrived. Kai looks a little lost. He goes to sit at one of the card tables, and waits with his hands in his lap. He doesn't want to be there. 'Duty' is written all over him.

"Derek leaves Laurie talking to Tommy and takes a plate at the buffet. Afrim the server stands at attention, eagle eyed for a chance to help. He is smiling; Derek is ignoring him. I watch as he fills his plate. I am amazed that he fits so much on it, and am sickened at the sight of bacon sitting on top of waffles, with syrup poured over both, beside a pile of scrambled eggs. I hate that syrup-on-savory habit. I nibble at my delicious chocolate pastry, and am glad that it's just sweet, though I can taste Laurie Cropper's perfume as she wafts past me to join Kai Pukui at the card table, smiling down at me as she goes. 'Not playing with your husband?' she asks. 'I don't play cards,' I reply, through crumbs. 'I never used to, though I'm learning a few important lessons,' she replies.

"I resume eating, and look at your face as you concentrate on shuffling a deck of cards on the table at which you have taken a seat. You're not finding it easy, though I can tell you've been shown how to do it properly, and are trying to make your hands work the cards into a truly random order. Looking past you I see Frannie Lang arrive. She's alone, and she's flushed. She's been hurrying. As she enters, she glances at Tommy and looks . . . apologetic? Yes, that's it. Tommy's being treated like a schoolmaster by you all. It's odd, but maybe it's to be expected.

"Frannie Lang joins Derek at the buffet table and allows Afrim to pour coffee for her, while she picks at the goodies on the buffet. She is now joined by Tommy who helps himself to a plate of bacon, sausage patties, and egg; Frannie takes a bran muffin and a black coffee to the table where Laurie and Kai are sitting.

"Tommy sits at his desk, away from everyone else, and begins to eat his food. He pulls a pot out of a holster thing he's slung on the back of his chair. It's a clear-ish plastic pot with a blue lid, and stepped sides. He unscrews the lid. The pot's about six inches tall, and seems to contain something he values. He dips his bacon into it and eats. His expression tells me he is enjoying the taste. I can see that the bacon has poi—a staple Hawaiian snack made out of mashed, fermented taro root—on it.

"Frannie leaves her food at the card table, walks to Tommy's desk, steps between me and him, and whispers in his ear. He doesn't stop eating as he listens. His expression is . . . angry. He's eating, but his jaw shows anger. Frannie rejoins the group at her table. What did she say to him that made him angry? No one joins you at your table, Bud, and you continue to concentrate on shuffling cards. At the table where Kai, Laurie, and now Frannie and Derek are seated, there's not a great deal of chatter; everyone is eating, except Kai, who bows his head slightly and stands.

"He walks to the buffet where he talks quietly to Afrim, who looks about, shakes his head, then dashes out of the room. Kai moves to stand near Tommy. He leans over him, and chats to him quietly. I cannot hear what is being said, but both men look relaxed, and I suspect general pleasantries are being exchanged, though Tommy is still eating, and doesn't stop to converse properly with Kai. Eventually Kai moves aside, and I watch as Derek nips over to have a quiet word with Tommy. The men seem tense, their voices too low for me to hear; it's not an easy conversation. Derek finally moves back to his wife at the card table.

"Moments later, Afrim returns with a large platter of bananas, one of which Kai takes and peels. Afrim places the platter at the end of the buffet nearest Tommy's desk, making room for it by rearranging the pastries. I uncurl myself, and move to replenish my coffee. Afrim serves me, and I am standing with my back to the door when there's the noisy arrival of Nigel and Janet Knicely. As they enter the door, Nigel Knicely is saying, 'You've never truly understood,' to his wife. I have no idea what he's talking about, because once through the door, they both shut up.

"The atmosphere in the room is like a library or a church. No one speaks loudly—except Nigel and Janet, who use their normal speaking voices. They sound raucous, but aren't shouting at all. Janet and Nigel greet Tommy; they approach him at his desk, and they all shake hands. I wouldn't say it's a warm greeting, but they huddle together for a few moments, exchanging polite morning pleasantries. Janet Knicely eventually waves at me as she moves toward you, then puts her hand on your shoulder, making you jump, and whispers to you. You look at me, smile, and raise your eyebrows slightly. As she moves away, your expression tells me you are glad she didn't stay longer, or say more. You roll your eyes at me, wink, and return your attention to your shuffling."

"Once she starts, she never shuts up," said Bud. "Oops—sorry. Didn't mean to interrupt."

I looked at Bud, and said, "Too late now."

Bud tutted. "She annoys me. You know what she's like. She's a woman who doesn't know when to stop. Very . . . intense, though almost vacuous. Strikes me as probably lonely, but doesn't seem to have the skills to get people to like her. She talks people away from her."

"And what do you think about her husband?" I asked.

Bud's smile was wry. "A man of few words. Necessarily, I suspect. Seems nice enough though. Typically English, I'd say—you know, reserved."

"Not all English are reserved," I replied, "in the same way that not all Canadians are beer-swilling Zamboni drivers with a penchant for being out and about in their boats."

"Touché," replied Bud, "though, being Welsh, I know you're not the greatest fan of the English. What is it you said once? The only three teams you support are Canada, Wales, and anyone playing against England?"

"And touché to you too," I replied. "That was in a weak moment, when Wales was playing England in the Six Nations Rugby on TV and I was shouting '*Cymru am byth*' for all I was worth. You know I'm not really that closed-minded when it comes to racial stereotypes. Indeed, much though it pains me to admit it, not all Welsh people are lovely innocents with hearts as big as the valleys. As we know only too well."

"True," replied Bud quietly, no doubt thinking back to our wedding weekend in Wales just a few months earlier. "Though, to be fair myself, Nigel Knicely is what most folks would call 'typically British,' meaning 'typically English,' in many respects. He's big on rank and form aboard ship, I've noticed. In fact, I saw him request the maître d' to come to his table at dinner a couple of nights ago so he could make some comment about his wife's food, rather than deal with a humble waiter."

"Interesting," I remarked. "Right, so back to it . . . I know I read my book for a while. I cannot be sure how long. I read about twenty pages, so I suppose about five minutes."

"Or maybe just three, given the speed at which you read," noted Bud, flirting with danger.

"Maybe three, then," I conceded, "but I know I missed some interactions and movement, because the next time I looked up, Tommy was bending over your back, shuffling the cards for you. I'll start again from there . . ."

"I am amazed at how the man's hands work. Tommy Trussler has remarkably long, slim fingers, and they are fast. I am not surprised that, if he has taught you how to shuffle this way on a previous occasion, you are having difficulties replicating his movements. He's very much at ease with a deck of cards. He leaves you and moves to the table where the Knicelys are sitting. He sits with them and again begins to shuffle a pack of cards. I can tell by the expression on his face that he enjoys this. He's dazzling the Knicelys—and he likes to do that. Interesting.

"Let me think more about Tommy, the victim. I can see him clearly now. The sun is on his face, and I can see his pale skin, and his wrinkles. His skin hangs beneath his chin. He's aggressively clean-shaven, almost glowing. His thinning hair is more gray than brown, and his eyes are a pale, washed-out greenish-blue. He avoids the sun. He's dressed in long khaki cargo pants, a golf shirt that's almost the same color as his eyes, and is wearing a pair of black flip-flops. *Dress* flip-flops? His hands are busy, but his face is impassive. His mind seems to be somewhere out on the ocean, not in the room or at the table. Certainly his motions are automatic. He snaps back to his surroundings, and I see his eyes focus on his hands. He stops, spreads the cards in a fan shape, and shows the Knicelys what he has done. Their faces show amazement. He has been shuffling the deck for a few minutes, but the cards are in perfect suit-order. He grins. The skin around his eyes crinkles. His skin is used to that. Does he smile a lot, or squint in the sunlight?

"Having entertained the Knicelys, for that is what he's been doing, Tommy rises, and gives each of them a pack of cards, which he encourages them to shuffle." ·

"Why did Tommy have you and the Knicelys shuffling cards all the time?" I asked Bud.

"He said I had to get to know the feel of the cards, the personality of the cards, if I was to be able to play with confidence. He said that, whatever the game, confidence was essential, even if a person wasn't playing for money."

"Hmm," was my only comment before I hummed again, this time in earnest.

"Tommy walks to the table with four players already playing poker. He moves around the table, looking at the hands the players are holding. Only Derek Cropper tries to hide his cards, but Tommy taps him gently on his shoulder and whispers in his ear. Derek shows him his cards.

"As he progresses around the table, Tommy bends and whispers to each person. I cannot hear what he says, but it's a technique that makes me feel uncomfortable. I wouldn't like him being that close to me. Why do I feel this? Does it reflect my own feelings about personal space? I note Kai Pukui's discomfort when Tommy whispers to him, and he wriggles in his seat. Kai's usually very self-possessed. Odd.

"Tommy sits with you at your table, and you two proceed to play gin rummy. Over his shoulder, I can see the hand he is holding. As I look across at you two, I can see Afrim beyond you. He's clearing and emptying plates. Wait—what does he do at Tommy's desk? I cannot see properly, because Tommy is now in the way, but I do not see Afrim leave Tommy's desk with anything in his hands. Why didn't he clear Tommy's desk?

"The Knicelys are shuffling cards silently. The chatter at the table with the Croppers, Kai, and Frannie Lang is all about how well Derek plays, and how poorly the rest of them play. Then Laurie Cropper shouts something about seeing dolphins. I can tell that, from her seat, she's able to look out at the ocean, so it's natural she'd spot the display first. Now I must concentrate even harder . . .

"Laurie is the first on her feet; she moves from the card table toward me, because I'm sitting close to the window, near Tommy's desk. Derek is right behind her and, as they arrive, I stand to give folks more space to get to the picture window. I pull my chair out of the way and back off. The Croppers are quickly joined by the Knicelys, who come around behind me, and Frannie Lang, who is rooting around in her tiny handbag for something. She produces her phone, which she uses to take photographs. She bumps into me and apologizes. Kai doesn't crowd forward, but does stand, and he looks out at the ocean. He's taller than everyone else in the room, so he can see over everybody's heads. I turn to move the chair farther out of the way, and you press against me when you arrive. I call to Tommy, who I'm aware isn't with us all, then turn to look at him. Afrim has moved to the far side of the room where he's bobbing about trying to see out of the window without getting in the way of the guests.

"Tommy Trussler is still at the card table where you and he were sitting, and all I can see is his back. If anyone outside the Games Room in the coffee bar is looking in, they will be able to see his face, but I can only see his convulsing back, and I whip around to be in front of him. I see his eyes bulge, his hands clench, his tongue ooze blood; then he collapses. I know he is dead. I call to you, you check for his pulse, then I turn to make the emergency phone call."

I fully opened my eyes. "Bud, did you see anything I haven't mentioned at this point in the proceedings?"

Bud looked thoughtful, then shook his head. "I was examining Tommy, then watching you on the phone. I did notice that heads jerked toward the card table when the announcement came over the intercom, then people turned and looked at Tommy's back—because they were all along the wall with the window in it, so behind him."

I gave the matter a little more thought. "If Tommy was poisoned, which I believe he was, he could have been dosed with something before he entered the room, or he must have ingested it in what he was eating and drinking at his desk. Yes, he took the bottle of water he was sipping with him from table to table, but that, and everything else he consumed, came from the common food and drink sources; others would, or could, have been affected."

"I saw him open the screw cap on the bottle of water when he pulled it from the big bucket full of ice on the buffet table," said Bud.

I nodded. "Yes, everything he consumed came from the buffet table—everything except his pot of poi. If he wasn't poisoned beforehand, and unless there's a poisoner on the ship who doesn't care who dies, any poison *must* have been in that."

"Poisoned poi?" said Bud. "That sounds utterly ridiculous."

"What does poi taste like, Bud?"

"Disgusting."

"Well, then—what a great way to hide the taste of something that could kill, eh?"

"You might have a point," replied Bud, "but don't 'eh?' me, right?"

I smiled. "So, if we use this as a hypothesis, that begs the question: Who had the chance to put poison in his poi in the first place?"

We stared at each other across our room, both coming to the same, horrifying conclusion. "Anyone," replied Bud. "Absolutely anyone on the ship—or even ashore, before we got on the ship. Oh no, this isn't good. Almost anyone could have killed him."

"Hang on a minute, Bud, I'm not finished yet. Let me recall a bit more . . ." I did a quick rethink of the last sweeping look I'd taken of the Games Room before we'd all been herded out. "Aha—got it! It wasn't there when we left, Bud. The pot of poi had disappeared. When we left the Games Room, there wasn't a pot on Tommy's desk anymore. I'm certain of it. Someone took the pot containing his poi. Only someone in the room at the time would have had the chance to take it. And why would they do that if they didn't know there was poison in it?"

Bud looked thoughtful. "You're right. Excellent work, Cait," he said, smiling and slapping his thigh. "If we're working on the idea of poisoned poi, that's the crux of the matter. In fact, to be perfectly accurate, someone—anyone—might have put the poison in the poi before we were all in the Games Room, but it could only have been removed by one of the people there at the time, so at least one person who was in the room when Tommy Trussler died had some hand in his demise."

"So we have an excellent focus for our inquiries,"

"Officer Eisen's inquiries, not ours, Cait," corrected Bud.

"Hmm . . . maybe he'll let us lend a hand."

"Who knows, Cait? But you must share your observations with him, and as soon as you can. The implications are significant."

An Officer and a Gentleman?

A KNOCK AT OUR STATEROOM door made both of us jump. Bud leapt to his feet in response and invited Ezra Eisen into our room. Once he was seated, the head of security accepted a bottle of water Bud had pulled from our little fridge, and drank deeply. Although not out of breath, I got the impression he'd been dashing about. Eisen took a moment to compose himself, then regarded us with a determined expression as we sat on the sofa across from the desk chair he had selected.

Eisen addressed Bud first. "Your record in Canada is exemplary, and I believe I might know of some of your work in Europe, Commander Anderson."

He's been digging into Bud's background. To which part of Bud's work was Eisen referring? Probably the stuff Bud had got up to in his last post that needed Canadian Security Intelligence Services (CSIS) clearances. Bud understood, which irritated me a little. *I hate that there are things he's not allowed to tell me.*

"You might," Bud said in a noncommittal tone. "I should mention that I am now retired. *Fully* retired." He emphasized the words. "My wife, Cait, and I are on our belated honeymoon, Officer Eisen."

"Please, call me Ezra, Commander Anderson." He finally cracked a smile.

Bud smiled. "No longer a commander, Ezra, and it's Bud, please."

"Very well then," replied Ezra. "I hope you don't mind if I speak frankly. I've checked you out as thoroughly as I am able, within such a short amount of time. I have also spoken to the captain about your presence here." He turned to look at me. "I understand you saw the man's face as he died, Professor Morgan. Tell me, what did you see?"

I decided to be equally professional. "I don't know exactly when they began, but when I turned from the window to look at Tommy Trussler, he was being racked by convulsions, which lasted for at least a couple of minutes. His face was contorted—he'd bitten his tongue, I believe. His eyes were bulging, and he didn't speak or cry out; it didn't seem that he could make any voluntary movements at all. Then his upper body fell forward onto the table. Bud tested for a pulse. There was none. That's when I called the emergency response number on the house telephone."

Ezra nodded, looking grim. "Thank you."

"We believe he was poisoned," said Bud.

"I suspect something that acted fast, and that was hidden in his poi," I added.

Ezra looked thoughtful, regarding us with an enigmatic expression. *He's tough to read.*

"I am sorry to say that everyone in the Games Room at the time of Tommy Trussler's death is someone I must investigate as a possible killer," he said bluntly. "I do not believe it is possible to hide this fact from you. I ask you to understand that you yourselves must be considered members of the suspect pool."

Bud spoke rapidly as he scratched his head, an action that always tells me he's under stress. "I understand exactly what you mean, Ezra, but I must ask you to take me at my professional word that neither Cait nor I had anything to do with the man's death—though Cait, especially, has some critical observations she'd like to share with you on the matter."

"You were the last person to be playing cards with him?" asked Ezra. *He's not following Bud's lead.*

"Tommy had spent most of the first hour of the day's session sitting at his little desk with people visiting him there," said Bud, "or else he popped over to their tables to give instruction. He happened to be at my table when the cry went up about a dolphin sighting. While everyone in the room was looking out at the ocean, Cait noticed that Tommy was in great distress."

Bud looked at me, and I took my cue. "Bud's right, Ezra. And you are too. I understand you're probably thinking that anyone in the room, or even anyone on the ship, could have poisoned him, but I can only add my assertion that it was neither of us. We'd only met the man here. We have no history with him. We would have no motive to kill him."

"Apparently *everyone* in the room had only met him on this cruise," said Ezra.

"I expect Kai Pukui, and maybe Afrim the server, might have traveled with him before," I added in what I hoped was a co-operative tone.

Ezra's glare told me he didn't consider my suggestion helpful.

"My investigation into everyone in that room will be most thorough," he said. He paused and sighed, his shoulders relaxing a fraction of an inch. Dropping his head slightly, he added, "I will admit that I believe it is highly unlikely that either of you were involved with this matter. As I have said, your records are solid, and I . . ." Ezra's expression as he paused for a long moment was complex, with what I judged to be resignation winning through. "I need to trust someone, Bud, Professor Morgan—or is it to be Professor Anderson from now on?"

"I'll be keeping Morgan," I replied with a smile at Bud, "as Bud and I have agreed. But I would prefer Cait, please. If you two boys are going to be on first-name terms, I don't want to feel left out."

Again, Ezra looked to be deep in thought. Then his shoulders straightened and he sat even more upright. *You've made a decision. I hope it's to trust us.*

"I have a good team on the ship," began Ezra. "In common parlance, I suppose you would call all our security responsibilities 'policing.' We do not usually have to investigate cases like this. My background has not been in this field. Military service, followed by post-service operations in security and security management, means I am well qualified to head up the security services needed onboard. I have received training in securing crime scenes, gathering evidence, assessing crime scenes and evidence, and have been taught about many sources of information to which I can turn when a possible, or alleged, crime has taken place. I'll be honest—I have never led a murder inquiry before, neither on land nor at sea. While most of my officers have also received the required training in crime scene management, none of them are trained investigators like you, Bud, and, as I happen to know, your lovely wife." He flashed a toothpaste-commercial smile at me, and I returned what I hoped was a winsome grin. *Charming*.

"Nurse Bartholomew Goodman alerted Rachel—Dr. White—immediately," he continued. "He's good at his job, and he was quite right to be suspicious. He has a background in this sort of thing."

I must have shown my surprise, because Ezra turned his attention to me and smiled. "All in good time," he said. Growing more serious, he added, "I apologize. I don't mean to be glib. Bud, your record is quite something. Your life of service to the cause of justice, both as a police officer, and," he paused and glanced in my direction, "in other roles, is admirable."

"I know something about Bud's 'other roles,'" I said.

Ezra looked relieved. "Good. Bud, I know that undertaking any work where national and international security clearances are required shows a determination to represent your country when it needs you most. Given our specific circumstances and the fact that your record suggests you are a man to be trusted, your investigative skills, and your ability to manage investigative teams and complex operations, are appealing."

"And what about me?" I asked, immediately regretting it, because I knew I sounded petulant.

Ezra looked at me and cocked his head. "Ah yes, you, Professor Cait Morgan."

I couldn't help but raise an eyebrow in anticipation.

"You have quite a reputation, don't you?" he continued. "A professor of criminal psychology at the University of Vancouver, adept at producing controversial academic papers about victim profiling, and helping the authorities apprehend criminals in various countries and locales, and with a solid track record of aiding an integrated homicide investigation team on your new home turf in Canada."

"It's hardly 'new' home turf, Ezra. I left the UK over a decade ago, and Wales many years before that. Canada is home now."

Ezra held my gaze then placed his water bottle on the coffee table between us. "It is your life in the UK that poses a problem though, you see," he said. *No easy grin this time?*

I knew what he meant, as did Bud, so I decided to tackle the matter head on. "I'm assuming you're referring to my being arrested on suspicion of killing my ex-boyfriend?"

"Yes," said Ezra.

"Well, if you'd dug all the way, you'd have discovered that I was exonerated. Since my arrival in Canada, I've been cleared by every organization and body that counts, and have subsequently worked on a number of sensitive police cases. As Bud mentioned, I consulted for the team he used to head up."

"I'm well aware of this, Cait. Still, I'm not convinced that your skill set would be of use on this occasion. I believe it will be the factual evidence that will crack the case."

Bud's expression shifted to one of determination; he was about to charge to my defense.

"I think it's exactly the sort of case where Cait could help, Ezra," he said proudly. "As a professional in homicide teams for many years, I know that most cases fall into two categories: targeted hits within the criminal community, and cases where someone close to the victim is the perpetrator. Random killings are rare. And that's where Cait's abilities have proved useful. If it's not a killing-to-order, and if there are no obvious family members or close friends in the frame as suspects, the victim profile that Cait builds can help focus the investigating officers so they are more likely to discern the perpetrator. What was the victim's lifestyle? What habits did they have? With whom did they come into contact on a regular, or even irregular, basis? To find a killer, one must first understand the victim. That is what Cait does—and it's what she could do for you, in this case. And as for me? I have run so many homicide investigations that setting up practical and productive lead-generating and investigation systems is a natural matter for me. I, *we*, would be happy to help, or advise, in any capacity."

Once again, Ezra fell silent. After a few moments of contemplation, he said, "I have spoken to the captain, and he has given me complete control in this matter. He trusts me. He and I have worked together on several occasions. Captain Andreas is an excellent Master. If this had to happen, I am glad it is under his command, because he will ensure that we do whatever is necessary to keep our guests and crew safe. Safety is our first concern. *If* poison is in play, I will need extra detection skills in my armory, which you could deliver. We have procedures onboard a ship, and I would only be inviting you to help me, not to take over."

"Question," said Bud. "What's your endgame? I'm guessing you won't be charging anyone while we're on the ship. If we manage to detect the killer, would you simply detain them until we reach Canada?"

"Essentially, yes," said Ezra. "We have just sailed from a US port. We operate under the Cruise Vessel Security and Safety Act of 2010. I have no authority to charge anyone. I can caution someone I might need to interrogate, but they would then have recourse to obtain appropriate legal advice; they could therefore choose, quite properly, to not answer any of my questions, which could be entirely counterproductive. The most I can do, effectively, is detain; we have minimal detention facilities. Alternately, we can place a guard outside a stateroom, so long as we are confident there is no way for the person we are detaining to leave the room. It's what we do when we need to place guests under

30

a curfew, or on an 'accompanied only' routine, when they are always accompanied by one of my officers when they need to leave their room. Neither the captain nor I are happy to detain everyone who was in the Games Room this morning in such a manner. We do not yet know if any one of them is responsible for Tommy Trussler's death. They are merely witnesses."

"But—" I began, but I was silenced by Ezra's steely gaze.

Bud sighed heavily. "Got it, Ezra. You lead the show. It's been some time since I've worked a case where proper procedure was involved, and much longer since it was an investigation that I was not in charge of. But I understand exactly what you mean. As does Cait, I'm sure. As a consultant to my team, she always played by the rules. I have no doubt we could both follow your direction, and add our own input, as appropriate."

"Only with my lead, and my say-so," said Ezra. "Procedures exist for a reason."

"Agreed and accepted," said Bud.

"As Bud said, agreed and accepted."

Room Service

AS SOON AS EZRA AGREED that Bud and I could be formally involved with the case, my spirits lifted. I reasoned that our last couple of days on the ship were bound to be marred by the tragic death, and I'd never been good at taking a backseat when a murderer was lurking in the shadows.

"Thanks for agreeing to include us, Ezra," I piped up. "As Bud said, although I have been known to work on cases where sleuthing was involved, I'm more than capable of following any procedural guidelines." I allowed myself a wistful smile as I looked over at my husband. "It could be quite like old times, Bud, with a team doing the information gathering while you and I investigate the victim and then the suspects, with the authority that comes from having a senior officer open doors for us."

"Yes, but bear in mind that such an approach brings its own challenges," said Bud. "Even if investigating a murder isn't something you've done before, Ezra, I'm sure you know that people's attitudes toward any type of law enforcement professional almost automatically affects their level of openness when it comes to sharing information."

It was Ezra's turn to smile. "I do indeed, Bud. My approach will be to keep our suspicions about murder confined to those who need to know, and to encourage the guests to share their knowledge about the victim on the basis that we are trying to fulfill irritating bureaucratic requirements because of a death at sea."

"Can we interview guests with you?" I asked. Bud shot me a warning glance.

"No, that is out of the question," replied Ezra. "I represent the cruise line; you do not."

I was disappointed. I thought it would be good for Bud to be involved, front and center, in a structured case again. The last police case he'd worked on, just before retiring from the force, was the investigation that led to his first wife's death. But even in retirement, his relentless pursuit of justice hadn't left him; I hoped, now that we were beginning to settle into our new life together, he might find further solace in tackling an inquiry that reflected his police work more closely than that of our sleuthing.

"As Ezra said, he has his procedures, Cait," said Bud. He spoke quietly, but I believed I could detect disappointment in his tone.

A knock at the door startled me.

Ezra stood. "I hope you don't mind—I took the liberty of ordering lunch for three to be delivered here. I don't think there'll be much chance to eat for the rest of the day; this gives me an opportunity to talk to you and have a meal from the guest menu."

Bud grinned. "I remember days when *all* Cait and I got to eat were a couple of slices of cold pizza at two in the morning." He winked at me. "Eating now, when we have the opportunity, is an excellent idea."

The next few minutes were taken up with sorting out who would eat what, and where they'd eat it. Although the stateroom was perfectly acceptable when two people wanted to eat, it became a little more problematic when three large trays arrived. We ended up putting all the trays on the bed, and pulling plates and dishes onto our laps as we went along.

Ezra rubbed his hands with glee when he saw the food. Bud and I insisted that he choose what he wanted first, and he selected the seafood ravioli with a lemon and saffron butter mousse. I pouted a bit; I'd rather fancied that for myself, but was happy to choose tender char-grilled lamb skewers, nestled on a bed of wild rice, infused with Mediterranean flavors. *Hey, when in doubt, meat on a stick is hard to beat.*

Bud tucked into the lemon and herb chicken breast, and looked happy enough. As he picked up his cutlery, Ezra looked at his watch, then wolfed down the plump ravioli as though he'd never eaten before. His plate was clear in about four minutes, whereas I took my time nibbling along the elegant little sticks of lamb, determined to get at every last morsel of the flavorsome meat before filling myself up with the rice.

Seeing that Ezra had finished, Bud said, "Why are you so sure it was poison? I mean, I saw the man, and agree that, with a background in homicide, that's where my mind flew. But what made your nurse practitioner—Bartholomew Goodman, right?—think that?"

"Yes, Bartholomew. He's a good man—" he paused and grinned at his own pun, "—who has a background in poisons."

"Really?" I asked. I couldn't help myself.

Ezra gave a wry smile. "Bartholomew has regaled us with many anecdotes about his time working at the British National Poisons Information Service in Birmingham, England, before he joined us here." With a more serious expression, he continued. "I won't tell you any of his stories, because they aren't appropriate given the circumstances, but he can bear witness that in Britain, an alarming number of people end up ingesting strange things. Then they phone the poisons center to find out if they are going to die, or at least what they should do about it. When Bartholomew saw Tommy Trussler's body, he immediately suspected poison. He told this to Rachel—Dr. White—on the phone when he called her; she then relayed this when she called me as she made her way to the Games Room from the officers' sun deck." He held up his mobile phone. "We all have these on the ship. They never leave our sides. Not even if we are off duty, as Rachel was when this call came in."

"As I told you, I saw Tommy Trussler's face as he was dying," I said. "I admit that I'm not an expert in poisons, but I have studied them to a certain extent, and it's certainly what came to mind. Will Dr. White be able to establish the exact nature of the poison? His convulsions were extreme and his death swift, which leads me to believe it was somehow introduced to the poi he was served. I saw him eat from the pot, but it wasn't there anymore when we left the Games Room. Someone removed it. Which means that—"

Ezra held up his hand, and I closed my mouth. "First of all, our procedures for managing a crime scene will establish what is and isn't in the Games Room, and we will do what we can to analyze everything at the scene at the time of Tommy's death. But remember—even though I am allowing you and Bud to help with this case, it doesn't mean I can simply take your word for something. The pot to which you refer might just be lying on the floor out of sight, or we might discover an obvious source of poison in the Games Room, or even in the victim's own stateroom."

Ezra had a point. The pot of poi could have been knocked off Tommy's desk and rolled out of sight, rather than lifted by someone on the scene. Or he could have been poisoned hours—even days—before we saw him die. I felt somewhat deflated at the thought, and I could tell that Bud did too.

Ezra sighed. "As for testing possible sources of poison, we have kits onboard used to detect illegal drugs, but Rachel is checking her supplies to see if she has anything we can use under these circumstances. What I can tell you right now is that she cannot perform an autopsy. Death must be properly certified at our next port, which, as you know, is Vancouver, in Canada. She and I will liaise with the authorities there, as well as with the US authorities, and those in our flag nation, the Republic of Malta. The death took place in international waters, so our paperwork will be time-consuming. We even have to bring the FBI in on the act; Tommy Trussler was an American, and the FBI likes to keep track of all US citizens, dead or alive. It is their job. We can store a body on the ship—we have a mortuary to allow for that—but that's all we can do."

I couldn't help but wonder how often it was used. As if reading my mind, Ezra said, "We don't have a lot of deaths on our ships. I think the average total for all cruise ships each year runs at about 200 unfortunate souls who die at sea. During the past few years, Stellar Cruise Lines has been trying to attract a younger average age of cruiser, and they seem to be succeeding. The truth is, when our guests were older, more died. Now that they are younger, fewer die. That said, few of those deaths are a result of anything other than natural causes. Yes, there are incidents where a brawl might be fueled by too much alcohol, which can cause injuries leading to death. I have witnessed this myself on two occasions during my seven years at sea. But this is the first time I have had to deal with a suspected case of an intentional killing."

"Now, on that point . . ." said Bud, but Ezra held up his hand. *A favorite gesture of his.*

"I know. Let us begin at the beginning, which is the correct procedure. First of all, are we sure this man did not intend to do himself harm? Is it a case of suicide? As I indicated, when I left you earlier I went directly to speak to Captain Andreas. But my team members have been hard at work. My second in command, the astute and efficient Officer Ocampo, whom I believe you met in the Games Room, has already searched Tommy Trussler's stateroom. The man did not leave a suicide note there—at least not one that has come to light. Rachel, Dr. White, has confirmed already that none has been found on his body. You were both there with him. So I shall ask you—did the man exhibit any signs that might now give either of you a reason to question his state of mind at the time of his death?"

I looked at Bud, and he took the lead. "Immediately prior to his death, Tommy Trussler was teaching me to play gin rummy, which doesn't seem like the swan song of a man who has deliberately imbibed poison. Prior to joining the rest of the occupants of the Games Room at the window—where, as I have said, we were all distracted by a passing pod of dolphins—I saw no signs that would indicate he was depressed, or resigned to his life ending momentarily." Bud stopped for a moment, and gave the matter some thought. "No—there was nothing to indicate that state of mind at all. I would say, in my professional opinion, that Tommy Trussler had no idea he was moments from death when we were playing cards. That said, he did look a little pale, and he was sweating more than I would have expected, given the temperature in the room. He looked . . ." Bud paused again, ". . . I'd have said he looked as though he might have had an upset stomach. Yes, that might be it. He was drinking a lot of water. Sipping it, as though to settle his stomach, though he didn't mention any discomfort. He was also breathing rather heavily, though that might have been normal for him. On previous occasions, when I'd met him at the gym, or while walking the deck, he was always breathing heavily, but in those situations it would be understandable. However, the poor guy might just have been suffering from the after-effects of a heavy night. I'm sure you see that often enough on the ship."

Ezra touched his forehead with two fingers and mimed tipping his hat at Bud. "With your record as a professional observer, Bud, I'll take all that you have said as valuable, and valid, insights. Thank you." He turned his attention to me. "And you, Cait—what did you note?"

He had no idea that he'd asked such a loaded question. I looked to Bud, silently seeking his advice.

Having wiped his mouth with a napkin, Bud said, "I think you should tell him, Cait."

Ezra looked puzzled, and I worked out how to begin.

"What Bud means," I said, "is that I have an unusual memory. An eidetic one. I've found it useful in cases in the past. Bud can testify to its accuracy and usefulness."

Ezra's dark eyes glinted with what I read to be uncertainty and suspicion. He looked to Bud for reassurance.

"Cait is telling the truth," said Bud. "Her abilities have been critical on many occasions, though we keep them as private as possible. Cait's not keen on being subjected to a host of laboratory tests any time soon, and I understand why not. We trust your discretion, Ezra."

Ezra nodded slowly. "So . . . you remember *everything*?" he asked.

I had piqued his interest, and knew from experience I'd have to take a few moments to explain myself. I tried not to sigh as I began.

"It's complicated, Ezra. Basically, all my senses pick up on the stimuli to which they are exposed, and grab onto them, never letting go. That's not terribly useful on its own, because, as human beings, we overlay every stimulus with our own interpretation, and that is colored by our experiences and attitudes. For example, I might smell something for the first time, and it could remind me of something I've smelled before, so I connect the new smell with the old one, and they become linked in my memory. When I try to recall the memory of the new smell, it will re-emerge with all the associations I have given it, some of which will have nothing to do with the circumstances under which I encountered the new smell. My skill set is only as reliable as my ability to interpret what I have retained. As human beings, we're not capable of experiencing the world as it is—we always experience it as we are, with all our faults, flaws, preconceptions, and prejudices filtering and infusing everything we perceive."

"Cait's pretty good at sorting out what her memories mean," added Bud, "but she does the best job when she's had a chance to mull it over for a while. It's not an instant thing. She's already recalled the time we were all in the Games Room this morning."

Ezra plucked a tangerine from the fruit platter he'd ordered and began to peel it as he spoke. The aroma of its zest filled the air, reminding me of a fancy restaurant in Las Vegas, until a breeze wafted it away.

"Did you see anything that might suggest that someone administered a poison to Tommy Trussler while he was in the Games Room this morning, Cait?" he asked.

"All I can say at this stage is that I do not recall seeing anyone doing anything that gave me cause for concern at the time, though I believe that everyone present would have had the *opportunity* to drop a poisonous substance into Tommy Trussler's pot of poi."

Ezra's expression told me that he didn't think I'd been helpful. "That's it?" he said, sounding unimpressed.

I bit, and gave Ezra two solid minutes of detailed recollection from the morning's events—just as I had for Bud, only much faster and with good deal more annoyance. Ezra's listening expression changed from skepticism, to alarm, to curiosity, to impatience. When I could tell I'd proved my point, I added, "I understand the comments you made about the idea that Tommy might have been poisoned before he entered the Games Room, and that the poi pot might still be in there, just out of sight somewhere. However, I believe you'll find the pot has gone, which means someone in the room knew there was poison in it. This is the most critical observation I have made."

Ezra looked resigned. "A rapid investigation is called for," he said tersely. "Following my initial report, the captain's decision was to continue our journey on to Vancouver because, as I'm sure you've already calculated, we are now closer to Canada than our last port of call in the US. He has instructed me that if Tommy Trussler was poisoned by someone on this ship—and that is the assumption I must make at this stage—I must apprehend that person. I must ensure the safety of everyone onboard. It's my duty. It's a big responsibility, and, while I face it every day in general terms, this is the first time I have felt it weigh so heavily upon my shoulders. I have never been aware of a murderer being on my ship before this. And I don't mind telling you that I do not care for that feeling at all."

He seemed a little overwhelmed.

"If Dr. White can establish the family of poison, she might be able to work out how long it would have taken to affect him," I said, having enjoyed my final mouthful of lunch.

"She is aware of that," Ezra snapped, "and will do all she can, without using any invasive techniques upon the body—and," he glanced at Bud, "without compromising any possible evidence that a future investigator might need to access. I have already informed her that she must take many photographs of the body before it is put into storage. We know the exact time of the onset of his symptoms, and we know when she pronounced death. But knowing all that doesn't help much, unless we can ascertain the type of poison used. Only *that* would allow us to calculate when the poison was ingested—if, in fact, it was ingested at all. Rachel will remove and protect the clothes of the deceased, check the body for any signs of a topical poison, and do her best to ascertain if it was injected into his person. She can tell me how she's getting on when I meet with her."

"When he was convulsing," I noted, "Tommy Trussler was having trouble breathing, and his whole body was affected. Like Bud, I'm no expert, but I'd have guessed at a cyanide type of poison—fast acting and painful. I could have been witnessing the endgame of a slower-acting toxin. Do you know if he'd sought any medical attention prior to today's incident?"

Ezra polished off his tangerine and shook his head. "No idea. That's something else I can ask Rachel when I visit her at the medical center. Which I should do as soon as possible." He looked at his watch again.

"Could we come with you?" asked Bud. "If we could see the doctor and the body, now, Cait might learn something that would help her begin to build a profile of the man and his life. That might help you frame any questions you want to ask the other guests who were in the Games Room. Or maybe, if Dr. White has discovered something concrete, it could completely change your investigation."

"You're right, and I have no problem with you joining me," replied Ezra. "Before we visit her together, I need to visit her alone." Ezra stood and addressed my agitated look. "Yes, Cait, you'll both have a chance to visit the medical facility with me, but though I am bending the procedural regulations in this instance, there are people who need to be brought onboard with that approach. I'll be as speedy as possible, and will telephone you here when it's convenient for you to join me on Deck 2, where the examination rooms and mortuary are located. Please, enjoy the rest of this wonderful food; give some more thought to the case, and I will call you as soon as I can."

After Ezra left, I said to Bud, "Right then—if I can't see the body or the dead man's cabin right away, I'm going to concentrate on what we know about him already, and start to build a profile that way. I'll make notes. What about you?"

"I'll do the same," said Bud.

How wonderful—a totally harmonious marriage.

As I sat on the bed, I realized I'd have to think right back to our arrival in Honolulu, and assess, with fresh eyes, everything that had happened. At the time, I'd simply been Cait Morgan, happy honeymooner. Now I'd have to reconsider everything in light of the fact that a man was dead, and that the killer was likely to be someone we'd met on our trip—someone who'd been in the Games Room. We'd met Nigel and Janet, and Derek and Laurie, for the first time in Honolulu, and had run into them several times before this morning—Bud more often than me, it seemed. Frannie had introduced herself to us on the day we'd embarked, when the three of us were feeding the exotic little fish that swam in the waters close to the Aloha Tower. Kai Pukui had seemed to appear at every event we'd attended on the ship, always accompanied—except for this morning—by his wife, Malia. Bud might have talked with Tommy on several occasions, but I'd only seen him in passing.

Yes, I'd take the time to reconnect with everything Bud and I had done, and consider how we'd intersected with the people who were now the prime suspects in a case of poisoning; I'd let Bud do the same. Maybe we'd even have time to compare notes before joining Ezra in the mortuary.

Aloha O'ahu

"CAIT, WAKE UP. WE'RE JUST starting our descent into Honolulu."

Bud's voice was gentle enough to not startle me, but firm enough to make me try to sit upright. My neck ached, and I knew I'd been snoring and drooling. It wasn't a surprise that I'd slept through the entire flight—I'd hardly managed a nap the night before, because I'd been mentally running through the lists of things I'd packed for our trip to the Hawaiian Islands.

Finally coming to grips with my surroundings, I realized that I'd managed the almost impossible feat of reducing our flight to a matter of no more than fifteen conscious minutes. I couldn't remember take off, and now here we were landing. *Wow—that's about as close to "Beam me up, Scotty" as you can get.* Other than an aching neck, I felt refreshed and excited. Again. The long spring semester was behind me. The snow had made my journey from our new home in Maple Ridge seem almost endless. I'd been used to a quick ten-minute sprint from my little house half way up Burnaby Mountain to my campus; now I was about forty-five minutes away, and that was when the traffic was light. It *was* worth it. The house that Bud and I were making our home was going to be wonderful—once we'd finished painting everything, replacing all the floors and window treatments, and extending the deck at the back of the house. Yes, it had been a slog, but it was beginning to come together.

I managed a glimpse of the island of O'ahu as we circled before landing, then we were down and off. I had to admit I was a bit disappointed when I wasn't immediately greeted by a woman wearing multiple Hawaiian *leis* upon our arrival in the baggage area, but when Bud came back from a quick "call of nature," I was thrilled to see he'd managed to find a beautiful garland to place around my neck. *Clever, wonderful Bud.*

The cab ride from the airport to our hotel was another delight. I'd grown up watching Jack Lord cracking down on criminals in Hawai'i, and now I had the chance to see the place for myself. From poring over tourist websites—and because Bud and I were avid fans of the new version of *Hawaii Five-O*—I already knew I'd be seeing a good number of gleaming tower blocks running along highways. What I hadn't been prepared for was how densely stacked those tower blocks would become as we headed into the downtown Honolulu area. I felt a bit disappointed until we approached our hotel, which looked as promising as it had on the screen of my laptop. Finally entering the magnificent main lobby from the white, colonnaded portico of the Moana Surfrider Hotel, I was enchanted by the dark wood flooring and delightfully "leafy" rugs, the gleaming white balconies above us, the traditional staircases and columns, and the wonderful ambience of the place; it seemed both formal and casual at the same time, and the view toward the sea from the main lanai, opposite the entrance, was breathtaking.

I acquired another lei at the check-in desk, as well as a delicious cookie, wrapped in its own little plastic bag and shaped like a tufted pineapple. Our room was small, and had the same mix of traditional elegance and beachside ease as the public areas of the hotel. The bellman, who'd followed us with our luggage, opened white wooden shutters to reveal a stunning view of the Pacific Ocean. He left Bud and me to hug beside the bed, which was dressed with suitably Hawaiian-themed linens, covered with magenta plumeria and vivid green palm fronds.

"Come on, unhand me, woman," said Bud laughing. "It's two o'clock already, and I know you want to have a good look around the place before the dinner we've booked at that fancy Beach House Restaurant at six."

Relinquishing my grip, I took a few moments to lean out of the window as far as I could. Our view was not just of the sea but of the hotel's private beach area, and off toward a few massive banyan trees, which were surrounded by a lounge and bar area. Suddenly the idea of a cold beer, or maybe my first Hawaiian mai tai, seemed appealing, but I knew we both needed a quick wash and brush-up before we ventured out.

Half an hour later, Bud and I were two of the appropriately attired guests sitting in comfy chairs, looking out to sea. I tackled a bottle of beer, knowing I'd otherwise sink an entire mai tai simply to quench my thirst. Sitting in the shade of the historic banyan trees, I couldn't have felt happier; Bud and I had waited quite some time for this, the first day of our proper honeymoon, and it seemed as though Hawai'i was going to be as beautiful and magical as I had hoped—certainly if our hotel was anything to go by.

Like all good tourists visiting Waikiki for the first time, we felt it necessary to kick off our shoes and walk along the world-famous beach. Leaving the bar and achieving this was easy—we just stepped over a rope that divided the hotel's property from the public beach, and we were off. The sun was hot, but the wind coming off the sea kept us cool. I was glad I'd applied my sun-gloop before we'd headed out, because it was the sort of weather that could easily lead to sunburn. We strolled along the pale, soft sand for quite some time. Even I, who hates the feeling of sand between my toes, enjoyed it. The beach was busy, and people were enjoying themselves in a myriad of ways, ranging from being fast asleep to almost alarmingly active.

It was the surfers who held our attention the most. Even though I'd seen the sight on television dozens of times, I found it difficult to believe that so many people, possibly hundreds, could all surf at the same time without causing each other some sort of serious injury. Many stood on longboards, paddling with oars; others lay down and propelled themselves with their tanned arms; most used the more familiar method of riding the waves. Bud and I laughed at the number of dogs people had with them on their surfboards. Marty, our loving, if a little tubby, black Lab, is strangely averse to bodies of water, so we agreed there'd be no way he'd be happy living the life of a surfing dog. These wet-furred creatures seemed to be part fish, happily leaping into the sea before being helped to scramble back onto their human's board. It was fascinating. Wonderful. Colorful. So vibrant it made me want to run along the beach and dive into the crashing waves, even though I can't swim a stroke.

We eventually decided to head away from the beach, toward the grassy area that ran the length of the bay, and we cut through what seemed to be a surfboard parking area. Dozens of boards stood in rows, all chained in place with colorful loops and locks. As we were washing off our feet at one of the many taps set up for that very purpose, a couple of boys who looked to be no more than twelve years old ran with joyful abandon from a bank of lockers where they'd stashed their clothes, and dragged their boards from the serried ranks. They looked so frail, and the boards so large, that I was surprised to see them handle the massive things so easily. They ran off toward the sea laughing with pure joy. *What an amazing thing to be able to do at the end of the school day.*

Within earshot of the endless stream of traffic that inched along the waterfront, Bud and I took in the sight of the impressive statue of Duke Kahanamoku, one of Hawai'i's most famous sons; the man who did more for Hawai'i's reputation as a world-renowned center for surfing than anyone else.

It was while we were making our way back toward the bar on the beach named for the man himself that we first ran into Janet and Nigel Knicely. Of course, we didn't know who they were at the time; all we knew was that we'd come upon a couple that looked pretty mismatched, comprised of a woman who couldn't stop crying and a man who seemed quite impatient with her distress. It was a situation Bud couldn't ignore.

"Anything we can do to help?" asked Bud in his calming voice as we drew parallel with them on the grassed area.

The man's head snapped around; he glared at Bud, his mouth an angry line. His large sunglasses, highlighted, well-trimmed hair, air of superiority, and collection of clothing that suggested he was color-blind all told me he must be English. *The pink golf shirt with the collar turned up is the real give away.* My supposition was proved correct when he answered Bud.

"We're managing perfectly well, thank you very much." *Bristol accent, poshed up a bit.*

"I can't find Nigel's sunblock stick for his lips," wailed the woman. She looked at me as though she'd lost her newborn child, tears streaming down her face from beneath her sunglasses. The backpack she'd dumped onto the floor was so big it could have taken her on a two-week camping trip. She was hunched over it, her hands stuck deep inside. "I know it's here, Nigel, honestly."

It seemed impractical to offer to help her search, so I thought the best thing to do was distract the annoyed man. "It's certainly the sort of weather that means you need a good sunblock, or maybe a hat," I said brightly.

"Forgot that as well, didn't you," was the man's surly reply, looking at his wife who was now bent double.

The woman looked up and said quietly, "I did mention it to you before we left the room. Maybe we should go back and get it?" She sounded uncertain.

Tutting loudly, the man snapped, "I suppose we'll have to. Though that seems like a terrible waste of time. I'm *not* buying a new one. I'm sure they'd rip us off as soon as look at us."

"Is it far for you to return to your room?" asked Bud. I could tell he'd spotted a situation he didn't like the look of, and was now in protective mode.

The man stood a little taller. "We're at the Moana Surfrider," he said proudly. "Lovely old place. Almost looks British."

Ugh—I could gag!

Bud slapped a professional smile on his face. "Great," he said, "we're staying there too. We'll walk with you. We were just heading back, weren't we?"

No, we weren't—you promised me ice cream, was what I thought; what I said was, "Absolutely!" and mimicked Bud's cheery grin.

"Bud Anderson, and my wife, Cait Morgan," said Bud, extending a hand to the man, who gave me a withering glance. He took Bud's hand and tried to shake it off the end of his arm.

"Nigel Knicely, with a K. The K is silent. Wife, Janet," said the man, his voice quivering as he continued to pump Bud's arm. "Janet *Knicely*," he emphasized, addressing me. *Oh, I see.*

Janet looked up from her stooped position, wiped away her tears, and rubbed her hands on her khaki cargo shorts. Once standing, she offered me her hand. "Nice to meet you," she said, smiling. Shaking her hand was like grasping a clump of wet lettuce.

Declining Bud's pointed offer to carry the backpack—Nigel didn't say a word—Janet fiddled about with the straps as we set off. It was impossible to walk four-abreast, so Bud took the lead with Nigel and I accompanied Janet.

"It's a lovely hotel, isn't it?" I began.

"Oh, it is. It's all so well done, isn't it? Poshest place I've ever stayed at. But it's only for one more night."

"You're leaving tomorrow?" *Please say yes.*

"No. Well, yes. We're going on a cruise." *Oh no.*

"Really? Which ship?" I tried to sound excited.

"We're going on the *Stellar Sol*. We're going to stay on it in the harbor tomorrow night, then we sail all around the Islands, then off to Canada. I'm so excited. We don't usually do things like this. Have you ever been on a cruise?"

As I replied, my heart sank. I had visions of this woman becoming a limpet for the whole of our honeymoon. "No, not yet. Bud and I are taking the same cruise. We live near Vancouver, where the ship arrives in Canada, so it's going to be an easy drive home for us when we get there."

Janet Knicely looked delighted. "How lovely! But that's not a Canadian accent, is it?"

This time my smile was genuine. "No, I'm Welsh, though I've been in Canada for more than a decade. It's my home now. Bud and I were married a few months ago. We're on our honeymoon." *Please take the hint!*

"Smashing," beamed Janet, sweating under her heavy load. "Nigel and I had two days in Ledbury when we got married, and that was that. Right back to work he went. We've been here renewing our vows, so that's almost as romantic, isn't it?"

I grappled with several emotions. Ledbury was where my parents had enjoyed their own two-day honeymoon back in the 1950s. Janet's unexpected mention of the place made me think of them, and how much I wished they'd lived to see me married and happy. Set against that was my astonishment that the Knicelys had been renewing their marriage vows; the dynamic between them wasn't at all romantic.

"Did you renew your vows today?" I asked. I couldn't imagine the answer would be yes.

"Yesterday," replied Janet happily. "They arranged it all at the hotel. Did it under that big banyan tree they have. It was a bit odd, people being all around us in swimsuits and such, but it was very nice, really. Nigel was the center of attention, like everyone was there for him. Well, us, you know. Nigel did look a picture, and I had a new frock for the occasion. You'll see it when I wear it on the ship for the formal nights. It's like something from a dream."

I had visions of Janet Knicely floating in for dinner amidst swathes of beige bridal chiffon, but I brushed such horrific thoughts aside and said, "So this will be like a honeymoon for you too?"

Janet nodded. "Funny, isn't it? I mean, we've got our first grandchild on the way, and here we are like teenagers."

I judged Janet Knicely to be around fifty. "How long have you been married?" I asked. It seemed like a natural question.

"Thirty years this year," she glowed.

"You married young," I said, as noncommittally as possible.

"Well, my mum said when you know, you know. And she was right. It's been a very settled marriage." *What an odd way to describe a life.*

Janet looked happy as she rattled on. "I knit. And now that we've got our first grandchild on the way, I have someone to knit for. It'll be a boy, so I'm doing lots of little jackets, and hats, and scarves. Due in September he is. Oh, I am so looking forward to it. It'll be lovely, won't it Nigel," she called at her husband's back, "to have a little one about the place again?"

The men paused and we stood beside them for a moment. Janet continued. "Not that you'll be there all the time, but you'll be at home a bit more than when ours were young, I hope. Nigel's retired, you see, but only half retired. Can't let go of him, they can't. They hired him back as an executive trainer at their Birmingham center, didn't they? So now he's still away a lot, but not quite as much as before. It'll be nice, a grandson."

"From what career have you almost retired?" I asked of Nigel, trying to sound interested.

Before he had a chance to answer, his wife jumped in with, "Drugs. He sells drugs!" She laughed almost manically. "That's what I always say. It makes me laugh, it does. Because he does sell drugs but, you know, not druggy drugs like drug addicts take—proper drugs that doctors prescribe. Worked for them all over the years, haven't you, Nigel? He's very good, you see, so all the big companies wanted him. They all kept buying each other up, so he'd end up leaving somewhere, then the new company would get bought up by the old one, and he's back at the beginning again. But they've all been good to you, haven't they, Nigel? Traveled all over, he has, all the years we've been married. It's been a funny old life, but it's suited me. The children kept me busy, and now they've gone off to do their own thing, I hope we get a bit more time together. And there are my charities too. Help out at a couple of shops near where we live, I do. Well, it's the least I can do for all those poor children around the world with less than nothing, isn't it? And there'll be our children's little ones for me to play with soon. Our Sophie—she's the one having the baby—she lives not far from us. We're just outside Bristol proper, in Westbury-on-Trym, and she's about half an hour's drive away. I hope I see a lot of the baby. We'll have fun babysitting, won't we, Nigel? And I know they'll be ever so grateful."

Nigel Knicely nodded. *I wonder if he's capable of conversation—or if he ever gets the chance.*

It was clear that Janet was the chatty type and, as we all headed up the steps under the portico of our hotel, I could see she was winding up to something.

"It would be nice to have some company for dinner tonight," she said, gushing. "Have you made any plans yet?"

I didn't know who looked more horrified—Bud or Nigel.

"We've planned a romantic dinner for two," Bud said firmly. Nigel's shoulders dropped in relief, but Janet looked disappointed.

"I'm sure we'll see you around on the ship," I said brightly. Bud's eyes widened.

"You're taking the same cruise as us?" asked Bud of Nigel.

"*Stellar Sol.* We embark tomorrow, but don't sail until the day after that," said Nigel brusquely.

Bud half-smiled. "Yes, same as us. Well, as Cait said, I'm sure we'll bump into each other onboard." We all shook hands and went our separate ways.

"Odd couple," said Bud.

"Peacock and peahen," I replied.

"And a very pecky peacock at that," said Bud, frowning. "I didn't feel at all comfortable with the way he was treating his wife when we first met them." I'd already spotted that, and had been comforted to see how Bud had acted under the circumstances. Comforted and proud.

"Hard to believe they were renewing their vows under the banyan tree over there," I said, waving my arm toward the bar area, beyond the lanai, "just yesterday."

"Really?" Bud sounded as surprised as I had been.

"If you and 'Mr. Knicely with a silent K' weren't talking about cruises and vow renewals, what were you talking about?"

"Cars." Bud sounded as bored as I guessed he must have been. "Why are so many men obsessed by cars? I mean, sure, they need to be able to get you from A to B, and I must admit I enjoy driving my truck, but to want to talk about engines and intakes and all that? Don't get it. Not for me."

"No, you'd rather be discussing the delicate balance of ingredients in a recipe, or the latest on the Paris runways for the man about town, wouldn't you?" I said, grinning.

"You know me so well," mugged Bud. "So, what about the ice cream I promised you? Time enough to think about the Knicelys when we're on the ship, eh?" He purposely pronounced the silent K with a wicked smirk, and we headed for the large man in a vivid orange shirt who was handing lurid blue shave ices in cups to two little girls.

"I hope he's got chocolate ice cream. I want something with a bit more substance than just frozen, flavored water," I said.

Mahalo Waikiki

THAT FIRST EVENING OF OUR honeymoon, Bud had arranged everything to perfection. We sat at the corner table of the open verandah attached to the Beach House Restaurant at our hotel, overlooking the sea. Bud dined on *poke*—saying it was the best ahi tuna he'd ever tasted—while I opted for the *foie gras* on a tiny corn cake, with caramelized sweet Maui onion and blackberry jam. My taste buds exploded at the first taste, and I was in heaven. I had the fish of the day—a meaty mahimahi, stuffed with crab and accompanied by a light, zesty salad containing a lot of ingredients I didn't recognize. Unsurprisingly, Bud chose the rack of lamb, and said it tasted wonderful. We sipped Veuve Clicquot Yellow Label champagne, which was insanely expensive, but Bud insisted we have it because he knew it was my favorite. I made sure I kept the cork and the cage to add to our little collection. We had the most perfect couple of hours, watching the sun go down and the stars appearing in the darkening sky.

A young man with a melodious voice and a talent with the ukulele strummed quietly at the end of the verandah farthest from us, and, just as the sun disappeared into a blood-red sea, he began to sing a song I'd never heard before, but that made me fill up with tears. Sung by a man to the woman he loves, it spoke of weaving a lei of stars for the love of his life to wear on such a beautiful night. Bud, who never, ever sings, began to hum along with the tune the moment he saw I was enjoying it. I told him to stop. It's not that I'm not a romantic at heart; it's just that I don't cope well with it, and it makes me blub. Then I feel like a fool.

Other than the blubbing, the evening was exactly what a honeymoon should be. After dinner, we decided to walk along the beach toward the Royal Hawaiian Hotel—also known as The Pink

Palace—and let our food settle while we partook of an after-dinner drink at the wonderful circular bar beside the beach. Once again, we managed to find a little table looking out toward the now-moonlit sea and, as we chatted, we could hear the rushing of the surf and the sounds of music and jollity coming from the bars along the bay. Along the sweep of Waikiki were dozens of flaming tiki torches, which gave the whole view a grand and unique atmosphere.

Just as we'd finished our drinks, a petite blond in her fifties, wearing a long gown and carrying a pair of spike heels, attempted to skip over the rope in front of us—which seemed to be the way all the beachfront properties separated themselves from the beach itself. She tripped and landed on her bottom in the sand with a squeal. A largish man hurried, as best he could, from the tideline toward the woman, who seemed to be having a fine old time sitting just where she was. I suspected a few cocktails might have something to do with her lack of sensitivity or concern.

"You alright there, princess?" called the man, as Bud rose from his seat to offer the woman a helping hand. *I wonder how many damsels in distress Bud will rescue before the day is out.*

"Sure am, honey," she called back, giggling.

Once Bud had managed to get her onto her feet, and safely over the rope links, she brushed herself down and dropped her shoes onto the ground. "Oh, my stars, I guess I should have drunk that last one a little more slowly, honey," she said. Then, looking up at Bud, she added, "Thank you, kind sir. Let me buy you a drink. And the lovely lady you're with. Derek? We must buy these wonderful folks a drink. You order. I'm off to the little girls' room." She pulled up the hem of her long, cotton gown into a ball, grasped it in one hand, then ran as lightly as a child toward the main body of the wonderful pink hotel. *Very lithe for her age.*

Taking his time to cross the rope with care, the man straightened himself up and held out a hand to Bud. "I'm Derek. Glad to make your acquaintance, sir. And thank you for helping out my good lady-wife. She's old enough to know better than to try to jump rope like that."

Bud smiled. "Bud Anderson. No problem at all, pleased to be able to help. But my wife and I were just leaving. No need for that drink. Another time, maybe?"

Turning to me, Derek held out his hand again. "Derek," he repeated.

"Cait," I replied. I didn't feel the need to add "Morgan."

"Good to meet you too, Cait. And the little lady won't take no for an answer, I'm afraid. Not used to it, ya see?" he winked at me as he spoke. "So, what'll it be?"

I hesitated for a millisecond, but when I locked eyes with Bud I knew that he, like me, would relent pretty easily. "How about we have one last mai tai?" I said.

"Two mai tais comin' up," said Derek as he weaved his way a little unsteadily toward the bar.

"Bud to the rescue, again," I said, smiling. He shrugged. "I love you, Husband. Have I told you that recently?"

"Not for at least ten minutes," he said with a pout.

Derek was back in a flash and plopped himself next to Bud. "Guy's gonna bring the drinks in a moment. I promised him you'd finished the ones you had, so you'd better drain 'em. Can't serve you no more than one at a time. Guess they don't trust folk to know when to stop around here. Some damn fool rules they have. Folks have to step over the rope to smoke a cigarette, even though they're standing no more than two inches from this side of the rope, but then they can't have a drink in their hand at the time. No drinking on the beach, no smoking on hotel property. And the guy at the bar told us they're gonna stop smoking on the beach altogether next year. I guess that's not the end of the world. But one drink at a time? We're not kids. Heck, wish I was!"

Despite his little rant, Derek seemed like a pretty happy chap, because he grinned as he spoke.

A waiter in a dapper outfit delivered our drinks and cleared away our empty glasses. I spotted Derek's wife waving toward us from the hotel. "I think your wife's trying to get your attention," I said to our "host."

He turned, straining to see. "Laurie? What's she up to?"

"She seems to be beckoning you," Bud said. "She's pointing at her feet, and calling you over. Maybe she wants you to bring her shoes?"

"Good idea if she's off to the ladies,'" I said.

Derek rose, smiling. "These shoes have been the bane of my life this evening. Had to be this pair with that outfit, but she couldn't walk in them more than five steps. It's why we came along the beach. Why do you women wear these things?" he said, looking at the four-inch heels he'd scooped up from the floor.

"I don't," I replied, waggling a ballet flat in his direction.

Smiling down at Bud, Derek said, "I see you've found yourself a sensible one. Hope she's fun, too, cause without that, there ain't no point in it."

"She's definitely fun," said Bud, returning Derek's smile. "Never a dull moment."

"Be thankful for it," said Derek as he tottered away with his wife's shoes. "I'll be right back. Talk among yourselves," he giggled.

"They seem nice," I said.

"They do indeed," said Bud.

"Maybe one cocktail over the top?"

"I'd say so."

"But that's what holidays are for—overdoing it a bit and having a silly time, right?"

Bud winked at me over the rim of his raised glass. "This is absolutely, definitely, my last drink of the day," he said.

As we clinked glasses, I said, "Me too." And it turned out that it was, because neither Derek nor Laurie ever appeared again. After half an hour, we took their drinks back to the bar, told the barman what was happening, and set off along the sand back to our own hotel.

The fiery necklace of tiki torches along the edge of the beach reminded us of civilization, but looking out across the ocean, everything was black velvet, trimmed with silver surf, moonlight, and stars.

Corpseman's Quarters

JUST AS I WAS WALLOWING in the recollection of our first wonderful night in Honolulu, the phone in our cabin rang.

Bud answered, listened, said, "Sure," a couple of times, then replaced the receiver. "Ezra says to meet him at the medical office as soon as we like," he said. "It's down on Deck 2, forward, so it shouldn't take us long to get there. Are you fit to make a move?"

"Just about," I said, pulling open the door to the bathroom. "Best to go before we go," I quipped.

Only one of the four elevators closest to our stateroom was capable of taking us as low as Deck 2. Waiting for the glass pod to arrive, Bud and I chatted through our initial meetings with the Knicelys and the Croppers. Well, I chatted, and he listened.

I summed up with, "So, at first meeting, we have a couple with a seemingly off-kilter relationship—and an unnecessary letter K in their surname—and another without an apparent care in the world, but a love of cocktails."

As we swept down the soaring atrium of the ship, I noted gaggles of folk in the other glass capsules, all oblivious to the fact that a man in their midst had met an untimely end. Smiling faces, family gripes, romantic couples—all on display, but unaware. The elevator cars were full of tales never to be told in full, only to be glimpsed in passing. *Fascinating.*

"After you, Cait," said Bud as he waved me out of our capsule into the somewhat gloomy corridor. Unlike all the decks above, this one was primarily reserved for the crew. Yes, sick guests would visit, and we had disembarked using this deck when we were at port, but otherwise, it was crew territory. We followed the signs giving directions to the medical center, and I noted the posters reminding crew members about the penalties for using or smuggling drugs, for abusing alcohol, or each other, and about the STAR! Program for crew members with the highest guest ratings each cruise.

In this part of the ship, below the waterline, the wave-patterned carpeting of the upper decks gave way to practical, durable linoleum that ran from the floor up to a waist-high grab rail. The uneven surface of the rail told me it had been rubbed down and repainted many times, unlike the sleek, brushed stainless steel found on the passenger decks. My nostrils told me we were nearing the medical area. *Nothing else ever smells quite like medical disinfectant.*

Bud and I entered through a wide doorway, and found ourselves standing in a tiny waiting area, with a hatch leading into a miniscule office. No one was in sight.

A moment later, Ezra appeared in the little office, having entered from a hidden corridor. He beckoned us to follow him.

Making our way along a short corridor, Ezra said, "I haven't managed to speak with Rachel yet, but I decided not to wait any longer before calling you. Time is of the essence."

Finally settling into a small medical consultation and examination room, I could feel the windowless, theoretically soothing pale green walls closing in about me as we awaited the imminent arrival of Dr. Rachel White. I tried to imagine how it would feel to put in multiple shifts in such enclosed quarters every week for months on end. Suddenly the life of a ship's doctor didn't seem quite as glamorous as I'd imagined.

After what felt like half an hour of silence—probably only five minutes—Bartholomew Goodman stuck his head into the room and exuberantly announced, "For once, callin' this the 'Corpseman's Quarters' is bang on! That's what they used to call it in the olden days. I never liked the term myself. There you go. She won't be long. Just washing up. You can *aks* her your questions. She'll tell you everything.

I'm outta here. Things to do, people to see." On this occasion, the nurse practitioner's London accent seemed to have given way to a distinctly Caribbean lilt, highlighted by his use of the word "*aks*" instead of "ask." *Odd. Maybe he feels more comfortable now, here, than when he was in charge of the crew at the scene of a death?*

Finally, the doctor appeared. As she entered the room, Ezra rose a little from his seat, and Bud followed suit. Clearly used to this display of good manners, Rachel White waved at the men, indicating that they should be seated. *You're deferring, Bud, you don't usually do that.*

A white coat covered the floral dress Rachel White had been wearing to enjoy her time off; the woman looked a little strained.

"Well, this is a right flamin' pain and no mistake," she said angrily.

I was surprised, as were Bud and Ezra.

Running her hand through her coppery hair, she added, "I'm sorry, I shouldn't have said that. I'm tired, and I've been looking forward to some time off. I'm terribly sorry for the deceased and his loved ones. I've done all I can to discharge my duty to the rest of the people on this ship." She clamped her lips together and pulled the edges of her mouth down with the forefinger and thumb of her left hand. Shaking her head, she added, "As promised, I can now make a preliminary report, Ezra. Would you rather wait until we're alone?"

Ezra motioned toward Bud and me. "Bud Anderson, retired homicide cop; Cait Morgan, professor of criminal psychology. On their honeymoon. Prepared to help out. Cleared with the captain. They will consult on this case, but I will run the investigation. You may speak freely in front of them."

Rachel White regarded us with the same blank, cold, cornflower eyes she'd cast over us in the Games Room. She was a tough one to read, so I decided to give as good as I was getting, and returned her steely gaze. As she noticed what I was doing, her expression changed to one of puzzlement, then she gave her attention to the digital pad she'd placed on the desk in front of her.

"Very well. I dare say we can use all the help we can get. Your Filipino Army won't be much use if there's a killer on the loose, will it, Ezra?"

Ezra cleared his throat. I got the impression that a line had been crossed. I judged that these two knew each other as more than colleagues, and that Rachel White had used a private term inappropriately.

"My security officers aren't trained investigators, as Bud and Cait are," said Ezra defensively. He smiled politely at us. "Pretty much every one of my officers is from the Philippines, as Rachel says, though I do have a couple of female officers from Jamaica."

Rachel almost smiled. "The Mamas?" she chuckled coldly. "I swear they're more intimidating than all the men put together." I was finding it difficult to get the measure of this woman. Was she essentially obnoxious, or was she just trying to flaunt that she was an insider, highlighting that Bud and I weren't? I suspected the latter, but wondered why she felt the need.

Bud seemed eager to please. "I think I've seen the two officers you're referring to. They had words with a couple of older teens the other evening up on the front deck. I understand what you mean about them having a presence." *Oil on choppy waters, Bud. Good job.*

"So, what can you tell us, Rachel?" Ezra asked the question we all wanted answered.

Prodding and sliding her finger across the device on her desk, Rachel read aloud the facts, and embellished them as she did so.

"I can't find any sign of trauma, other than a bitten tongue. No signs of an injection site, or any other puncture wounds. Luckily for us he did, indeed, bite his tongue, because I was able to get some blood samples without having to do anything invasive. I'm still having a think about how exactly I can use the supplies on hand so I can work out what killed him, but at least I have something to work with. That said, don't hold your breath. I'm not equipped for such work here, and the samples are small. I might be better off holding onto whatever I have to test any possible sources of poison you might find. It's unlikely that we'd find a source of poison A if he was killed with poison B, so . . . we'll see. His body is telling me it could have been any one of a number of things. Cyanide, ricin, strychnine, arsenic—it could even have been a massive dose of something not usually lethal, like antihistamine, or any number of over-the-counter, or even prescribed drugs. They are all possibilities. I suppose the most worrying would be ricin, especially if he inhaled it."

Ezra and Bud stiffened as she said these final words, both well-versed in the implications of an airborne variety of ricin. We relaxed somewhat when Rachel added, "I checked, and his nasal membrane shows no indications of inhalation of a toxic substance."

"That's some good news at least," said Ezra. He looked relieved.

"Had the deceased shown any symptoms of nausea, vomiting, or diarrhea in the past couple of days?" I asked. Quite pleasantly, I thought.

Rachel rearranged her shoulders and replied tartly, "I was coming to that. No, he hadn't reported any, but that's not unusual. Tommy Trussler had cruised on many occasions, and he would have been well aware that the exhibition of such symptoms can result in a person being quarantined. Since he was here to provide a service to our guests, he might have thought that his chances of being requested to do so again in the future would be compromised by his being unable to fulfil his duties on this trip. I see it too often: crew members don't report sickness until they are very poorly. We have an active campaign informing them that admitting to sickness is preferred, but, especially for the bar servers, it means fewer tips, so they keep going until they all but drop. Stupid. It's why we have to work so hard to contain illness on ships. That said, my money's on ninety-nine percent of the bugs we get here being brought onboard by guests, who also lie about not feeling sick, just so they don't miss their holiday."

Her acid tone was beginning to grate on me. I decided to wade in. "So, does his corpse tell you anything his living self didn't?" *Well, someone had to push her along.*

Bud and Ezra seemed oblivious to the tension growing between Rachel and myself. I already knew I didn't play well with others, but she was really irritating me. I suspected she felt the same way.

Rachel's voice had a hard edge. "*Professor* Morgan," she said, emphasizing my title, "as a psychologist, you will not have received any formal medical training, so you cannot be expected to understand the thoroughness of my examination of the body—" I heard Bud inhale as he waited for me to explode, "—so I shall get straight to the point." Bud hardly breathed. "Tommy Trussler died from a lethal dose of an unknown poison that was not injected into him, and that he did not inhale. I believe, therefore, that he either ingested it, or the toxin was introduced to his bloodstream by some type of topical application. His body showed no signs, however, of any patches of skin that were inflamed or discolored, so my tendency is to suggest he ingested the poison. There is no non-invasive way to establish this beyond all doubt, though I can also tell you that I saw no signs of a corrosive substance in his mouth. Although not discolored, either in patches or in total, his skin was somewhat desiccated—more than I would expect so soon after death. It suggests to me that he was dehydrated. This might have been a result of any number of factors, but I have discounted sunburn, at least. He might have been vomiting for days, or simply have drunk a great deal of alcohol last night. He did not smell of alcohol, nor did he give off the odor of almonds, often associated, though not always present, when cyanide has been introduced into the body. He did smell somewhat of garlic, which might suggest the use of arsenic, or that he'd recently eaten garlic. His forehead was slightly grazed, which I believe happened when his head hit the card table. I have sent Bartholomew to Tommy's stateroom and have instructed him to bring any and all potions and devices that might have contained a toxin here, so they can be stored securely until we dock." She looked away from her tablet and toward her little phone with disdain. Then, seemingly finished with her report, Rachel White folded her hands.

"So, there's no clear information on a possible poison. No way to tell if the man did this to himself, except for the lack of a suicide note, but no alarm that there's an airborne toxin on the ship," said Ezra. "The captain will be relieved about that last point, at least. Is there anything else you can tell us, Rachel?" He was almost pleading.

Rachel nodded. "It's probably completely irrelevant, but I can tell you that, at some point in his adult life, Tommy Trussler sustained a severe trauma to his left thigh. There are clear indications of a skin graft, taken from his right thigh, having been used to aid with the management of a trauma that resulted in the removal of a relatively large part of his *vastus lateralis*, the long muscle on the outside of the thigh of his left leg. I have no way of knowing how, or when, he was injured, but the skin graft suggests it was an external trauma rather than a disease. The area affected seems too large for any planned medical procedure I know of. It might have been any sort of an injury. The only other mark on him is from what I judge to be an appendectomy. I suspect it was performed within the past decade as it looks to me as though laparoscopic procedures have been used."

"Would he have been in pain because of his leg injury, doctor?" asked Bud.

"It's likely. For a man of fifty-four years of age, his muscle tone suggests to me that he exercised regularly, though not strenuously. That would have helped with the general pain, but he would have tired easily. Does anyone know what he did ashore? Ezra? I have his boarding file, which lists his emergency contact as someone who lives in the same complex as he did, just outside Honolulu, but doesn't share his name. I've put out the word, but can't seem to find anyone onboard who really knew the man."

Ezra shook his head. "I will take care of that aspect, Rachel. I understand that you are medically responsible for the well-being of everyone on this vessel, but I have expertise you don't—and the manpower. I am conducting a thorough inquiry about his known associates on the ship, and my department has connected with the authorities in Honolulu, who have agreed to send a patrol officer to the address of his stated emergency contact. Tommy Trussler was hired through our usual agency. They have also been contacted. Maybe I'll get something from them."

He pressed his hand against the table in front of him signifying to me his sense of frustration, and continued. "So, back to your areas of concern, doctor: We know he was poisoned, though we don't know with what, or when. We know he had an old injury, but we don't know what it was, when it was sustained, or even if it's relevant. We do not believe he died at his own hand. All we really know is that someone, somehow, got him to eat or drink a toxic substance at some point—most likely on the ship. All of us around this table know enough about poisons to realize that whatever killed him so violently today must have been administered at some time within the last forty-eight hours, while we've been at sea. That's it."

"I would say much closer to the time of death, because of the ferocity of the symptoms," said Rachel, "though that's merely an opinion."

"Opinions don't help; what we need are facts," said Ezra.

At Ezra's words, Rachel's expression hardened even more; I could tell her teeth were clenched, and her jaw muscles twitched.

"It's better than nothing," I said as helpfully as possible.

"But not much," she snapped, launching herself from her chair in anger. "I feel so useless!" *Ah, she's frustrated with herself, and the situation.*

Bud and Ezra once again raised themselves from their seats.

"Oh, sit down," wailed Rachel impatiently. She turned to me. "Why do men always do that?" she asked.

"I don't know. I would make the most of it if I were you. They never seem to do it for me," I replied.

It was as though a dam had burst. Rachel let out a long belly laugh, which escalated until she was all but crying. Her almost-manic laughter was infectious, and we couldn't help but join in. It was this sight—two senior officers and two guests laughing almost uncontrollably—that met Captain Andreas's eyes as he entered the room.

"I'm here to evaluate the progress of the investigation into a probable murder on my ship," he said sternly.

His expression made it abundantly clear our laughter wasn't what he'd expected—or condoned.

ICU

AFTER EZRA HAD BROUGHT THE captain up to speed, which took a matter of mere moments, the master of the ship informed us he would have to take his leave of us because many other duties were pressing. Ezra seemed to have convinced him that matters were being handled adequately, but the captain's micro-expressions told me he was still feeling the weight of a suspicious death on his shoulders. As he left, he muttered something about the Aloha Spirit being in pretty short supply.

I turned to Rachel, who seemed much more approachable after her outburst. "Is there any chance of Bud and me being able to take a look at the body?" I asked.

The doctor reverted to being on her guard. I suspected a territorial issue was about to raise its head, and it seemed that Bud also sensed a potential problem. "Cait's a well-respected victim profiler, doctor," he offered. "She's worked on many cases for the integrated homicide investigation unit I used to head up. If she could begin by familiarizing herself with the victim's body, then move on to his stateroom," he raised an eyebrow toward Ezra, "I think that would be most helpful."

Ezra responded first. "I think that would be a very good plan," he said. I noted he didn't tell Rachel to accede to my request. I wondered about these two; did they have a personal relationship? I got the impression that they were of equal rank, or maybe the doctor held a slightly higher one than our head of security. I told myself to check, when it was appropriate.

"Very well," said Rachel with some reluctance. "The body is still in our intensive care unit. Follow me."

We walked down a particularly long corridor that eventually opened on one side into some large rooms. As we walked, I noted a sign on one closed door that said X-RAY EQUIPMENT, a few private rooms with half-glass doors containing one traditional hospital bed each, another door with a DISPENSARY sign, and another with the word SLUICE beside it. Finally, Dr. White swiped her card at a double-width doorway, and we entered a large room containing two beds, arranged on either side of some substantial equipment. On one bed lay an array of clear plastic bags containing the personal effects of the dead man. I looked them over. His outer clothing, his underwear, what would likely have been the contents of his pockets—a few playing cards with ripped corners, a keycard, a nest of tissues, a stick of sunblock for lips—and a wristwatch.

On the other bed lay the figure of the late Mr. Tommy Trussler himself; his body had been covered with a sheet. Dr. White pulled back the covering—with real respect, I noted—and since I have an aversion to viewing dead, naked bodies, I steeled myself, making sure I was in a totally professional state of mind.

Rachel spoke as she gestured toward parts of the cadaver, showing us the lack of any medically relevant indications. She was right about the healed wound on the man's thigh; it was substantial.

I peered at the man's forehead, hands, feet, scars, and arms, which I noted were fleshy, flaccid. Eventually I thanked Rachel, and suggested we leave the chilly room. Even though almost everything in it was white, and lit with high wattage lights, it felt gloomy. *I need to see the sky.*

Making our way back toward the waiting room, which was the only entry point to the long corridor, I stopped outside the dispensary and asked, "Is this always locked?"

Rachel glanced at Ezra. "Every room in the medical facility is kept locked at all times. We use these to open the doors," she said, pointing to a swipe-card on a lariat around her neck. "Only six of us have these cards—myself, Bartholomew, my three other nurses, and my junior doctor. Though I dare say Ezra has something that would also allow him to enter any room on the ship."

"I have a master-override card," Ezra explained.

Rachel smiled. "Access, all areas," she said enigmatically. Ezra looked uncomfortable, and almost blushed.

I allowed their private exchange to pass. "And what about the drugs in here? How do you account for their use?"

"Most of the supplies on the ship are replaced when we turn-around," replied Rachel. "You know, when the guests leave, and we embark new guests for a new cruise. It's not the end of the world if a particular type of yogurt is used up during a cruise; other alternatives are available. But that's not the way it works for medical supplies. We cannot risk running out of anything. That means we have a strict record-keeping system, and we re-order supplies ahead of arriving at a port. We have a list of approved medical supply companies at each port, so Bartholomew arranges for deliveries to be made and safely secured here in the dispensary before he ever takes time off at any port. He's a reliable chap, thank goodness."

"Is Bartholomew the only person who can do that?" I asked.

"I do have a junior doctor reporting to me, but we're both reliant on Bartholomew for this one particular service. It means at least one of us can rotate off at each port, and get away from—" she waved an arm "—our glamorous surroundings. I am the senior doctor, so I usually attend to the needs of the passengers and officers. Under normal circumstances, the junior doctor deals with the crew, though we take it in turns to allow the other as much time off as possible when we're in port." Once again drawing her right forefinger and thumb down her face, pulling her lips as she did so—a signal that she was stressed and frustrated, I judged—she added, "My junior doctor has been confined to his quarters since the ship left Hilo. He's quite sick. Vomiting and so forth. I can't allow him to be anywhere near anyone until he's been clear of his symptoms for forty-eight hours, so it's just me until we reach Vancouver. The twenty minutes I had on the officers' deck this morning, after surgery hours, was the first break I've had for some time. And now this."

Rachel White sounded tired.

"Given the circumstances of Tommy Trussler's death, do you firmly believe that your junior doctor's symptoms are the normal result of a stomach upset or a virus?" I asked.

Rachel looked thoughtful. "I'd say yes. He presented with classic symptoms, and we've had a few other cases of guests being ill since we left Hilo. As I said, these bugs are usually brought onto the ship from some land-based source. The sick guests are also quarantined."

I shrugged. It was her world, not mine, and she was the one with the medical degree after all, as she'd been at pains to point out.

"Bartholomew is a great help," Rachel added, "but he's not a doctor, and a doctor must be available whenever needed, and must oversee and approve anything he does. Bartholomew usually attends all Star Code calls, but it's been just me on 'Doctor Call' since Hilo. It's been a busy time. We've had quite a few falls, bumps, and a good deal of seasickness since we headed away from the Islands. I'm dealing with a challenging number of cases of cabin cough too."

"Cabin cough?" asked Bud.

"A dry, hacking cough. It can become very painful," she replied in a matter-of-fact tone. "The crew members get it quite a lot, and some guests as well. The air conditioning in the interior cabins is largely to blame. Guests with balconies don't tend to suffer as much."

"Rachel will be relieved to reach your country," Ezra told us quietly. "It's the end of her contract, so, from there, she heads back to England for six weeks."

I tried to take the chance to find out something about her. "Where are you from, Rachel?"

The medic half-smiled. "Here and there. My father was a doctor for the Royal Navy, so my family moved about a good deal while I was growing up. I did my training in London, and then stayed on at my training hospital, St. Mary's, for a couple of years. Eventually I joined a practice in Islington as a G P. I hated it so I ran away to sea." Her smile dimmed even more. "It's not all it's cracked up to be. Though, to be fair, my dad did try to warn me."

"Will you come back after this break?" I asked.

A significant look flew between Ezra and Rachel. "I've signed up for another five months on this very ship." She didn't sound as though she was looking forward to it. "I have a couple of weeks to change my mind, if I want," she added with forced nonchalance.

"I have every faith that Rachel will return," said Ezra with a charged smile, "and we'll be lucky to have her. She is an excellent doctor, with just the right amount of experience needed to make the perfect ship's senior medical officer. She has earned her half-star, and no mistake."

"Half-star?" I asked.

"Ezra's referring to the fact that I was made up—promoted—half a star about a month ago. That makes me a three-and-a-half-star officer. Not bad."

"I'm guessing you have only three stars?" I said to Ezra.

He shrugged. "What can I say? It is the most stars allowed for my function on this ship. However good I might be at my job, they cannot give me more. But three stars are good too. Once they were even good enough for Rachel." His gaze rested upon her face for a couple of seconds longer than a professional glance would have allowed.

Encouraging us to continue our walk along the corridor, which led to the exit, Ezra added, "I suggest I take Bud and Cait to see the stateroom of the deceased, and allow you to make the arrangements to store the body. By the way, Cait, did you see anything that we should know about? On the victim's body, I mean."

By now, we were back in the waiting room, though this time the door to the outer corridor was closed, so I felt comfortable saying, "Thanks, Ezra. I do have one question for the doctor. There were some playing cards among Tommy's effects. Where did they come from?"

"He was clutching them when he died," replied Rachel. "It appears that his convulsions had forced his hand into a spasm that gripped the cards when he died. I had to rip them out of his fingers, because his muscles had remained rigid."

"Isn't that rather unusual?" asked Bud.

"It is, and it isn't," she said. "Cadaveric spasm, or instantaneous rigor mortis, can happen when a death occurs during an extreme physical episode. Your description of the man's convulsions would likely explain it, Cait. It doesn't always happen, and it certainly doesn't happen as often as those who create fiction would have us believe, but it seems to have happened here. I'm sure you all saw how his left hand and fingers were curled into a claw-like shape, and maybe you noted that the toes on his left foot were also curled. I would suggest these signs were the result of his manner of death."

"Thank you Rachel, that's all fascinating," I said.

"You're welcome," she said. "The human body is an amazing thing, don't you think?"

I nodded politely. "It certainly is, but that wasn't what I was thinking about."

No Guests Beyond This Door

AS EZRA LED US TOWARD Tommy Trussler's stateroom, I refused to answer any of Bud's questions about what I'd found so interesting. Luckily he knew my methods well enough to stop pushing for an answer.

We'd walked up one flight of stairs and entered the main foyer area, above which soared the four-storey atrium. The imposing, angular sculptures, the swathes of diaphanous draperies, the sweep of the stunningly under-lit marble staircase, and the elegantly simple classical music of the string quartet—four Russian girls in their twenties, all blond, and all very good—told me that life onboard was proceeding as usual. On the decks above us I imagined people ordering specialty coffees while comparing handmade leis, or else enjoying the thrill of the glittering casino while bedecked in silk shirts covered in colorful plumeria and hibiscus. Some would be wandering through the shopping arcade, while others would already be planning to head back to their rooms to prepare for the main seating of the final formal dinner of the cruise. I noted that the photography team was already setting up its equipment at the foot of the imposing central staircase—a popular choice for group photographs.

Bud and I were due to dine at eight thirty, and I'd brought a suitably posh, glittery midnight-blue dress for the occasion—a brave departure from my usual black. I wondered if I'd have the chance to wear it, or if Bud and I would be "otherwise engaged" for the entire night. I hoped not. I also hoped that the dress in question would still fit me after two weeks of overindulgence—it had been a little snug when I'd packed it. And now? I told myself off. *Priorities, Cait, there's a murder to solve!*

Leaving the hubbub of the guest relations area and the central lounge behind us, we padded forward along the deep carpeting of

Deck 3 toward a door clearly marked NO GUESTS BEYOND THIS DOOR—CREW ONLY. Ezra pushed the heavy door, and we entered yet another restricted area onboard the cruise ship.

Instead of wide, carpeted corridors with tastefully veneered doors on either side, we were now faced with a much narrower passage. Following Ezra as he wound along between a warren of rooms, I noticed that the linoleum covered the floor and came halfway up the walls, just as it had on Deck 2. Scuffed and dinged, these walls bore testament to having taken some heavy traffic. We seemed to be walking in a loop, and Ezra shook his head. "We should have come the other way," he said. "He was in 3519. It's a cabin reserved for guest entertainers, speakers, and so forth. It's a big step up from a crew cabin. There are three on each side of the ship. Nearly there."

As we rounded yet another corner, I spotted the security officer named Ocampo outside a room on the outside of the ship. She stood to attention as she caught sight of her boss, and knocked lightly on the door to the dead man's room.

Bartholomew Goodman stepped into the doorway to greet us. He was, rather surprisingly, wearing a surgical facemask and a paper over-garment, the type surgeons wear in the operating theater. The latex gloves I found more understandable.

He peeled off one glove, removed his face mask, and extended a hand toward Ezra, who took it, and shook it heartily. "Nothing in here anymore that could present a danger," announced Bartholomew. Beginning to pull off all his remaining protective gear, he added, "You can't be too careful when unknown substances are concerned." He rolled his eyes toward the cabins we'd just passed. "Lot of interest about this, sir. Cabin chatter's running amok. The crew will need some information soon, or they'll fill in the blanks themselves."

"I'm aware," said Ezra gravely. "When you say 'nothing,' what do you mean, exactly?"

Bartholomew drew closer to Ezra and spoke in low tones. Luckily, on this occasion, I caught every word. "Checked everywhere. Nothing out of the ordinary. Some painkillers, but I'd expect them, given his leg issues. I've bagged anything that could be poisoned, and I'll take it all with me." He held up three sealed plastic bags.

"May I?" I asked, leaning forward and reaching for the bags.

Bartholomew snatched them away from my grasp. He looked at Ezra for guidance. Ezra nodded, and I was handed the bags, one at a time. I checked the first two bags quickly, but gave more attention to the third. I rolled and flipped the bottles it contained. Three bottles of prescription medications in the dead man's name, all for pain management, each more potent than the other. A bottle of over-the-counter antihistamines, some laxatives, multivitamins designed for men over the age of fifty, an additional bottle of vitamin C capsules, and a box of statins.

"Thanks," I said, returning the final bag to the nurse.

"I don't think there's much more I can do here," said Bartholomew. "I've briefed all the members of your team who are guarding the people who were in the Games Room this morning to be vigilant, and to alert me if anyone feels unwell at all. But I would now like to be able to check the Games Room for any substances that shouldn't be there, as Dr. White asked. I suppose you have a person on duty there who can let me in, to make sure I don't do anything I shouldn't?"

"Indeed," Ezra said. "Officer Ocampo, I'd like you to accompany Nurse Goodman, and you will be in charge of the management of the scene. Understood?"

"Yessir," said the woman with the slick, black hair. I noticed she had intelligent eyes, and she seemed proud to be given such a responsibility.

I hated feeling as though I wanted to be in two places at once, then I realized I could be—well, as good as. "Could Bud go along too?" I asked.

"Will you stay here with me and begin to build your impressions of Tommy from his quarters, Cait?" asked Ezra.

"I will."

Bud looked a little taken aback, then said, "Of course I'll go, if it's okay with you, Ezra."

"It certainly is," said Ezra.

"It's been a while since I've worked a crime scene, but I reckon it's like riding a bike," continued Bud. He felt his pockets. "If Officer Ocampo is to take the official photographs, I'll use my phone's camera to take shots before we move anything, so you can see them right away, Cait. I dare say you'll be taking everything that needs to be removed from the scene to the medical facility, right?"

Ezra agreed. "It seems to be the best place to gather everything together."

Bud added, "I assume there's refrigeration there we can use for any perishables. We'll have to keep all the food from the buffet, if nothing else, for example."

Bartholomew looked at the small plastic bags in his hand. "We'll need bigger bags than these."

Officer Ocampo looked at Ezra with uncertainty. "I don't think we have big enough evidence bags for this job," she said.

"How about garbage bags, with ties we can seal and sign?" asked Bud.

"We've got medical waste bags. How about them? I don't know how many we've got, but I know some of them are pretty big. Why don't we go and grab some supplies from the medical center and the security office, then tackle the Games Room?" Bartholomew Goodman seemed to be a practical man.

Bud, Bartholomew, and Officer Ocampo left, allowing Ezra and myself to enter Tommy Trussler's stateroom alone. We both donned latex gloves, and, after allowing the door to close behind us, I stood for a moment and took in the scene.

The stateroom was not dissimilar to the one Bud and I had; it was about the same size, had a slightly different layout of essentially all the same elements, but was a little narrower, and had a round porthole where our balcony door would have been. To my immediate right was the door to what I knew would be the bathroom. Without moving, I pulled it open. It was tiny—a far cry from the one we had. Our bathroom was large, with a marble-tiled floor, a large shower capsule with semi-circular sliding doors, and two washbasins separated by a decent counter space. There was even a little privacy screen dividing the loo from the rest of the room. Tommy Trussler's bathroom was so small he could have taken a shower while sitting on the toilet and brushing his teeth at the miniscule sink, all at the same time.

Along the wall housing the bathroom was the closet area. One sliding door was open, revealing what, at first glance, seemed to be a paltry amount of clothing when compared with how much Bud and I had brought with us on the trip. As I'd expected, the bed was made up, there were fresh towels in the bathroom, and the room had been cleaned after Tommy had left it that morning.

"We'll need to talk to the attendant and his or her assistant to check on what was taken from the room during their cleaning this morning," I said to Ezra. "Is there some way you can find out what would have happened to any rubbish they removed?"

Ezra looked at his watch. "By now, anything taken from here would have been dealt with as a part of the general garbage sorting operation. I don't think we stand any chance of getting our hands on it, but I'll check. Let me make a call."

I thanked him as he punched a number into his phone and began to speak to someone in Greek. *Multilingual too.*

I walked to the farthest wall of the room and peered onto the windowsill above the head of the bed. I picked up a couple of paperback books and flicked through the pages. A receipt from the Sundowner Bar for a bottle of San Pellegrino water was being used as a bookmark. It was dated two days earlier. Turning it over, I could see a penciled list on the back:

I put it on the bed so I could pop it into one of Ezra's evidence bags. I replaced the books, which told me that the dead man had enjoyed reading a good thriller. I'd read them both, and applauded his taste.

One little shelf to the right side of the bed was bare; the one on the left held an old-fashioned fold-out traveling alarm clock, with the alarm set for 6:10 AM.

I picked up the pillows and pulled back the coverings. As I'd expected, nothing. I knelt on the floor and looked under the bed. A suitcase was wedged in there, so I wriggled it out of its storage place, plopped it onto the bed, and unzipped it. It had seen a lot of miles, but was completely empty. I pushed it back under the bed where it joined a lifejacket, stuffed against the outer wall. On the other side of the bed I spotted a rectangular aluminum case. I grappled with the bedcovers that dangled down, and finally pulled it out. Unclipping it, I found it contained a large collection of multicolored gambling chips, all neatly fitted into recesses—a few were missing—and some beakers and dice. *Odd.*

I turned to the sofa and coffee table. There was nothing at all on the coffee table. The cushions on the sofa were, I noted, the same as in our room, but, whereas the theme color in our quarters was blue, here it was green. Same pattern, same fabric, different hues. It was the same with the carpeting; some decks were blue, others green. I reasoned that the décor of such a ship had to be equally at home in the Pacific, the Caribbean, Australasian waters, or sitting beside an Alaskan glacier. Thus, the predominant theme throughout the ship, other than being sumptuous, was the one thing the ship was always close to—the sea. Wavy lines, foaming patterns, blues, greens, grays, sandy yellows, and even corals, all repeated throughout the vessel. It made for a pleasing atmosphere.

I dug my fingers into the recesses of the sofa, but, again, found nothing. Similarly, the desk had nothing upon it except the books and supplies provided by the ship. Tommy hadn't allowed anything personal to spill into the room at all. I pictured the mess in our room and told myself it was much more difficult for two people to remain contained in such a small space.

Ezra finished his phone call and announced, "Everything he might have disposed of is gone, as I suspected. Already sorted into recyclables and garbage. Garbage sorted and already crushed, or else mixed in with garbage from the rest of the ship, ready to be crushed."

"Well, thanks for trying," I said, smiling.

"Find out anything about him yet?" asked Ezra. His tone was hopeful.

"He's neat," I replied with a sigh. "Onto his closet space next," I added more cheerily.

I looked into the open part of the closet to begin with. Given how little he'd brought with him, it was easy to see why he'd chosen to place everything on a hanger, rather than folded on a shelf—he had the space to be able to do so. Shorts, work-out shorts, golf shirts, T-shirts, a couple of short-sleeved dressier shirts, a dark suit, and a white long-sleeved shirt. That was it. Five pairs of flip-flops were neatly lined up on the floor of the closet beside a worn pair of training shoes and one pair of black dress shoes.

"He liked his slippers," I said. "He lived in Hawai'i, so I expect that's what he called them, though I've always called them flip-flops."

"Slops," said Ezra. "That's what we called them when I was a boy. Though I know they have many names around the world. I've heard them called thongs, slides, *tsinelas*, and other names."

I took my chance. "Where did you grow up, Ezra? You have an interesting accent."

"Born in South Africa, moved to the States when I was seven. Pasadena. Nice place. My mother died when I was fourteen, so I went to live with her brother in Israel. Tel Aviv. Did my service there, then joined this company. In the last seven years, I've visited every continent, even Antarctica, on one of our ships. I guess that would explain my strange accent." He smiled, but his eyes hardened a little.

"Sounds like you've had an interesting life so far. Do you think you'll remain at sea for long?" I tried to sound as though I was having a chatty, fussy moment, because I've found that puts people at ease. It didn't work on Ezra Eisen.

"I have no plans to leave the company," was his guarded reply.

"I hope they treat you well," I said, almost, but not quite, gushing. "You seem to be experienced in matters pertaining to security." *Will he bite?*

"It is my profession, and, I believe, it is my nature," he said with finality. "What do Trussler's clothes tell you about the man, Cait?" *Well deflected.*

I decided to be as professional as he. "He was a man with few needs," I said. "His clothing isn't expensive, though the formal suit, which is old, was probably a fair price when he bought it. His clothing is well-used, but not worn out, so he took some pride in his appearance. His flip-flops suggest he wanted comfort rather than style, though the lack of support they offer is puzzling; he could have chosen footwear that might have offered more comfort for his problem leg. I noticed he had a bunion on his right foot, so maybe that explains his choices. That, and his life in Hawai'i. There is nothing unnecessary here. Maybe he was an efficient packer when he traveled, but I suspect his home would look similar to this. Is there a laundry that he could have used onboard? Or would he have used the same laundry service as the guests? His clothes all look clean and pressed, as though the only items he had worn are those in plastic bags in the mortuary. I suppose he could have hand-washed them in his little bathroom, but I know that no irons are allowed in staterooms. Is it different here in the crew area of the ship?"

"No, it is not," said Ezra, his voice sharp. "No irons, no naked flames allowed in cabins. Fire onboard a ship is one of our greatest dangers. He'd have had a choice for his laundry. There is a crew laundry area, below us, where crew members can look after their own clothing—and where there are pressing facilities—or he could have used the same system as the guests where you bag up your items for them to be taken away, washed or dry cleaned, pressed, and returned to your room, for a fee. He'd have received a discount on such services. I'll find out if he sent any items for cleaning this morning. Another phone call. Excuse me. I'll allow you to continue."

I nodded, and turned my attention to the bathroom.

Above the minute sink a mirrored cabinet protruded from the wall. I guessed this was where he'd stored his medications. Now it was empty. Bartholomew had even taken away the bottles of body wash and shampoo that had been housed in dispensers on the wall of the shower unit. I wouldn't learn much in there.

I moved back into the main room and opened the drawers in the cabinet beneath the flat-screen television, which, as in our quarters, was mounted on an arm on the wall. A couple of pairs of socks—both black—some underwear, two pairs of swimming shorts, and a baseball cap were in the top drawer. In the drawer below that, nothing, and in the deepest drawer at the bottom, two more hats—the floppy type that give good shade from the sun.

I pulled open the little fridge, which seemed to contain the same standard array of bottles and cans that ours did. There was nothing in there of a personal nature. *No more pots of poi?*

"Are you able to open the safe?" I asked Ezra, who'd now finished his phone calls. "If he's anything like Bud and me, he'd have stored his personal valuables in there. They could give me some useful insights."

"Yes, I can do that," he replied, bending to do so. "By the way, he sent off a pair of shorts, a T-shirt, and two Hawaiian-style shirts to be washed this morning. That's it. Nothing else in the system. There—" he pulled open the door to the little safe, which sat at waist-height, and I bent down to peer inside. I poked my hand in and realized it wasn't just dark in there; it was full. I pulled out my hand and took a proper look. I was surprised by what met my eyes. "Oh dear. I think you should take a look at this, Ezra, before I move anything. I think we should take some photographs too."

Ezra and I both knelt on the floor and stared into the safe. Like the one in the room I was temporarily calling home, it was about a foot wide and nine inches high. I suspected it went back about a foot as well, as did ours. Whereas we'd used our safe to secure our passports, the credit cards we didn't need onboard, our car and house keys, and cash, in Tommy Trussler's room the safe was full, and I mean *full*, of wallets.

"Oh no," said Ezra heavily. When he looked at me, he was clearly horrified. "That explains it."

"Explains what?" I asked apprehensively.

"I've had a lot of reports of guests losing wallets, cash, and credit cards while they've been ashore. More than is usual. I've got to be honest and say I put it down to the fact that times are tough; cruise ship guests always stick out like a sore thumb on the Islands, and I thought maybe they were simply being targeted by local gangs as we island-hopped. But this makes much more sense. The thieves weren't on each island—there was one thief, and he was traveling with us." He sat back on his haunches and shook his head. "It's a nightmare," he said quietly. "I should have known. Tommy Trussler was a pickpocket."

Ezra looked as though someone had smacked him in the face with a halibut. His upright bearing collapsed.

I felt compelled to try to comfort him. "Well, first of all, Ezra, I don't know how you *could* have known, if he wasn't spotted and reported. And that's rather beside the point, now. We'd better take all these items out of the safe, so you can identify their owners by their contents—where that's possible—and check that against reports made to you," I suggested. "First, let's get some photos."

I snapped away with my phone's camera, then we emptied the contents of Tommy Trussler's safe onto his bed. There were fifteen wallets, which all seemed to be full of credit cards and various other valuable items, like family photos. Some looked as though they might have belonged to women, some to men. Along with them was an impressively large roll of cash. There was also a little carrier bag with the logo of a jewelry store on Maui. It contained two pairs of diamond earrings and a receipt for three pairs. *Odd.*

Ezra whistled when he saw the earrings, each set fixed in a presentation box. "They're quite something," he said. "Look—excellent color, complex cut, seem to have great clarity, and I reckon they're about half a carat each earring." Ezra checked the receipt. "Whoever bought these got a good price. Not as good as they'd get in the Caribbean, of course, but not bad for Hawai'i."

I felt my multipurpose right eyebrow shoot up as I said, "Very interesting."

"Okay, I see why he'd hang onto these, and the cash. But why would he keep everything else in his safe like this?" said Ezra. "He could have just taken the cash, then dumped the rest of the stuff before he came back onboard. Heck of a lot easier than getting items back onto the ship." Ezra gave the matter some thought. "I guess if he went off the ship with no wallet of his own he could easily get back on and run a couple through the X-ray machine at a time without raising any queries. Folks often have a couple of places where they keep their valuables when they go ashore. My guys would be used to seeing someone carrying more than one wallet-type item. But what's the point of bringing it all back to the ship anyway?" He seemed dumbfounded.

"Yes, it's curious," I observed. "Maybe it wasn't about the money. Maybe he wanted to study the contents of the items he stole, and to do that in the privacy of his stateroom, in his own time."

Ezra's tone was almost dismissive as he replied, "But why?"

"That's an interesting question, Ezra. And it means that Mr. Tommy Trussler, however much his personal possessions suggest otherwise, was clearly a fascinating man. I tell you what, I'll leave you to check through these, but if you could find his wallet among all the others, would you keep that separate so I can look through it later?"

Ezra sighed heavily. "Sure. But where are you going?"

"I want to see what Bud has discovered in the Games Room, if anything."

Deck 5, Amidships

I LEFT EZRA TO TAKE photographs of each of the items that now adorned the late Tommy Trussler's bed, and set about matching them to the descriptions he'd received from the guests of items they'd lost. Heading toward the Games Room two decks up, I decided to take the scenic route, and grab some much-needed fresh air along the way. Not having the patience to wait for the elevator, I climbed the two flights of stairs and pushed open the heavy door that allowed access onto the open deck. I wandered along the line of wooden steamer chairs, which were usually occupied by those seeking shade and some peace and quiet.

Looking up at one of the ship's clocks, I was surprised to discover that it was only 1:11 PM. Tommy Trussler had been dead for less than two hours, and I already knew a little about the man, but I wanted to discover more. Clearly his proclivity for relieving folks of their cash and credit cards meant that any number of people might have a reason to want him dead, but only if they knew he'd stolen from them. But why would anyone kill him when they could simply tell a security guard of their suspicions, or knowledge, in order to become reunited with their stolen items?

"You alright there?" An elderly gentleman in a panama hat and a Hawaiian shirt so vivid that it made me wish I was wearing sunglasses peered up at me from his deck chair. *Have I been muttering aloud?*

"Yes, fine thanks," I said in a curt tone, and went on my way. The breeze was invigorating, the warmth of the sun tempting, but I needed to get back to business. I hoped that Bud would have lots of information for me, and that I could get a good look at the crime scene for the first time without dozens of people in the way.

Stepping back into the air-conditioned interior of the ship, I oriented myself. I was in the posh bit of the shopping area where all the designer labels were proudly displayed. The aromas of expensive perfumes jostled with each other for dominance in the cosmetics area, and I almost gagged as I rushed away.

Moments later, one of Ezra's security guards opened the door to the Games Room for me. Officer Ocampo stood looking down at Bud and Bartholomew, who were both on their hands and knees, their noses close to the carpet near the card table at which Bud and Tommy had been seated. The table had been moved aside, presumably to allow them to act like bloodhounds with space to spare.

"Manage to sniff out any clues?" I asked in a cavalier fashion.

Bud knelt up like a meerkat and said snappily, "Ha, Ha. I just might have. Come and smell this, Wife. But put on some gloves first."

I shot him a withering look as I took a pair of surgical gloves from Officer Ocampo and wrestled them on. "Okay, if I must."

"Yes, you should," said Bartholomew, looking uncomfortable in his keeling pose. "Bud thinks it's—"

"No! Don't tell her what I think it is," interrupted Bud. "Let's see what Cait thinks."

I knelt down and sniffed the area they indicated. "Okay," I said noncommittally.

"Now smell over there a bit," said Bud, waving to another part of the carpet which was, I assumed, not contaminated with whatever they thought they could smell in the first area.

I hauled myself up and sniffed. "Quite different," I said.

"So?" said Bartholomew, his eyes wide with anticipation.

I got up and brushed down my knees. I waved toward the spot I'd just smelled. "I'm guessing that this is the 'control' area?"

"It is," said Bud.

"And all the rest of the carpet smells the same?"

"It does," said Bartholomew.

"But the first area I examined, close to where Tommy died, is the only area that smells different?"

"Yes," answered Bud.

"Well, the critical area smells of coffee grounds. Not coffee, but coffee grounds. There are even some in the fibers of the carpet. They're clearly visible. Why is that important? Couldn't someone have simply spilled their coffee there?"

Bud shook his head. "Tommy and I were the first to enter here this morning. He had the guy come along to unlock the room for us. Officer Ocampo, Grace," Bud nodded at the woman, who grinned toothily back, "told us that if anything had been spilled on the carpet yesterday, even late last night, the overnight cleaning crew would have got rid of it. Each room is inspected by one of the housekeeping managers at the end of the night shift, around six in the morning, and the room was then locked until Tommy and I entered it. I even saw them deliver all the supplies for the buffet, and I can tell you that nothing at all was spilled. No coffee, no coffee grounds, nothing."

"Okay," was what I said; *odd* was what I thought. "Why would Tommy purposely drop coffee grounds onto the floor where he was sitting?" I said.

"Smugglers use coffee grounds in drug shipments to try to confuse the sniffer dogs," said Bud.

"But there aren't any sniffer dogs on the ship," I replied as patiently as I could. My mind was racing. "What can coffee grounds be used for? Other than for making coffee, of course."

"My mum mixes them in with the potting soil on her balcony," said Bartholomew.

I nodded. "They add acidity to the soil, as well as a good color, and help repel slugs," I said. Bud looked surprised. "You'll be glad I know all this stuff when we begin to work on our five acres at the new house," I added.

"I dare say I will be," said Bud with uncertainty in every syllable, rising to his feet. "But that's for when we get home. Not for now. I, for one, have no bright ideas, other than the grounds being used by drug traffickers. But why are they here? It's a mystery."

"To add to all the rest of them," I pondered. "Anything else? Other than the white powder on the carpet, of course."

Both men were now fully upright, and looking a lot less like naughty puppies. "White powder?" Bud replied. "What white powder? Where? What have we missed?"

"Stand here and look across all the carpeting in the room. Can you make out anything odd?"

"It's tough to tell," said Bud. "The wavy pattern makes it difficult to spot anything other than the waves and the colors. What do you mean?"

I moved toward the area where Tommy Trussler's little desk stood. Without getting too close, I bent down and brushed my hand across a part of the floor covering. A little spray of glistening white granules sprang up.

"Careful!" called Bartholomew. "That could be toxic."

"Yes, you shouldn't do that," agreed Grace Ocampo.

"It looks like salt," I said.

"A lot of things do," said Bartholomew in a worried voice. "Many dangerous things can look like salt. Out of the way. Alright with you if I take a sample, Grace?"

The security guard grunted her agreement, and I stood back and allowed Bartholomew to do his work. Bud peered at me, looking worried.

"You shouldn't have done that, Cait," he scolded.

"Excuse me, you were the one telling me to join you on my hands and knees to sniff the carpet," I replied quietly.

Bud looked deflated. "Maybe that wasn't the wisest thing to do, under the circumstances," he admitted.

"You don't say," was, I felt, my best possible reply.

Finally happy with the amount of the white powder he'd managed to get out of the carpet with some sticking tape, Bartholomew joined us again, all four of us standing in a row close to the door. "At least we can test this to see if it's anything illegal," he said, lifting the little baggy in his hand. "You both feeling quite well?"

Bud and I nodded.

"So, Cait," said Bud, "since we all seem to have survived the white powder, show me again, from here, where you can see it on the carpet, because I'm having trouble."

I indicated what I believed to be swathes of the stuff, almost all around the room. Bud finally said, "Yeah," when he spotted it.

"I see it," said Grace.

"Very strange," said Bartholomew.

"That it is," I said. "So, other than missing that, how did you get on?"

Bud answered, "We supervised the bagging of all the foodstuffs, all the equipment, crockery, and so on. Most of it's already been taken to the medical facility for refrigerated storage. Both Grace and I took photographs before anything was moved. You and I can look at them later on my laptop, Cait. Maybe that powder will be more obvious on a screen image. Everything the victim definitely used, or could have touched, has been bagged separately; this final bag," Bud cast a glance at a plastic sack beside the door, "contains everything that was on his desk, and the table where he and I were playing gin rummy. I know I don't have your memory for details, Cait so I've listed everything in this bag, here." He held out a list, written in pencil on one of the little pads that had been dotted on each of the card tables.

Turning to the nurse, Bud said, "Bartholomew's been a great help, Cait. Highly professional. I know he's keen to liaise with Dr. White, and I also know that we need to have a few moments together, alone. Why don't we let him get back to the medical facility?"

"Good idea," I replied. "Feel free to take this last bag with you—and could you ask Rachel to try to establish if the dead man's hands had recently been in contact with coffee grounds, please? And could you check if he had any in his possession? You know, in the corners of his pockets, for example. Thanks."

"Sure t'ing," said Bartholomew, reverting to his natural accent. He looked bemused, but happy enough to be taking his leave of us. "You comin' wit' me, Grace?"

"I am," she said. "You'll get the guard to lock up when you leave, right, Mr. Anderson?" she added as they departed, in such a way that the guard knew what was expected of him.

"Will do," said Bud, waving. As the door closed, he turned to me and said, "Cait, what were you thinking, bending down and touching that white powder without knowing what it was? You're not the most cautious of people, are you?"

"You married me," I replied coyly. "You should know."

Bud sighed and returned my smile. "You're right; I did, and I do. But enough about us. What have you discovered? Anything more telling than a hint of coffee grounds and a mystery white powder in the carpet?"

"You have no idea," I replied. I told him about the discoveries Ezra and I had made in the dead man's stateroom.

"Whoa, that opens up a large can of worms."

"Yes, Bud, but pickpocketing is hardly a good reason for murder. Not that anything really should be, but you know what I mean."

Bud mused for a moment. "The sad truth is, Cait, both you and I have witnessed circumstances where murder has been committed for what any right-minded person would consider absolutely no reason at all. I don't mean a violent outburst over a five-dollar bill, or a bar brawl because of a spilt drink that gets out of hand—oh!" Bud paused, and grabbed my hand. "Sorry, Cait, I didn't mean to remind you of how Angus died."

I patted Bud's hand, "It's okay, Husband. Don't worry. I've got a dead ex-boyfriend in my past, and you have a dead wife in yours. We cannot go tiptoeing through life, especially *our* lives, without something coming up to remind us about them, and how they died. So we have to each deal with it in our own ways, and keep moving on."

Bud nodded and rubbed my back.

"But you see," I continued, "my point isn't that a pickpocket might not steal something valuable enough to make someone want to kill them to get it back, however insignificant it might seem. What I mean is that, because pickpocketing is an illegal activity, there are options other than murder available to the person who's been robbed."

"Unless they don't want anyone to *know* they were originally in possession of whatever the pickpocket stole from them," said Bud.

"Yes, the theft of something compromising might mean the target wouldn't report it to the authorities. But I saw what was in his safe— well, not properly, of course—and it seemed to just be wallets, cash, and so forth. Nothing else, except a bit of jewelry."

"Besides," mused Bud, following a slightly different train of thought, "there are much easier ways to kill someone, especially on a cruise ship. Just push him over the side in the dead of night, for example. None of this messing about with poisons."

I probably shouldn't have said it aloud, but I did. "But pushing someone over the side of the ship would take strength. Poison doesn't. It just takes knowledge, cunning, nerves of steel, and maybe patience."

"So a woman?" said Bud, without missing a beat.

I sighed. "I'm not going to chastise you for making a sexist remark, because we both know that statistics tell us that women are more likely, when they kill, to use methods that allow for a 'peaceful' rather than 'violent' death. We have to consider that Tommy wasn't a large man—maybe his old leg injury meant he would have been a relatively easy target for tipping over a railing, since his balance wouldn't have been good. So, no, not necessarily a woman. But a person with a knowledge of poisons, and an ability to get their hands on something deadly on the ship, someone possibly averse to using overtly violent methods to kill. That suggests to me someone who is comfortable with, and knowledgeable about, poisons."

"Bartholomew?" Bud blurted out the man's name. "It couldn't be him. He wasn't even here until Tommy was dead."

"True," I replied. "Without knowing what sort of poison was used, and how long it takes to act, how can we be sure when the poison was ingested? And, without testing all the foodstuffs that were in here, we can't even be certain how it was administered—though my money is on the poi."

Bud brightened. "You'll be delighted to know that there was no pot containing poi in this room, by the way. You were right, and now we can encourage Ezra to take our theory seriously."

I felt my shoulders relax. "Good. That makes a huge difference. Now I'm ready to push forward down that path—someone in this room must have been involved in Tommy's death, and they must have known the poison was in the poi. Now the question is, who could have removed the pot without being observed?"

"Yep, you're right," said Bud.

Rather than worrying about that for a moment, I added, "We need to convince Ezra to let us sit in with him as he interviews everyone who was in this room when Tommy died, because they should be our focus."

"He was quite clear that he didn't want us to do that, Cait," replied Bud, "and I can understand why. When I allowed you to observe me interrogating suspects back in Vancouver, I was able to do so in controlled surroundings where the suspect was unaware of your presence. I cannot imagine there is any way Ezra would allow us to be a part of his questioning process. Besides, if we let him get on with the interviews, you'd be free to do your recollection thing again—you can concentrate on whether anyone picked up the pot—"

I interrupted. "I don't have to concentrate on that. I've recollected this morning's events, and I *know* I didn't see anyone pick it up—I know it was there, and then it wasn't. I am also quite certain that it would have been almost impossible for anyone to take it from the room without being spotted by everyone."

"What do you mean?"

"The pot was about six inches tall, and a few inches in diameter. It wouldn't have fitted into a pocket, and none of the women had a purse large enough to accommodate it."

Bud scratched his head. "So you're saying it was definitely taken, but that no one could have taken it?"

I nodded. "Hmm. Yes. Not an easy one to work out, is it?"

"Right, well, let's not dwell on that problem for now," said Bud. He looked deflated. "Let me call Ezra; we can find out what his plans are, and if he's got any more information—about anything." He pulled Ezra's card from his pocket.

"I wonder how Action Man's interrogation skills are," I said as Bud crossed the room.

"'Action Man?'"

"Ezra. What do you reckon? Mossad?"

"Possibly," mused the man with full CSIS clearance who had headed up an international anti-gang task force, and had a history of undertaking covert operations. "I don't have any way of checking while I'm on this ship, and I cannot see Ezra and me sitting down any time soon to compare dark-ops stories."

"You'd have some to compare?" I teased.

"You know I can't tell you that, Wife, because then I'd have to kill you. And, even though our belated honeymoon isn't going quite as we'd hoped, I am looking forward to a post-honeymoon life together."

Bud shot me a wicked grin, picked up the house telephone, and punched numbers into it. *I love you*, I mouthed silently, and listened while he spoke briefly.

Replacing the handset, he said, "Ezra is on his way here. He wants to talk to us first, then he's off to see the Croppers. But we are absolutely *not* invited."

We didn't have to wait long for Ezra. He entered the Games Room bearing a plastic bag containing a wallet, and was holding two pairs of surgical gloves.

"Here you are," he said, holding out the gloves for Bud and me to put on, before handing me the bagged wallet. "This is Tommy Trussler's own wallet. I've checked it; there's nothing unusual in there, but you said you wanted to inspect it. I realize that's a good idea if you're trying to build up a picture of the guy. You might also want these," he added, pulling some papers from under his arm. "The dead man's file from the cruise director's office, and his embarkation and registration paperwork. Now you'll have to excuse me. I'm off to interview the Croppers. They've cruised with the Stellar line on more than forty previous occasions, and often stay in the ship's most exclusive and expensive suite. Of course, all guests are treated equally well on this ship, though some are—" he paused and shrugged, allowing us to infer the rest of the Orwellian reference, which both Bud and I did.

"Just before you go, Ezra—a couple of things," I said. "First, we can now confirm that the pot that both Bud and I saw Tommy using, and in which he appeared to have his own supply of poi, was not found among the items here in the Games Room. Someone must have removed it, and that backs up our theory that someone here this morning knew the poi was poisoned."

Ezra was silent for a moment. "That's significant," he said. Bud and I agreed.

"Also," I continued, "how many of the items we found in Tommy's room were stolen from guests on this ship? And were any of them stolen from the people who were in this room this morning?"

Ezra consulted a notepad he pulled from his breast pocket. "I have a total of ten items that match descriptions of items lost by—or as we now know, *stolen from*—guests on this ship. I have no idea if the other items belong to guests on other ships, or people Tommy Trussler targeted who were visiting, or lived on, the Islands. I can tell you that every single time something went missing from one of our guests, the incident happened ashore, but that's to be expected. Guests don't usually, nor do they need to, carry their wallets and credit cards with them on the ship. It's why we use the charge-card/key-card system. It's simple, it's cash free, and much more secure. The fewer occasions that cash is around, the better. No one who was in this room this morning had reported anything missing, and I didn't find any items that I could directly link to any of them. Now, I really must go." He looked at his watch. "I hope to be finished in one hour, so would you telephone me then, and we can make arrangements?" He dashed off, leaving us standing in the middle of the Games Room.

"Nothing belonging to anyone who was here? So that's one possible motive gone." I must have sounded low because Bud gave me a hug, lifting my spirits right away.

"Okay, let's have a look at what a pickpocket keeps in their own wallet," I said, pulling on yet another pair of protective gloves before peeling open the plastic bag Ezra had given me. It was a disappointment. Tommy Trussler's wallet contained a fifty-dollar bill, his drivers' license, one solitary credit card, and nothing else. The paperwork from the cruise director's office was also uninformative. It gave contact details for Tommy ashore, an emergency contact, and the name of the agency in Miami that had hired him.

I stuffed everything back where it belonged, then grumpily shoved it into my bag.

Bud, using his most encouraging tone, said, "Tell you what—why don't we get outside, find a quiet spot, and give some more thought to our interactions with the folks who were here this morning. It's a good use of time, right?"

"You're right, and I could do with feeling the wind on my face. Sundowner Bar?"

It wasn't long before Bud and I were sitting in a sunny, windy spot on the top deck, each with a cold drink in hand, and taking the time to give some more thought to how our paths had crossed with the others who'd shared that morning's tragic scene.

'A'ole Pilikia

THAT FIRST NIGHT IN HAWAI'I, Bud and I had slept with the window open, wanting to hear the surf on the beach outside our hotel window. It was an incredibly soothing sound, and we both slept deeply. When I awoke, I did so with a start, but I couldn't work out what had disturbed me. Sitting up, still swathed in bedding, I peered out toward the glittering sea; it was obvious that the "noise" was the joyous sound of people for whom an early morning romp in the waves was the normal start to their day. *Good for them.* I snuggled back under the bedclothes and allowed my body to wake up slowly.

If we hadn't needed to get cleaned up, repack, have breakfast, and checkout by eleven o'clock, I think Bud and I could have slept in until noon. As it was, we were installing ourselves in a cab to be whisked away to the Aloha Tower Pier, and our waiting cruise ship, by a little after half past eleven.

Neither Bud nor I had cruised before, so we had no idea what to expect when we arrived at the ship. I was in awe. I've seen cruise ships—albeit from a distance—docked at Canada Place in Vancouver, but to stand right next to one for the first time is quite something. It's like peering up at an apartment building that's twenty floors high, clad in white metal, and studded with hundreds of glassed-in balconies that reflect every ray of the sun. It's huge, dazzling, a little overwhelming, and very inviting.

Our bags were taken from us on the dockside by impressively large men in vibrant shirts who lifted my mammoth suitcase with an ease borne of great experience. Bud and I strolled into the cavernous embarkation area following the arrows on signs, and were waved ahead by welcoming staff members. Massive reproductions of Hawaiian travel posters from the middle of the twentieth century, as well as representations of some of the most photogenic flora, fauna, and locales in the Islands, bedecked the walls. The only hold-up was a short line in front of the security scanning machines. Bud and I emptied our pockets and stuffed things into carry-on bags as we moved closer to the inevitable conveyer belt. A good-looking couple stood behind us, and chatter about security screenings ensued.

My first impression of Kai Pukui and his wife, Malia, as they introduced themselves to us, was that they were a couple with a special bond; they seemed to carry a stillness within them. Each was physically beautiful—evenly bronzed skin gleamed, perfect white teeth shone, dark eyes smiled, graceful gestures made every movement balletic. They seemed to be at peace with themselves and the world. My only less-than-positive reaction reflected more on me than them; Malia was shorter than me by a head, about half my girth, and looked entirely comfortable within her skin. I, on the other hand, was already sweaty, my orange linen shirt looked as though I'd slept in it, and the gray in my hair was a stark contrast to her lustrous, long dark locks. I'd felt rather good about my crisp, white linen pants and vivid overshirt when we'd left the hotel, but now I felt like a rumpled mess. I wanted to hide behind my sunglasses, but I'd already relinquished them to the voracious X-ray machine. Bud grasped my hand and squeezed it tight just before he walked through the security arch—almost as though he knew how insecure I felt in that moment. The Pukuis didn't notice my momentary lapse of self-confidence, and they spoke slowly and happily about the joys of honeymooning on the Hawaiian Islands.

By the time we'd all moved to the next line to check in and get our ship pass-cards, I'd gathered that the Pukuis were retained by the Stellar Cruise Line to act as our onboard Hawaiian cultural ambassadors, and would be offering a wide range of culturally appropriate activities and talks as our cruise progressed from one island to the next. They kindly gave us some helpful tips, suggesting we head for the Sundowner Bar as soon as we embarked, because we'd get the best view of both sea and land from there while we waited for our rooms to be opened. They also cleared up the question I had about when our luggage would be likely to arrive at our room; I'd purposely worn something that I had thought would serve me well for a full afternoon and evening ashore before returning to the ship to sleep for the night. Now that I was beginning to wonder if that was the case. The Pukuis were able to tell me that our luggage would likely arrive at our stateroom by five o'clock at the latest, and that, once we had our pass-card, we'd be able to embark and disembark as we wished. They did point out, however, that because the ship was to be docked for this one night, guests might be checking in at all times of the day, right up until midnight.

I was grateful to gather such useful information from experienced cruisers. I'd read up on the Cruise Critic website before we'd left home, but it never hurts to get information from someone standing right in front of you, with specific knowledge about that ship, sailing a specific route at a certain time. I thanked them in their own language, my "Mahalo," receiving smiles and bowed heads.

"'A'ole pilikia," said Kai. "That's 'you're welcome.'" He paused, then added, "I don't know anyone Welsh, nor anything about the Welsh language. How do you say 'Thank you' in your language?"

"Diolch yn fawr," I replied. We all giggled as the Pukuis tried to make the guttural sound required to pronounce the words, and our conversation shifted to how the Hawaiian culture was managing to thrive anew on the Islands, in much the same way that the Welsh culture was seeing a rebirth in Wales. The Pukuis demonstrated a deep-seated and warm connection with their native cultural history. With a little hug of gratitude from me—please don't snap in two when I embrace you!—for Malia, and a hearty handshake for Bud and Kai, we went on our separate ways to complete the embarkation process.

"Delightful couple, and so helpful," said Bud as we mugged for the photographer who was offering to capture our excited arrival. We were now at the final exit from the harbormaster's realm and were about to take our first step on the ship, where the captain reigned supreme.

"I hope they got a good shot of us," I added, as we climbed the not insignificant rake of the embarkation ramp.

Bud looked surprised, with good cause. "You usually hate having your photo taken," he said.

"This is the thinnest I'm going to be for about the next month," I replied ruefully. "Me, fifteen restaurants, twelve bars, and no bills to pay for any of it for eleven days? I suspect I might pack on a few extra pounds. Then there'll be the battle to lose it all, of course. Yep—I am now the thinnest I'm going to be for some time."

"Hey, Cait, if you want it, have it. And if you're having it, enjoy it. And if you're enjoying it, don't worry about what will happen when we get home. I love you as you are now, as you have been, and as you will be. I love the you that's inside that body." He blushed a little, "Which is not to say I don't love the body you're in too." It was my turn to blush. "But please, don't make every mouthful a trial."

I relaxed, and Bud did too. "I promise that when they deliver a side of guilt with every dish, I'll thank them to take it away with them," I said, grinning.

"Mahalo, Wife," said Bud, picking up his bag.

"And mahalo to you too, Husband. I know I'll overindulge, but I'll do it *and* enjoy it."

"And we can buy shares in the Greek yogurt business when we get back home, okay?" called Bud over his shoulder, almost at the top of the ramp.

"The yogurt can be on you," I replied, which seemed to amuse the short Filipino woman who took my sea-pass from me. She swiped it through the large machine, which made a "bonging" sound as I stepped aboard.

"Champagne?" asked a gloved server in a burgundy jacket.

"Thank you. Of course, I only ever drink it if there's a 'y' in the day," I quipped as I took the glass.

Star Signature Salon Suite, Deck 12

THAT MOMENT OF EMBARKATION SEEMED like a long time ago, as I reminisced about our first encounter with the Pukuis while sitting at the Sundowner Bar. Our time aboard had been joyful—up to the point when Tommy Trussler dropped dead, of course. But I felt a bit guilty that we weren't doing more about his death. Saying as much to Bud, he nodded, finished the last gulp of his beer, and said, "How about we make our way down to the guest relations area on Deck 3, then call Ezra from there and find out how he's doing?"

I agreed, and we strolled, in as carefree a manner as possible, toward the elevator pods. As the doors opened, they revealed Derek Cropper, who reacted to us as though we were catnip, and he a cat. He didn't get out of the elevator; instead he remained with us and rode down. It was clear that he was keen to talk, but the presence of another couple prevented him from doing so. When they got out on Deck 5, he almost exploded with excitement.

"Have you seen the security guy yet? Ezra. Nice guy. Bit scary, I reckon. He just left us. Hey—come on," he punched the button for Deck 12 before Bud and I could get out on Deck 3, "Come and have a quick drink with me and my honey. She'd love to see you."

As soon as he invited us to join him and Laurie for a drink in their suite, I agreed. Bud tried to stop me, but I dragged him out onto the Cropper's floor. Derek led the way while Bud hissed, "Ezra will not like this."

"Tough. I know we've run into them a couple of times, but I want to know more about the Croppers," was all I managed before I had to return my attention to our "host."

Deck 12 was laid out in much the same way as our own deck, except there was a beautifully etched glass wall around the midship point. Derek used his security card to open a sliding door. It swooshed back, sounding almost like something you'd hear on Star Trek. Beyond it was another part of the ship that Bud and I would never have seen without the need for this inquiry; the Salon Suites area. Even thicker carpeting, more elaborately flamed veneers, and double-width doorways were arranged along this short, sumptuous corridor. The space between the doorways signified the size of the suites. Big. There were two sets of doors to the left, and two to the right, with just one ahead of us, which Derek opened with his card.

Walking through that door was like entering a different world. The stateroom that Bud and I had called home for the better part of two weeks was very pleasant. It had everything we wanted and more, and was delightfully appointed. But this suite was something else. The first thing that struck me was the view. From my position at the doorway, I looked straight ahead at a glass wall, with sliders, that gave a view of the ocean at the rear of the ship. Our wake foamed in the distance, and everything was sea, sky, and openness. Between the sliders and the sea was an expansive deck, set with lounge chairs, and a table that seated eight. The room in which we were standing was clearly a sitting room, with two sofas and four elegant chairs, but it also had another dining table that seated eight, and there was a grand piano in the corner. *Who needs a grand piano in their room on a cruise ship?* I realized my mouth was open, and shut it.

I felt like a complete twit until Bud whispered, "Who needs their very own grand piano on a boat?"

I grinned, though I couldn't help but hiss back, "It's a ship—if you can put a boat on it, it's a ship. If you can't, it's a boat."

Derek was the perfect host, encouraging us to enter, but I dared take no more than a few steps across the thick pile of the carpet. Like everything else in the room it was a symphony of blues, greens, grays, and creams. Modern, elegant, not quite minimalist, but airy and spacious, the room was delightful. As Bud and I hovered, a man emerged from a door to our right. We both turned, startled.

"Is there anything I can do to be of service?" The small, neat man wore a navy suit, a brilliant white dress shirt, a bow tie, and shiny black shoes. He looked to be about thirty. His badge told me his name was Michael and that he was from Goa. He had good, white teeth; I suspected he had to smile a great deal in his job as a butler, which was another piece of information on his badge.

"Thank you, Michael. Yes—let's have some drinks on the deck. And some nibbles too. Hors d'oeuvres, please." Turning to Bud and me, Derek asked, "And how about some sangria?"

"That sounds lovely," I said.

Bud shrugged and said, "And maybe something soft?"

"There you go, then. Thanks, Michael," concluded Derek.

"Momentarily, sir," said the smiling butler as he disappeared through the door from whence he had emerged.

"Just give me a moment to check that Laurie is receiving," said Derek, striding across the acres of carpet toward the deck. "Make yourselves at home," he added airily. *I couldn't have imagined anything less like home if I'd tried.*

One particularly imposing piece in the room was a glass-topped coffee table, standing between two sofas, the base of which was a pair of breaching dolphins, frolicking in the foam, which was silver-tipped marble. A couple of $100 poker chips, yellow with a red border, lay forlornly on the edge of the table beside a pack of well-worn playing cards.

Derek reappeared at the slider. "Why not come out and join us here?"

Bud and I complied, and headed for the deck.

Once in the open air, it was clear that what we'd been able to see from the sitting room was just half the deck. The rest of it swept away to the left, and housed a large hot tub, out of which Laurie Cropper had just emerged. Swathed in a long, luxurious white velour robe, she smiled and waved.

"I'll just dry off, and be right there," she said, then disappeared into another set of sliders, which I assumed led to the bedroom and, more likely than not, the bathroom.

Derek waved at the loungers, inviting us to relax, but I knew I'd feel more comfortable at the dining table, as did Bud, who pulled out a chair for me. Luckily we were shaded from the sun by a white canvas awning, which wriggled in its stainless steel housings in the stiff sea breeze. I scrabbled around in the overstuffed shoulder bag I was carrying, trying to find my sunglasses.

"Been one heck of a day," smiled Derek, settling himself at the table, his back to the fabulous view. "Has that security guy been to see y'all yet?"

"He just released us from our room," I lied.

"I guess he must'a come to you when he left here. All a load o'hooey, if you ask me. Course, I'm sorry that poor Tommy's gone but, you know, it's gonna be everyone's turn one day, and this ain't a bad place to be when it happens, I reckon. He went quick at least, lucky guy."

Derek's comment struck me as rather heartless, but I decided to take my chance. "Did you and Laurie know Tommy Trussler well?" I asked. Bud glared at me.

"Nope, like I told the guy earlier, hardly knew him, really."

That seemed to be that, so I thought I'd try a different approach. "Did you enjoy the Islands, Derek? Is that why you came—to see them? Or is the ship the destination for you and Laurie?"

"The ship's as good as ever. First time to Hawai'i. We enjoyed the Islands. I think my favorite was Maui, but the wife seemed to prefer O'ahu, especially Honolulu. They're well set up, aren't they? All the right stores, great beaches, some excellent hotels, and I have to say that I enjoyed the cleanliness of the place. I guess that's the rain. Stops everything looking dusty. And I might not be a great gardener, but I sure did enjoy the plants they have everywhere. Great colors, even just the leaves. And the flowers? Laurie liked the hibiscus and enjoyed wearing a plumeria flower in her hair every day. It suited her. Ah yes, I could take to the Island Life, as they call it." He waggled his thumb and little finger in the sign seen across the Islands, "Hang loose," he grinned, "though, again, sorry for abandoning you guys that night at the Royal Hawaiian."

"No need at all," said Bud. "The ground's been covered, as Laurie explained when we ran into you the first formal night."

The first time we met, you were both plastered, was what I thought, quickly followed by, *but what of it?* "Derek, it's totally understandable; the travel, the time change, and probably a bit of dehydration—it's going to make a person feel quite out of sorts," was what came out of my mouth, though Bud's expression led me to suspect he was doing a bit of mind reading.

Laurie Cropper made her entrance to the deck from her boudoir. Her neat, slim figure was now encased in a fitted crimson top and white pedal pushers, and she wore crimson kitten heel mules. Her expensively highlighted hair was still damp and she peered over her giant sunglasses, which covered most of her small face, at a manicure I suspected wasn't up to standard.

"How wonderful to see you folks again!" she gushed in a genuine, if overly friendly, manner. "Derek—did you tell Michael we have guests?"

"I sure did!"

"Good. Just time for a little drinkie-poo before I head off to the spa. I don't know what time it is, but I have to be there for five o'clock. It's formal tonight and we're dining at the captain's table. He's so dashing, so I want to look my best." She grinned at her husband, who smirked back at her. They seemed to be a genuinely affectionate couple.

Michael the butler appeared, as if by magic, and laid out platters of succulent treats along with jugs, glasses, and ice buckets. Derek allowed Michael to present him with a drink that appeared to be almost entirely vodka, with the tiniest drop of cola added at the last minute. He smiled greedily, then gulped.

"Thanks, Michael, very refreshing," he said. "Help yourselves, won't you? Michael will tell you what he's brought."

Michael nodded and listed the hors d'oeuvres in front of us. "Today we have a selection of blue cream cheese with celery, smoked salmon mousseline on a miniature bagel crisp, cherry tomatoes stuffed with basil-infused mascarpone, frozen grapes, and fresh strawberries dipped in chocolate; the drinks are ginger lemonade with citrus fruits, and guava punch with red berries, as well as the sangria. I can also bring anything else anyone might desire in no more than a moment."

He sounded proud of his offerings, and I got the impression he'd been selected and trained to be a butler in the most expensive suite on the ship because he was the best at his job. When it came to being civil without obsequiousness, he nailed it.

Laurie sipped heartily from the exceptionally large mai tai placed on the table in front of her with a final flourish by Michael. "A little less orange juice next time, Michael, but otherwise, very good."

While the butler was still within earshot, she turned to me and said, "I guess he'll get it just right the morning we're getting off the ship."

I replied with, "mai tais for breakfast, you mean?"

Laurie's good-natured, tinkling laugh stopped only when she sipped again.

As I poured soft drinks for Bud and myself—*best to keep a clear head*—Derek spoke quietly. "This is all very tragic, and I know we can't talk about it, other than with the folks who were there this morning. Did Eisen tell you how he died? Do they know yet? He was a kinda cagey about it when he talked to us."

I suspected that Derek and Laurie had discussed little else—until she'd decided to dunk herself in their private hot tub, that is.

Bud shook his head. "He didn't say." He sounded quite convincing.

"It was sudden, we all know that," I added. "And you're right, it's very tragic. Though I only met the man for the first time this morning, he seemed pleasant. Derek said you didn't know him well, either, Laurie."

Laurie sucked her drink through a straw. "Derek and I ran into him when we were visiting the USS *Arizona* Memorial at Pearl Harbor," she said. "We'd been in Honolulu for a few days before that, but hadn't got about much. It was a long trip from Nashville, and we were pretty tired after, weren't we, Derek?" She looked at her husband with gentle eyes.

"I ain't as young as I once was." He winked at Bud. "But none of us will admit that, right?"

I felt bad for Bud, who was probably a decade younger than the bald, flaccid man sitting opposite us.

"I guess I should'a taken a couple'a days off work before we traveled, but, for all that I've 'retired,' I just don't seem to be able to keep my nose outta my businesses," added Derek wryly.

"What line are you in?" I asked. I hadn't broached the topic with the couple during our previous meetings, so it seemed like a natural question.

Beaming, our host answered, "Cars, my dear. New, used, rebuilt, yet to be designed. Been in the game my whole life. *Cropper's Cars* is a sign you see in many places around the state. Seven dealerships, five more outlets for used cars only, several repair shops."

Squirming from being referred to as "my dear," I replied with, "I expect you've noticed the change in the economy over the past few years." I heard Bud inhale deeply.

Derek smiled in a way that suggested he thought me to be rather dimwitted. "In Tennessee, everyone needs to drive something, anything. If we can't sell 'em a new one, we sell 'em an old 'un. And if they can't afford that, we fix up the one they've got. Some of the small guys have gone under, but we were big enough to muscle our way through. We're doing just fine, thank you ma'am."

Our surroundings bore testament to the truth of his statement, so I shut up and allowed Derek to continue, which, thankfully, he did. He sipped his drink, then said thoughtfully, "Tommy *was* a pleasant guy, but didn't know squat about cars. He knew a lot of historical stuff about Hawai'i, though, I'll say that for him. Usually Laurie and I hire a guide for the sort of thing we were doing the day we met him, but we'd been planning to go somewhere else, some palace or museum or other because it was raining. But then it cleared up, so we told our driver to take us to Pearl Harbor instead. She watched a movie about it on her pad on the airplane, so she was full of it, and I like to please her when I can." He winked at his wife, who nibbled on a strawberry. "It's been a long time since we've gone off on our own like that, me and the lady-wife, so we kinda palled up with Tommy. Then we found out he was going to be on this cruise with us, and we got to chatting about ships and different cruise lines. We hung out with him a few hours, then we left. It's quite a place, that memorial site. Makes you think. Makes you realize we sometimes don't know when it's our time. Didn't see him again until we were on the ship, which was when I found out about him being the card-playing guy here. He hadn't mentioned that when we first met. I just thought he cruised a lot."

So Tommy Trussler had portrayed himself as more of an equal than he really was when he'd met the Croppers. I wondered if he'd been sizing them up as possible marks. I judged that places like Pearl Harbor would be an ideal spot for a pickpocket to operate. Lots of people passed through, all with their minds on something else, something so big, dark, and terrible that they might not notice a light-fingered, ordinary looking man with a bit of a limp.

"And what about after you'd met up with him again here, on the ship, and ashore as we cruised—did you mix much with him then?" I asked.

Dropping the end of her strawberry onto a little plate and wiping her fingers on a napkin, Laurie replied, "Before we got on the ship, he was at the *luau* the last night at our hotel."

"I didn't see him at the luau," responded her husband, sounding puzzled. "You didn't tell me about that, and you certainly didn't mention it to Ezra." He sounded sure of himself.

"Of course I didn't mention it to him. Nothing of any consequence happened there. But I told you, dear." Laurie Cropper didn't sound cross or impatient; she just spoke with a certainty that matched her husband's. "I told you he was carrying his own little plastic pot of poi in a fanny pack." She looked at me as if sharing a confidence when she added, "Tommy told me he always did that because the poi they served at luaus was dreadful. Which it was. I mean, I don't want to sound like that French queen, or whoever it was, but why can't they eat relish, or mustard, or ketchup? That gray stuff is just disgusting."

So here was someone who knew something about Tommy and poi. It was an interesting lead, but I thought it best not to reveal my fascination immediately. "What did you think of him, Laurie?" I asked. "Was Tommy Trussler a pleasant man?"

Bud glared at me.

Laurie Cropper's fingers hovered above the plate of snacks as she gave my question some thought. She nibbled the smoked salmon mousseline on top of a chip, depositing the chip itself on her plate before she answered. *Terrible waste of a perfectly good chip.*

Finally she said, "He was the sort of man who made me want to count the rings on my fingers after shaking hands with him." She cocked her head slightly as she spoke. Her sunglasses made it impossible for me to read her expression, but it surprised me that she'd said something that hinted at an ability to read a person's true nature. I was immediately more interested in Laurie Cropper. I wondered what role, if any, she'd played in her husband's business success; he'd referred to the business as a joint effort, not merely his own, which was unusual. Then again, the old adage about every successful man having a strong or successful woman behind him is not one that's appeared out of thin air.

I decided to follow up by saying, "That's a very curious comment to make, Laurie. Could you maybe explain what he did to make you think that of him?"

Laurie removed her sunglasses and rubbed her eyes with small fists. She wasn't wearing a scrap of makeup—she'd been plastered with the stuff every time I'd met her before—and she looked about ten years younger than I'd imagined her to be. I reckoned Derek was in his late sixties, and had guessed at Laurie being his junior by a decade. Now I thought she might be in her early fifties. *Interesting.*

As I was revising my assessment of her age, Laurie regarded me calmly. She began to wriggle in her seat, then pulled a long tube from her pants pocket and shoved it into her mouth. A second or two later, a trail of white vapor poured from her lips.

"An electronic cigarette?" asked Bud.

Laurie nodded and smiled. "No flammables, no smoke. I know that smoking isn't allowed in staterooms or on private decks, but this ain't smoking, right?"

Tilting her head coquettishly toward her husband while exhaling a plume of vapor into the air above her, Laurie Cropper said, "By way of an answer to your question, I'll tell you this: Derek and I have worked together for thirty years to fill what we like to call our 'Cropper Coffers.' We always had a plan, and that plan meant working our socks off until we could afford to live like this all the time—or at least whenever we wanted. I started work at Derek's first-ever dealership back when I was right out of high school. I meet a lot of girls these days who moan about how women don't get a fair shake. Well, I just up and beat all those men I was working with, sold more cars than any of 'em and became Derek's best asset within a year. No help from anyone. No whining. Eventually we married, and we've worked together ever since. A true partnership, in every sense of the word. I don't see why women can't have everything, but there's nothing says they can have it all at the same time. We chose not to have children. It didn't make me popular with other women in the area, but I took the whispering and the gossip, and I ate it up. Now we live like this, and the ones with children run around after their grandkids, and I'm sure they just love 'em to bits.

But we prefer this. One of the things I've learned to be good at is sizing up a man and knowing what he really wants. Tommy Trussler was a slippery sort. Not to be trusted. I saw that in him eventually."

"She's never wrong," added Derek. "She's warned me off writing finance agreements with people in the past, and I've always been grateful. She's known when to upsell, and when to walk away. She's guided me to do deals with people I haven't known well, but whose aims have coincided with my own. Though I must admit I didn't get the same feeling about Tommy that she did, not until she told me how she felt about him, in any case. He struck me as . . ." he took a long draught of his drink, almost polishing it off, ". . . a little sad. Kinda invisible, but wanting to puff himself up a bit. He was a good teacher at the card table, I'll say that. He pointed out a tell I have that I've never known about." He chuckled. "I won't be doing that again."

"Did you mix with Tommy outside the Games Room?" asked Bud. "I saw him around the place a fair bit, but he didn't seem to have any particular friends onboard."

Laurie and Derek both shook their heads. "To be honest, we don't leave our suite a great deal," said Laurie. "Why would we?" *I probably wouldn't*, I silently agreed. "The pool is always busy, and we certainly don't need or want to shop onboard. I guess I go to the spa every day, for something or another. We do like our massages, don't we, Derek? And we would pop into the Games Room early in the day if we wanted. As he said, Derek's been brushing up on his poker there. I think it's helped him at the tables after dinner."

Derek grinned. "I'm getting better at bluffing out the amateurs," he smiled. "But the casino crowd on a ship ain't like the folks you find in Vegas, for example. The high rollers here wouldn't stand a chance there. I'm doing fine. About forty thousand up to date." He leaned toward Bud and added, "I might come away from this trip with enough money to cover my costs. I like sticking it to the Man and getting a freebie when I can." He looked pleased with himself, but not smug.

"I wish you all the best with that," said Bud evenly. I was still grappling with the idea that someone would risk enough to win forty thousand dollars, and that that was how much their trip had cost them. A university professor's pay means I'm used to a different category of price ranges, and I never, ever, gamble; my eidetic memory might mean I could count cards at will, if I chose to do so, but my moral compass, and my love of justice and fair play, mean I'll never do it.

"Such a shame," said Laurie. "No one deserves to go so fast, just like that, on the spot."

"There are worse ways," said Derek.

"Oh, I know, honey," replied his wife soothingly, "but, still . . . I guess it must have been his heart. They just pop, don't they? Sometimes, I mean. Remember Big Lou, Derek? Dropped dead on the thirteenth hole at the golf club, didn't he? The Board even had a meeting about changing the numbers of the holes after that. You know," she turned to me, "like they don't have a Deck 13 on the ship? I think it's best not to tempt fate." She sucked at her drink again.

"Did you ever see Tommy playing in the casino?" asked Bud, surprising me.

Derek shook his head. "Told me he wasn't allowed to. Said no one who works in any capacity on the ship is allowed to play in the casino. Not even the video poker or the slot machines. It wouldn't look good if they won."

"Except when the officers have their tournament against the guests, right?" said Laurie, smiling.

Derek's response was cheerful. "Except then, yes. The chief engineer and I had quite the battle," he added by way of explanation to Bud and me. He slapped the table as he laughed. "Good man, nerves of steel, but I got him in the end."

"But it was only for chips, not money, honey," said Laurie, still smiling.

"It's the principle," said Derek. "That was a sweet victory, and a real crowd pleaser. We were quite the draw that evening, no mistake."

Laurie chimed in with, "That's the one night I've stayed to watch you play, honey. Tommy was there that night, standing right behind the chief engineer. What's his name again?"

"His name is Aetios Papadakis, known as Chief Papa," said Derek.

"Of course," Laurie said, looking relieved. "I knew it was something like that. I might be good at judging people, but I'm hopeless with names, especially the foreign ones. They're all Greek on this ship, aren't they?"

"The people who run the ship as a vessel, rather than the hotel or entertainment parts of the operation, tend to be Greek, as are the owners of the Stellar Cruise Line," I replied. "Greeks have a long and traditional relationship with the sea."

"It's all well and good to be treated like royalty, but we want to be safe when we're in the middle of the ocean," said Derek. "That's why we like this line: great safety record. We check these things out, right, Laurie?"

"We sure do. I want to look my best, and they do have a great spa here, but it's no good to you in a life raft. Poor Tommy. So sad to die at sea. I guess it'll be complicated—dealing with the body and all. I didn't like to ask Ezra, but he seemed to have a lot of paperwork to fill out."

"I expect they're tracking down his family right now," I said as innocently as I could.

"He didn't have any family," said Laurie. "He told me his mom and dad had passed, and that he was an only child. Never married, he said. Looked kinda sad when he said that."

"When did he tell you all that?" asked Derek, puzzled.

"When I got chatting with him at the luau. He said it must be nice to have folks come to a place like Pearl Harbor to remember you when you've gone, because people like him, with no one left, would never be remembered at all."

"Now we'll remember him as the guy who died on this ship, in that room, right in front of us all," said Derek. "Maybe not the way he'd want to be recalled, but he'll be the talk of the rest of this cruise, and many in the future, I bet. From the days when we used to share a dinner table with other people, I know the topic of how people had been evacuated off a ship, or how many people had died on a cruise, would become the sole conversation at a table, each person or couple trying to outdo another. Grisly. It's why we only go to the dining room if we're at the captain's table, like tonight. Ha! For once we have the best story of all, though I guess it would be kinda impolite to bring it up."

"Ezra was keen to suggest it's something to keep off the list of topics tonight," said Bud.

"Oh, he did with us too, didn't he, Derek?" said Laurie. "That's why it's so nice to have the chance to talk to you about it, because I'm just fit to bust with something if I know it's a secret."

Bud and I had both finished our drinks, and I'd done my best to nibble only healthy snacks, like celery and strawberries.

"I'm pleased to see you didn't serve us poi," I noted, glad to find a way back to the critical topic.

Laurie pulled a face. "Horrible stuff. Tommy talked to me about poi like some people talk about coffee. But there's no way I'll ever eat it again. Slimy stuff, right honey?" She looked at her husband who was staring into his drink as though it were an abyss.

Snapping up his head, he grinned. "Yep, slime. Not fit for a dog. Now, what time is it, and when do you have to leave, honey?"

I felt as though Bud and I were about to be dismissed, and that was what happened, but in a polite way, and with a promise that we'd all try to meet up for a drink before dinner.

As Bud and I padded across the sumptuous carpet toward the door that led back to the "normal" luxury of the rest of the ship, I whispered, "Didn't want to talk poi, did he?"

To which Bud replied, "I cannot imagine that most people would."

Stateroom 3749, Aft

MAKING OUR WAY BACK TO our stateroom made me realize how far the people who worked on board the ship had to walk every day, just to get from one place to another. Bud and I had made every effort to get off at each port and we'd strolled a good deal on land, but we'd been fairly static since the ship had been at sea. Well, *I* had, though Bud had enjoyed his laps of the Promenade Deck after his visit to the gym every morning.

As we descended the stairs—*walking down counts as exercise in my book*—we had to navigate gaggles of folks taking the self-directed walking tour of the artworks onboard. We kept running into couples gazing at a piece of art in the stairwell with headsets plugged in, expressions of rapt interest on their faces. Bud and I had done it the second morning we were at Lahaina, killing time until we could get on a tender boat to take us ashore. It was a better choice than sitting about waiting, and I'd enjoyed it a great deal. Until then, it hadn't dawned on me that the sheer amount of art purchased for each of these gleaming vessels meant that the companies that own cruise ships are among today's largest commissioners and purchasers of art produced by living artists. And that's not even counting the artworks being sold at auction on the ship, which was another thing that surprised me; I couldn't imagine buying a piece by Salvador Dalí, or Peter Max for that matter, on a ship, then getting it delivered to Canada. The paperwork must be nightmarish.

"What are we going to say to Ezra about the time we've just spent with the Croppers?" asked Bud guiltily, as we reached Deck 8.

I gave it some thought. "I think we have to be honest about it. Derek was insistent that we join them. It wasn't our fault. We didn't initiate the contact."

"So spin it, don't lie?" replied Bud.

I nodded.

Turning toward our stateroom, I heard a reedy voice call my name. It was Janet Knicely. My heart sank.

"I thought it was you," she said, beaming as she approached. Her eyes were almost shut in her usual, off-putting manner. *How does she not bump into things when she's on the move?* "We just got the all-clear to leave our cabin by the security chap. Has he seen you too?"

"He has," I answered.

"Oh, it's like on the telly, isn't it, when they grill people. Though he wasn't that bad, I suppose. I was just going to fetch Nigel so we could go for a stroll on the top deck, but I wanted to swap my library book first. Sitting about waiting for that chap, I finished the one I had. And I like to take the stairs when I can. Why don't you come with, and we could all take a stroll together?"

Bud demurred, but I agreed. Bud was holding my hand when I did so, and gave me a hard squeeze.

"Oh, lovely," squealed Janet. "Nigel will be pleased. Likes the company of men, does Nigel. Come on—oh, let's take the lift down to Deck 3, or my feet'll get sore."

As Bud and I tagged along, dawdling a little, he hissed, "This is a very bad idea."

"It's too good a chance to pass up," I replied, as Janet blindly grinned at us. She kept hitting the down button on the elevator, as though that would make it arrive more quickly.

Once inside, she asked, "So where are you from in Wales, Cait?"

"I'm from Swansea. Do you know it?"

"Not really. It's quite close to Bristol, I know, but I've only been there once. Nigel and I went to the Brangwyn Hall for a concert many years back. They've put in a new Severn Bridge now, haven't they? I don't think I've even been to Wales since it opened. I'm always so busy."

"But it opened back in 1996," I said, surprised that a woman from Bristol, which is about thirty miles from the Severn Crossing, wouldn't have ventured across it in over fifteen years.

"Really?" Janet Knicely sounded genuinely astonished. "I didn't think it was that long ago. My, how time flies." I suspected that our time with the Knicelys would do anything but.

When we arrived at their stateroom, Janet knocked, which surprised me. Nigel pulled open their door, and looked taken aback. Nevertheless, he invited us to enter. Bud and I hesitated. I could see that their room was exactly the same as ours, except that where we had a balcony door, they had a wall with a round, backlit mirror, giving the room at least the illusion that it had some natural light, but the entire place suggested claustrophobia.

"I thought we could all take a turn on the top deck, dear," Janet said quickly.

Nigel looked relieved. "Good idea. Close quarters in here. I'll just get my bits and pieces."

"I wonder, would it be rude of me to use your loo before we leave?" I asked.

Bud gave me one of his looks as Janet gushed, "Of course you can. I expect all these rooms are the same, so you'll know where it is. Not that there's a lot of choice, given the overall dimensions of the place. Come on in, Bud. I'll just get a hat."

Bud hovered near the door while I nipped into the Knicelys' bathroom. I poked about a bit, noted the contents of their medicine cabinet and the toiletries that lay on their countertops, then flushed the loo and ran some water. Given that Nigel had been a pharmaceutical sales rep, and was now still training those who sold drugs, I had been half hoping for a bathroom overflowing with exotic pills, any of which might have been used to kill Tommy Trussler, but my hope for an easy solution to our problem was dashed.

Reemerging, trying to look suitably refreshed, I said, "Ready when you are."

We all trooped out, smiling like old chums, and headed toward the top deck. Once we got there I lingered with Janet, and Bud strode out with Nigel. I was sure he'd do some investigating, and began my own.

"So, how did you first meet poor Tommy Trussler?" I began.

Janet Knicely seemed happy enough to chat, though I struggled with having a one-to-one conversation with a woman whose face made all the appropriate expressions, but who never looked at me because she insisted on not properly opening her eyes. It was incredibly disconcerting.

"I know I told you all about us renewing our vows," she began, "and how this cruise is like a second honeymoon, but I can't remember if I told you it was all Nigel's idea. He's so good to me. I've always wanted to visit Hawai'i. It's so exotic. No Tom Selleck, though, more's the pity." She grinned blindly at me. "We met Tommy on one of those tours around Maui," she continued. "You know, one of the ones arranged by the ship? We only did those ones. They won't leave without you, even if you're late back, you know. But they can just go, sail off without you, if you're not back onboard in time otherwise. Imagine that? Being stuck with just nothing? I wouldn't want to risk it. 'The Maui Experience' the trip was called. Did you do it?"

I shook my head. "Bud and I rented a car the first day on Maui and drove the Hana Highway, then the second day we caught the little bus to Kaanapali Beach."

"Oh, isn't that a lovely place?" gushed Janet. "I loved the way that fat grass came all the way down to the sand. It's all so green everywhere there, and so colorful too, don't you think? I can't believe what they manage to grow in their gardens. Even just around their front doors. Houseplants, most of those things are for us. And so clean. Mind you, sometimes it felt a bit too . . . American. You know, not really Hawaiian."

Janet pronounced the word *Hawaiian* as though it was spelled

High-Why-Ann. I didn't comment. However, I couldn't resist saying, "But it *is* America."

Janet giggled. "Well, you say that, but it's not really, is it? I mean, it's so foreign."

Not knowing quite what to say—unusual for me—I said nothing except, "So Tommy was your guide on the trip?"

Janet shook her head. "No, he was a sort of assistant to the guide. Very helpful. Knew a lot. Did you say you and Bud drove along that really twisty road?"

"Yes, we did."

"We did too, in the bus. Terrifying, wasn't it? And we went to Hana. Then drove past some pool place."

"The pools of Ohe'o?" I asked.

Janet nodded. "Very nice, but it looked busy there and we didn't stop, you know, we just went past. I'd had enough by then. It was hot. Not as hot as in Lahaina, of course, but they say it's a remorselessly sunny place, don't they?"

"It was once known as *Lele*, which means 'relentless sun,'" I replied patiently. Desperately trying to get the woman back on track, I added, "Did Tommy tell you about that too?"

Janet nodded. "Yes, that and lots of other stuff. It all got a bit much to take in, to be honest with you. And when he told us what he did here on the boat, we said we'd see him in the Games Room to play cards. I've always wanted to learn to play poker. I don't know why. It just sounded interesting. It turns out it isn't, but it was nice to mix. Nice man, Tommy. A bit like a bird. Always picking at something. You know, food, cards, that sort of thing."

And a lot more too, I thought. I worked hard to focus on what Janet Knicely was saying, rather than how she was saying it; firstly there was the eye thing—her spectacles glinted, but there was nothing behind them except eyelids—and then there was the fact that her accent reminded me of Angus, my dead ex-boyfriend who'd also

116

hailed from Bristol. The burr of the rolled *r* and the West Country twang has always lulled me into a false sense of security. It's almost mesmerizing.

Janet continued to chatter on. "He was patient. Never told me off when I did something wrong with my cards, and I got it in the end. Mind you, I don't know what all the fuss is about. I can't understand why people get hooked on it. They do, don't they? They say it's the buzz. I didn't feel any buzz. But then I wasn't playing for real money. Maybe it's different then. I think I'm still too slow to play for real in the casino, though I might have a try tonight. Maybe people will be nice to me. They all seem very nice here. There's only tomorrow night left after tonight, and I did say I'd have a go. Maybe to remember poor Tommy I'll do it." We'd caught up with Bud and Nigel. "What do you think, Nigel?" said Janet to her husband. "Can I have a go at poker in the casino tonight? I wouldn't bet much. Maybe ten pounds? Would that be alright?"

"Yes, dear, perfectly acceptable." Nigel Knicely didn't seem to be listening to his wife. "We're eating at six o'clock, and then I'd like us to see the show, but there'll be plenty of time after that. Unless you need to get back to the room to finish your knitting, that is."

His manner toward his wife was far from warm. His words were polite, but his tone was disdainful.

Janet seemed oblivious to his dismissive inflection, and replied cheerily, "No need, I've been making excellent progress. Our grandson will have lots of little outfits ready for him when he comes. Would you like to see some photos of the family?" Without waiting for me to answer, she whipped a camera out of her backpack and began to show me tiny images on a screen. I pulled my reading cheats from my bag and peered at the photos. Rather unsurprisingly, Janet Knicely had her eyes closed in every one of them. I oohed and aahed in all the right places, I felt, and, after scrolling through dozens of pictures of their completely over-the-top recommitment ceremony, we eventually reached other photos taken in the Hawaiian Islands.

"Look, there we are in Maui, with Tommy," she said brightly. "Ah, poor thing." I perked up immediately, and paid more attention.

Bud took his cue. "Nigel was telling me about the tour you guys took with Tommy, weren't you, Nigel?"

It was like someone had turned on a switch; Nigel Knicely squared his shoulders, and lifted his chin. He looked as though he was going to dive into a deep pool—against his will.

"Poor Tommy, yes. We had an interesting day with him, didn't we Janet?" His wife nodded, and continued to click through photographs. "We joined the bus, along with our fellow guests, just yards beyond where we alighted from our tender boat, in Lahaina, Maui. I'm sure you know the place—hard to miss it, really, with dozens of coaches lined up just waiting for us all to get into them and be whisked away. We like to be on time. For us, ten minutes early is half an hour late, so we were first onto the vehicle and we sat at the front, with Tommy across the aisle from us. We chatted the whole time. And chat he did. Neither Janet nor I managed to get much of a word in sideways, did we, dear?"

I found it hard to imagine that Janet Knicely wouldn't eventually be able to dominate any conversation with her fussy nattering, but she nodded her agreement with her husband. Listening to Nigel, and seeing Janet's endless photographs, I couldn't help but compare the Knicelys with the Croppers. The British woman was dressed in another beige ensemble and her husband sported a hideous mixture of lime green and powder blue, whereas the Tennessee couple weren't just more wealthy, but more classy too—in their dress, their lifestyle, and their personalities. I couldn't imagine either of the Knicelys heartily enjoying an afternoon drink, no matter how well padded their bank accounts might become. They just didn't seem the type.

Nigel Knicely seemed to be running on autopilot. As he related the trip he and his wife had enjoyed with Tommy, he said all the right words about the lushness of the Iao Valley, about how they'd been alarmed, then fascinated by, the ability of the men who husked coconuts; he even spoke about the beauty of the tropical gardens they'd been to, but underneath it all was . . . what was it? *He's selling me something—that's it! But why?*

"You sound as though you had a good trip," observed Bud. I wondered if he'd been taken in by Nigel's technique, but I needn't have worried. What Bud said next spoke volumes: "I wonder how such a good beginning ended up with you not liking Tommy very much."

"Nigel didn't *not* like Tommy," said Janet, a little confusingly.

I knew Bud had something up his sleeve. He continued. "When Tommy and I were playing gin rummy this morning, he mentioned that Nigel and he had had a little falling out. Over something to do with a drinks recommendation?" *Good job, Bud.*

The robotic Nigel spat, "Stupid man offered to buy us a drink at the little bar where we stopped for lunch on the trip. Of course I refused. He was acting as a guide; there were two of us and only one of him, so I insisted we bought him one instead. Only polite. He ordered a really expensive one, whereas Janet and I just had a bottle of water each. I tried to hide that I was a bit cross. One doesn't like to speak of money, of course, but, well, there you are. I didn't dislike the man, I just thought he made a selfish decision on that one occasion, which maybe meant I was a little more guarded around him."

"Oh Nigel—you never said," Janet said, sounding surprised. "Oh dear, I hope it wasn't an expensive drink like the ones they have here in that bar that are all frozen, and they have those things that have herbs in them and they froth and foam and stuff. Did you know that some of those drinks are twenty dollars? Each!" She'd turned her attention to me as she finished, so I nodded. "I can't imagine why anyone would drink them. I'd be afraid I wouldn't like it, or I'd spill it," she concluded.

"No need to worry, dear," replied Nigel, who seemed to be reverting to his original, inanimate self. "We're on holiday, after all."

"And what a place for it," I said. "Your second honeymoon. Janet's been showing me all your photos. You've been fortunate to have had thirty years together."

"Haven't we," replied Nigel with an unexpected burst of positivity. His voice took on a surprising warmth. Now that he'd ceased his robotic recitation of what amounted to no more than a tourism brochure's copy, he sounded, and looked, genuinely enthusiastic. He was glowing as he said, "It was a lovely ceremony, renewing our vows. Not like the first one in church with dozens of guests, but just the two of us. The children would have liked to have come, but of course, it was all very expensive. Hawai'i is such a long way from Bristol. You cannot beat a wedding, but the vow renewal ceremony was almost as good. We did the whole thing, didn't we, dear? Cake, fancy outfits, wonderful music. We even danced to the Hawaiian Wedding Song afterward. People made such a fuss of us, didn't they? It was like being famous for a little while. The photographer was very good, and we got the whole thing filmed. They're going to edit it all in professional studios, then add some music, and we'll be able to show it to everyone back home. It was quite magical."

Nigel Knicely's entire person was suffused with passion and energy. The man was completely transformed. *Odd.*

Janet hung on her husband's every word, glowing alongside him.

"How romantic," I said.

"Oh yes, he's good at romance, is Nigel," said Janet blushing. *Really?*

"Will you fly home from Vancouver when we dock, or will you spend some time there too? You know, extend the celebration?" asked Bud.

"We don't travel a lot," said Janet, "and we were a bit nervous about getting from the ship to the airport, so we're taking one of the tours of Vancouver that ends up at the airport. They'll take our luggage from the ship to the plane, and check us in and everything. It'll be lovely, won't it? Much easier for us, Nigel? And we get to see another place without having to leave the bus."

Nigel's response of a fairly sullen, "Yes dear," signified to me that the romantic, enthusiastic Nigel had crawled back into his shell. *Very odd.*

I realized that Janet was still showing me photographs, and I spotted the white colonial-style architecture of the historic Moana Surfrider Hotel.

"Did you like the hotel?" I asked.

Janet looked shocked. "Yes, but I didn't like the whole place. Waikiki. It's very busy, isn't it? Nice sands, but big waves. Dangerous, I should think."

I stopped myself from saying it was the big waves that had made Waikiki world famous for surfing, because I didn't want to sound glib, so I satisfied myself with, "That's a very nice bracelet you're wearing in all the photos, Janet. It's a real pop of color." Given that she was wearing a mixture of various shades of beige in almost every shot, including the vow renewal ceremony, a red bracelet rather stood out.

Janet pouted. "I know. It was my favorite one. I've had it for years, but it broke a couple of days ago, didn't it Nigel?"

Awakened from his stupor, Nigel replied quietly, "Yes, dear, it did. Shame." The loss of the bracelet didn't seem to have impacted Nigel at all.

"You found beads all over the floor, didn't you?" continued Janet. "Did his best to pick them all up before the cleaning man came in the next morning. He's put everything he could find in a little bag. I might be able to get it fixed when we get home."

"I cannot imagine it's worth bothering with," said Nigel in a sullen voice. "It's a mere trinket. Worthless."

"But it was a gift, a special gift, from Leslie. You know that." Coming close to me, she added, "Poor Leslie—she's gone now. Breast cancer. Over a year ago. That's why it was special. She used to do some shifts with me at the charity shop, and she gave me the bracelet as a memento of our time together, when she had to stop working."

A little bell rang inside my head, and I asked Janet if I could take a closer look at her photos. She was delighted. Unfortunately, because the camera wasn't a new model, I couldn't enlarge the parts of the photo that showed the bracelet. My mind whirred. "I tell you what, I'm not bad with craft projects. How about I see if I can reconstruct your bracelet for you?"

Janet looked delighted, Nigel uncomfortable, and Bud utterly astonished.

"There's really no need," said Nigel, but I allowed Janet's "Thanks!" to win the day. I ignored Bud looking at me as though I'd lost my mind.

"If we could head back to your stateroom now and get the bits you have left, that would be great. Bud and I need a fair bit of time to get ready for tonight."

Janet looked up at a ship's clock we were passing, as we continued to wander the lap-walk on the topmost deck while enjoying the stiff breeze. "It's getting on, Nigel, and I could do with a bit longer to get dressed and so forth before dinner." Looking at me, seeking reassurance, she added, "You're wearing long?"

I nodded. Janet looked relieved. "Me too. I thought you had to, but two ladies at our table wore short dresses on the first formal night, and I felt a bit overdone. I hope they dress up a bit more tonight."

"I was astonished that I was the only one in a proper dinner jacket at our table, and I wore a hand-tied bowtie," moaned Nigel. He winked at Bud. "Nifty little number. Very appropriate for here. I picked it up at a place at that pink hotel on the seafront there, in Waikiki. The Royal Hawaiian, I believe?" Bud nodded, since Nigel was addressing only him. "Newt's, it was called. Lot of hats. Stupid name. Pretty wide selection they had there, and I thought I'd treat myself to a floral tie and cummerbund set. I must admit, I'll probably never wear it after tonight. Certainly not the done thing back home. Best to stick to black there. The number of men who wear their cummerbunds upside down on this ship is quite amazing, you know. They were called 'crumb catchers' for a reason." With that, he headed off toward the doors, which would take him back to the elevators.

Janet and I hurried after him, and Bud trailed behind, shaking his head.

Stateroom 8221, Forward

FIFTEEN MINUTES LATER, AS BUD and I sat on the sofa in our own stateroom, Bud phoned Ezra.

"He'll be here in five minutes," said Bud, replacing the handset. "So tell me, what on earth is all this business with the bracelet? You're no good at crafts of any sort. What did we have to bring those beads here for?"

"I think they're significant."

"You *think*? You mean you're not certain?"

I smiled. "Yes. I quite readily admit that I don't know *everything*. I *think* I know about these beads, but, like I said, I wanted to get my hands on them so I could check."

"And?"

"They are what I thought they might be."

"Which is?"

A knock at the door interrupted us. Bud invited Ezra inside. After entering, he sat down on the edge of the desk chair. He looked drawn.

"How's it going?" ventured Bud.

"Good and bad," replied Ezra. "Good in that I have interviewed everyone who was in the Games Room at the time of Tommy Trussler's death, and have now been given a good deal more information about Tommy Trussler. But some of that is bad news."

"Worse than that he's dead?" I'd meant to just think it.

Ezra shrugged. "In a way. For the Stellar Cruise Line, in any case. And possibly for me. The captain is beside himself, with good reason."

Bud and I waited. I couldn't imagine what Ezra was going to tell us.

"Tommy Trussler was a decorated war hero. Purple Heart. Silver Star. He pulled members of his unit from a burning vehicle during

Desert Storm, despite being wounded himself. I suppose that's what happened to his leg. The man in the refrigerated unit on Deck 2 is an honest-to-goodness war hero and he died on my ship, on my watch. Not that it should matter that he was a war hero, but it will."

I felt terribly sorry for Ezra. "The death of anyone before their time, because somebody wants it so, is a tragedy," I said softly. "Justice needs to be served. And I know that both Bud and I feel strongly about seeking justice for Tommy Trussler simply because he was a fellow human being—no matter his station in life, his being a criminal or a hero. However, I can see this is a public relations nightmare waiting to happen."

Ezra nodded. "Let's just say the captain is even more insistent that I 'get to the bottom of it,' as he put it. And fast. My job, my entire career, could be on the line. The company will need someone to blame, and if it all becomes high profile—which it will in the case of a murdered hero who pickpocketed our guests while working for the company—then they'll need to make a public announcement of my termination."

I understood why Ezra was so angry and upset. "We'll do our best to help you solve this," I said.

"I hope it's good enough," replied Ezra.

"So, did someone poison him because he was a war hero, or in spite of that? Did they poison him because he was a pickpocket, or in spite of that?" I said.

"Or did someone poison the man for a completely unknown reason?" added Bud.

"I don't know," said Ezra shaking his head.

"Then let's find out," said Bud. "We're a team, Ezra. Is there anything else you can tell us? For example, if you've interviewed everyone, is everybody who they say they are?"

I shouldn't have been so surprised that Bud had asked such a basic question. It served a dual purpose; Ezra focused on the case, and he seemed a lot calmer.

Squaring his shoulders, Ezra said, "Everyone checks out. They're all who they say they are. I spoke with the Croppers—they saw nothing, they know nothing, they hardly knew Tommy. Same with the Knicelys, though it took me longer to find out. Frannie Lang seems to have spent a fair amount of time with Tommy in Hilo, but wasn't able to tell me anything about the man. I've interviewed Kai Pukui, who didn't mix with Tommy at all, it seems. I have yet to speak to the server Afrim. That, and the background I've just given you on Tommy, is all I have so far. I have the Hawai'i Police Department tackling Tommy's home in Honolulu right now, and they have promised to report to me as soon as possible. What about you two? Anything in the Games Room?"

Bud cleared his throat rather dramatically. "We found some unexplained coffee grounds and a white substance on the carpet. Bartholomew removed some of the white powder so it could be tested," he offered, "and we happened to run into the Croppers and the Knicelys, didn't we, Cait?"

Ezra looked dismayed. "Procedures. You promised you would follow them," he said, his low voice sounding angry.

Bud sighed. "You know what, Ezra, I understand how tough this is for you. Believe me, I've been in your shoes often enough to appreciate the pressure you're feeling right now. But although Cait colors outside the lines sometimes, she usually turns up something useful, don't you, Cait?"

Bud was throwing me the chance to make our findings clear to Ezra, so I decided to do just that. I reached over, squeezed my husband's large, tanned hand and smiled. "You're right, Bud, I do. So, Ezra, let's address the Croppers first. They've got a lot of money, and they worked hard for it. They seem a pretty well-balanced couple, focused on each other and enjoying their hard-earned wealth. I believe they've had a lot of money for quite a while—they're both used to service, and they know what they want and how to get it politely, without a fuss. That means they've been receiving high-end services for some time. They both like a drink, he's good at taking risks, and I believe she manages and grounds that tendency in him. I got the impression they were both telling the truth about their encounters with the victim, largely speaking, though Laurie omitted telling you that she met Tommy at a luau in Honolulu, where she certainly had a chance to learn of his penchant for poi. I suspect some sort of precipitating event led Laurie Cropper to mistrust Tommy, and I believe that Derek knows about it, whatever it might be. I believe she must have told him about it directly, because Derek Cropper doesn't always 'tune in' to what his wife's saying. He seems distracted by—something. The Knicelys are another matter. She's focused on home life, but he's been on the road selling and is distant from his wife. Initially I suspected that she pushed for them to renew their vows to reassure herself that he still loves her, but the way Nigel spoke about the ceremony, and how much he enjoyed the whole process, has made me question that. He was transformed as he spoke about their experiences. His wife seems to be sure that his attitude reflects a romantic nature, though I'm not as convinced. He, too, is in his own little world sometimes, and again doesn't 'tune in' to his wife. I'm hoping that's not a trend I see being repeated in our marriage."

"What's that?" Bud retorted with a grin.

I smiled sweetly. "Very funny, Husband," I said, punching him gently on the arm.

"So?" said Ezra pointedly.

"I also discovered that both couples had access to enough poison to kill Tommy, and had the opportunity to do so without having to work hard at it."

Both Bud and Ezra looked curious.

"My only problem is I don't know *why* they might do it," I continued. "And I cannot work out how anyone removed the poi pot from the Games Room."

"I beg your pardon?" Ezra sounded cross.

"We've agreed that anyone in the Games Room this morning had the chance to put poison in Tommy's poi, and that it was the only thing in the room that *he alone* ate. We've also agreed that the only person who *would* have removed the poi pot from the room must have known about the poison. But no one could have secreted such a large object about their person without it being obvious. Now, when it comes to sources of poison, the Croppers have access to more than lethal quantities of liquid nicotine, and the Knicelys had these." I held the little clear plastic bag of beads toward Ezra for him to see.

"And these are?" he asked.

"They are called rosary peas, among other names. When Janet Knicely told me she'd been given this bracelet by a friend connected with a charity shop, I remembered a story I'd once read about potentially lethal bracelets being sold as fundraisers a few years ago. They were recalled, but I can't imagine Janet Knicely either knowing about that, or even caring. The bracelet was an important item to her."

Ezra stood, frustrated.

"I find this hard to believe. That this is true, or that you happen to know about it," he said bluntly. "You seem to know a great deal about a wide variety of topics."

Bud tried to not roll his eyes. "You're right, she does," he said.

I hurled a warning eyebrow in Bud's direction, then explained. "As you know, I build profiles of victims. A few years ago, I wrote a paper about the sort of person who falls for Internet fraud. Are you familiar with the whole 'I'm a Nigerian with millions of dollars and I'll pay you x to allow me to put it into your bank account, so long as you send me y right now' sort of thing?"

"I am," Ezra said.

"Well, people who actively support charities are terribly vulnerable to all sorts of scams, I discovered. Their psychological profile is often of someone who wants to believe the best of people, and is therefore less likely to be cynical when it comes to assessing what seems, on the face of it, to be an offer that can benefit a cause in which they believe. Of course, the Nigerian money-laundering scam, or just plain fleecing, is as old as the hills, but there are new variations all the time. It was while I was working on that particular paper that I found out about the rosary pea bracelets; they weren't a scam, just an unfortunate error on the part of some well-meaning person who saw a way to buy trinkets from a part of the world that needed the money, and sell them to support their own charity." I peered inside the bag at the vivid red beads with their little black "eyes." "I'm sure these are those beads," I added.

Ezra sighed heavily. "Would someone have to make Tommy eat the whole bean, or pea, or bead—or what?"

I shook my head. "No. They are relatively safe when they are whole, and can pass through the human body without causing death. They are the deadly seed of the plant *abrus precatorius*, and if they are punctured, drilled, or powdered, the inside of the bean is lethal. They contain *abrin*, a toxin that is much more lethal than ricin. People have been known to die by pricking their fingers when they are making holes in them to make them up into jewelry."

Bud looked amazed, and raked his hand through his hair. "Don't you dare open that bag, Cait," he snapped. "What on earth are people doing making jewelry out of lethal seeds? And why are they able to export them from where they grow, anyway? It makes no sense."

"They're used in many countries around the world for a variety of folklore-inspired purposes, from being a symbol of love to warding off evil spirits." I smiled brightly, and handed the bag to Ezra. "There you go. Tell Rachel to be careful with them, if she does anything to them at all. These are already drilled, and the powder from them could be lethal. I realize Janet's been wearing the bracelet for some time without any side-effects—as many unsuspecting people do—but that doesn't mean they aren't dangerous. She's been very fortunate. I didn't mention any of this to the Knicelys, by the way. I thought you should make that call—after all, one of them, or even both of them, might have known about the beads and used them as a weapon to kill."

Ezra put the bag into his pocket. "And the liquid nicotine you mentioned?" he asked.

"Electronic cigarette," said Bud quickly. I smiled at him, and let him continue. "Laurie Cropper uses one. She was 'vaping' on her deck when we had drinks with the Croppers in their suite." Bud tried to make it sound as though we'd been having a casual social interaction, but Ezra wasn't buying it.

"I thought I'd been perfectly clear about you two not interviewing the guests," he almost growled, though he leaned back onto the chair, rather undermining his attempt at angry indignation.

"We're a team," said Bud. "Your instincts were right, Ezra; if Cait and I had accompanied you when you questioned the guests, it would have compromised our possible ability to get to know them a little better, and to be able to talk to them as 'one of them' rather than as 'one of you.' You know exactly what I mean, right?" The men exchanged a significant glance, and I knew that Ezra would soon be on-side again. "So that's what we've been doing. We've managed to turn up two possible sources of poison already, and we haven't even talked to Frannie Lang, Kai Pukui, or Afrim yet. But I hope we now have your permission to do so."

Ezra nodded grudgingly. "What if they all find out we've been working together on this? That you've been pumping them as suspects, rather than merely being witnesses?"

"Justice needs to be served," said Bud quietly.

"We don't care about what people might think of us, Ezra, not when there's a killer to be caught," I added.

Ezra smiled wryly. "I like you two," he said, standing up. "Do as you must, and do it fast, and well. But please, keep me informed."

"We will," I said.

"Phone me in an hour. I hope to have some concrete news from Tommy's home by then. Agreed?"

"Agreed," said Bud.

I looked at my watch. "We've just got time to get hold of Frannie Lang and Kai Pukui in that case," I said, "if we're quick about it."

"How will we find them?" asked Bud.

"I can help with that," said Ezra just before he left. "Frannie Lang said she wasn't leaving her stateroom until dinner—late seating. She's in 8739, on this deck. I'm pretty sure you could come up with some reason for visiting her in her room." He smiled. "As for Kai? He'll be giving a presentation about Hawaiian flora and fauna in the cinema at 6:00 PM. He's always there twenty minutes early. You have my blessing to speak to them both. Now I must go. Good luck, and phone me."

The Ezra Eisen who left our stateroom looked more confident and buoyant than the one who'd entered, and I was pleased about that. I was more pleased that he'd seen how Bud and I could complement his efforts, if only we were left to get on with things for ourselves. After all, I like bending the procedures, on occasion.

Stateroom 8739

FIVE MINUTES LATER, BUD AND I knocked on Frannie Lang's door bearing a fruit basket that we had left over from lunch. When she invited us inside, I was happy to see that her room was delightfully messy. Earlier in the day, knowing that Ezra was going to visit ours, I'd done some hurried clearing of all the bits and pieces that Bud and I had allowed to accumulate on the various surfaces in our stateroom. Frannie Lang hadn't felt the need to tidy. Carrier bags bearing the ABC Store logo were piled on the back of the sofa, and mounded on the deep windowsill. Her closet door was open and displayed almost as many hanging garments as Bud and I had between us. A glance into the bathroom showed me three swimsuits draped over the frame of the shower door. Enough toiletries to stock a small drugstore littered the entire length of the marble counter. The sliding doors were open, so the air in her room was sea-breeze fresh mixed with the scent of pineapples. *Very Hawaiian.*

Cheerfully welcoming us, Frannie pushed items that looked like bits of garbage to one side on the bed and the sofa so that we could all sit down. She placed the detritus down with such care that I peered at it. She noticed.

"I scrapbook," she explained. "I like to keep lots of little things that mean something to me, then I can decorate pages in a really personal way. Do you scrapbook?"

I shook my head.

Picking up the hairdryer from the chair next to the desk, Frannie stood holding it awkwardly, not knowing where to put it. In the end, she dumped it on the floor beneath the seat upon which she then sat.

"It's so nice to have company," she said, smiling. "Can I offer anyone a drink?"

We declined. "We just wanted to make sure that you were doing okay," I said as convincingly as possible. "It was such a shock this morning."

"Yes, it's very sad," said Frannie. "I've been thinking about Tommy a lot since he died."

"Did you get to know him on the cruise?" I asked directly.

"Yes. Well, no. I didn't get to know him well, but I did meet him before I knew what he did on the ship. I met him at the Pacific Tsunami Museum in Hilo. Outside it, to be exact," she replied. "I'd walked off the ship alone, and I'd taken the little shuttle bus into downtown Hilo, if that's what you can call it. I have to say, it wasn't what I was expecting. It's a bit . . ." she paused and searched for the right word, ". . . run down? The restaurants all looked a bit grubby, and I hadn't expected thrift stores. Anyway, I found the place I was looking for, and Tommy was outside. We were both carrying Stellar Cruise totes, so we got talking, and we both went in. It was interesting. We battled each other on the tsunami simulator thingy there. It was fun. He was ever so knowledgeable. Then we went off to the Lyman House and Museum. He knew the way, which was good, because the map wasn't helpful and it was a lot farther than I'd thought. The rain had stopped by then, but my shoes were wet through."

Bud interrupted her flow with, "Did Tommy Trussler talk to you about his life at all? We hardly knew the man."

Frannie looked guilty. "I've thought about that, but he didn't really talk about himself, just about stuff. I must admit, I do like the chance to talk about my boys, and I think I did rather a lot of that. One thing he was insistent about was that I should understand all about Isabella Bird."

"Who's she?" asked Bud, suddenly alert.

"She died over a hundred years ago," I said softly, just so he didn't think he was on the trail of a viable suspect.

Frannie's expression told me she was curious why I'd know about the woman. "Yes, she did, Cait," she said quietly. "Did you two go to the Lyman Mission House too?" We nodded. Frannie brightened. "She stayed there, you know. The guide went on and on about Mark Twain visiting there, but didn't mention her at all. Tommy told me all about her. She did a lot, Isabella Bird—a lot that women weren't expected to do back in the day. Maybe not even today. And she wrote about it all. That's when I told Tommy about my journaling. I've joined a writers' group in Edmonton, and I read from my journals sometimes. One of the women who runs it thinks I could write a memoir. I'm going to read Isabella Bird's books when I get home."

To keep Frannie from getting sidetracked, I said, "As a female explorer, traveler, and the first woman to be elected a Fellow of the Royal Geographical Society, she was a pioneer; no question about it—she was a fascinating woman. Why do you think Tommy was so keen to tell you about her?"

Frannie gave it some thought. "He said everyone should be free to be who they really wanted to be. Who they were meant to be." Her pale face looked a little more drawn when she added, "We talked about my husband, you see, and he was very sympathetic."

Her gaze wandered off into silent remembrances, though I didn't know if they might be of her husband or the deceased card tutor. I decided to ask. "Is your husband dead, Frannie?" *Best to be forthright.*

The woman's head shot up and her eyes blazed. "I wish! He should be. If I could just get my hands on him—but he's the father of my children, so I shouldn't say such things." She flushed. "I'm sorry, I didn't mean to sound so angry. I have learned some techniques to manage all that in my counseling sessions. No, my husband is not dead. He's living in Calgary with a widow and her daughter. I found out he'd been carrying on with her for years. They even had a dog." She spat out the word *dog* as though this were the final straw.

She took a deep breath and squeezed her fists, then added, "I didn't tell the security man, Ezra, because it's not really relevant. I don't know why I told Tommy. He just seemed like a good listener, and I was feeling a bit angry. I think it was the exhibit about Burma at the museum."

"You remember, Bud," I said, as I struggled to make a connection. "There was that lovely display of photographs at the museum, showing the concept of kind acts made real."

Bud nodded vaguely.

The photographs had been touching, and had captured a real grace in giving, and receiving, acts of kindness across the troubled little nation of Burma. I couldn't fathom what that had to do with Frannie Lang's ex-husband, but I made a guess.

"*Sasana*?" I asked.

Frannie nodded. *Good guess!*

"Yes, *Sasana*, the Buddhist idea that all living things have a mutual obligation," she said quietly. "Barry, my ex-husband, never felt any obligation to me for the life I gave up to be his wife and raise our children. It was unfair of him. He was a long-distance truck driver, you see, so he was away a great deal. I couldn't work; I had to give it up. I'd been a good nurse, and I could have been promoted, but he didn't like the shifts. So I packed it in. I did everything for them—him and the boys. And the boys have turned out to be just super. Really they have. I think I managed to teach them right from wrong, and how to treat their wives. They don't speak to their father anymore, which is sad for them—and for him, I hope."

"It was an impactful exhibit," I said. "It's amazing how small acts of kindness can move through a community."

"Only looked at the kind side, didn't they? I think mutual obligation should work all ways," said Frannie Lang sharply. *Telling.*

I recalled that Frannie had told Dr. White that her sons had sent her on this cruise as a gift for her birthday. I guessed that must be her fiftieth birthday, so she was the same age as Janet Knicely, and just a couple of years younger than Laurie Cropper. How very different these three women were: one flush with cash she'd earned in partnership with her other half, and happy to spend it; one living frugally in the shadow of a quixotic husband; the other a discarded, unfulfilled wife with a penchant for history and philosophical thinking. Suddenly I saw myself in the same light as the three of them. I'd celebrated my own forty-ninth birthday just a few days earlier, so was pretty much their contemporary. If I could summon a caricature for each of them, what would the equivalent be for me? *Stop it, Cait, think about the case.*

"I'm sorry to hear that things didn't go well for you in your marriage," said Bud gently. "But I wonder, would it be rude of me to ask if you can remember anything that Tommy said or did, either when you spent time with him in Hilo, or when you spent time with him here on the ship, that might help us understand the man?" Bud's calming voice worked well. "We've been wondering if we should organize something to remember him, but we don't know what to do." *Bud was working hard.*

Almost smiling, Frannie replied, "No. Not really. The only thing he seemed truly passionate about was his poi."

"His poi?" I tried not to pounce.

"Yes," she said, "he always had it with him. In a big pot. He told me about it in Hilo, when we were walking to the museum. He loved poi, he said, couldn't get enough of it. He preferred it sour. He explained to me how it was made, and he said he liked it a day or two old, so that the flavor changed and it got sour. He offered me some when we shared a sandwich on the waterfront in Hilo, but I knew I didn't like the stuff; just looking at it was enough for me."

"But you say he always carried a pot of it with him?" pressed Bud.

"Yes, he told me he bought it on every island, from a particular place on each. I went to the place in Hilo with him." Frannie Lang rolled her eyes. "It wasn't very clean there, but he seemed to know the guy who ran the place. He looked to be about a hundred years old, like the store. He bought a big plastic tub of it, his last stock for the trip. He wasn't looking forward to being without poi on his way back to the islands on the return trip, but he said he'd manage. He was funny about it. Said he'd miss it like *sake*. I suppose he didn't drink for some reason. Or didn't drink sake anymore, anyhow."

Why would Tommy Trussler miss drinking sake, rice wine, so much? An alcoholic as well as a pickpocket?

"You two didn't hang out on the ship at all—other than this morning in the Games Room?" asked Bud.

"I was there yesterday as well," replied Frannie. "But I left when the argument broke out. I don't like it when men raise their voices."

"What argument?" asked Bud.

Frannie looked thoughtful. "Maybe it was something and nothing. You know how men can be. The young man serving the buffet yesterday had just gone off to get some hard-boiled eggs for that American who has all the nice clothes. Laurie, yes, Laurie. Anyway, the English man, Nigel, who was there today, told Laurie's husband that he could have got the eggs for her himself, and Derek—that's her husband—began shouting at Nigel. Derek left, and then Tommy and Nigel got into it. Tommy said something about Nigel knowing how to take care of his wife, and Nigel—well, he sort of went nuts. Weird. Anyhow, I didn't like it, so I left. I wasn't really playing a game at the time, just watching, so it didn't matter."

I could tell that Bud was thinking the same as me: Why had neither Nigel Knicely nor Derek Cropper mentioned their little contretemps the previous day?

"We'd better be going," said Bud, looking at his watch. "We're glad you seem so . . . *together* about all this. We were concerned for you."

Frannie smiled. "No need to be. I'm used to death, and being on my own." As she spoke, I noticed that she touched a locket that hung at her throat, and glanced toward a picture frame placed next to her bed.

I looked at the photo in the frame as Bud and I stood to take our leave. "Yours?" I asked, nodding at the photo.

Frannie brightened, and passed the frame to me.

"I like the Hawaiian word *ohana*. Me and my boys," she said proudly.

I took in the shot of her with two strapping young men who beamed at her with wide grins. Neither of them looked anything like her at all.

Once again, Frannie stroked the locket she wore, looking sad—wistful.

"And I am guessing that locket contains a photo of someone close to you too," I said, not meaning to.

"That's right," replied Frannie, a strange light in her eyes. "Fay, my kid sister. Gone now."

"I'm sorry," I said quietly.

Frannie smiled. "Oh, it's alright, really. She died many years ago, so I've come to terms with it quite well, now . . ." Frannie Lang paused, and the faraway look returned to her gaze. "She was on holiday in Honolulu with her boyfriend, and their car went off the road. She died instantly, they said. This trip was my first chance to visit the place where she died. It didn't feel like I thought it would."

I touched Frannie Lang gently on the shoulder. "I'm so sorry. I lost both my parents in a smash, and it does get a little easier to bear, with time. But it's such a shock, isn't it? And there's no real closure when you don't get to say goodbye, I know."

Frannie nodded. I could see the sadness and loss in her eyes. It seemed pretty raw. "Such a terrible way to go."

There seemed to be nowhere to take the conversation, and we left Frannie's room, all the more saddened by remembrances of family losses instead of concerned about Tommy Trussler's death.

"Any signs of poisons?" asked Bud once we were halfway along the corridor.

"I think the woman must either be allergic to almost everything, or a complete hypochondriac," I whispered. "She had enough antihistamines and sleep aids in her bathroom to either kill a herd of elephants, or at least give them a deep sleep for a month."

"And having been a nurse, she'd know how to use them—*and* she knew about his poi," replied Bud sagely.

Galaxy Cinema, Deck 4

"TOMMY TRUSSLER SOUNDS LIKE SEVERAL different people," said Bud pithily as we made our way to the elevators, heading for the cinema and Kai Pukui.

"Everyone has a multifaceted personality," I replied as we walked, "but his seems to be a little less cohesive than most. Being a war hero *and* being interested in feminism and Buddhism doesn't seem to fit with his being a pickpocket."

If we could get something out of Kai Pukui, I hoped I might stand a better chance of understanding what Tommy Trussler was like as a whole person, not just the little glimpses we'd been getting of him. I was hoping that the two men, both having responsibilities for Stellar Cruises, would have mixed with each other more than Tommy had with the guests. To find out, we had to come up with a ruse to make Kai open up about the man in a way he hadn't to Ezra.

Arriving at the cinema, I could see Kai hovering outside the door. Inside, one of the ship's engineers was talking about the ballast systems, using some complex diagrams as a part of a PowerPoint presentation, and his audience of about a dozen seemed rapt.

Kai managed to look graceful even when doing nothing more than standing still. When he saw us approach, his smile was wide, and his expressive hands fluttered as he spoke. His accent was American, but, as with Ezra, there was a formality in his manner of speech as a result of his different cultural background.

"Aloha. Have you come to listen to me speak about the natural beauty of my Islands?" he said hopefully.

"I'm afraid not," I said honestly. "We've had quite a day of it, and I really need to pay some attention to myself before dinner tonight."

"I understand," said Kai. "This is not a well-attended session, but I enjoy speaking about my home, and quite a few people choose not to go to the formal dinners. They do not care for all the dressing up."

"Do you cruise a great deal?" I asked.

"When it's the right season. The ships don't come to the Islands as much as they used to, but they usually still run the route in May and September. Then they take different routes. Malia and I do this when we can."

"And what do you do back at home?" asked Bud.

"We make toiletries," said Kai, rather surprising both Bud and myself, though I wondered if that was why he always smelled so fragrant. He reacted to our expressions with, "Yes, it sounds odd, but Malia's brother grows kukui nuts and castor plants, so we use the nuts and the oil to make organic spa products and toiletries. It's just a little business, but we enjoy it, and it allows us to live close to, and work with, our family."

"*Ohana*," I said.

Kai nodded graciously and smiled. "Exactly," he replied. "Ohana is very important to us."

"This business today must have shaken you up," said Bud, dropping his voice to a quiet whisper. "Was Tommy Trussler ohana to you? I understand the term is also used to refer to good, long-term friends, as well as blood relatives."

Kai tilted his head and spoke slowly. "I've been counting the times that Tommy and I have cruised together, which isn't easy, since one cruise can merge with another, and one season with another also. He'd usually do two sets of back-to-backs—one cruise after another—twice a year, spring and fall . . . so, about a total of about sixteen weeks a year. But, although we always smiled and were pleasant toward each other, and had the odd chat now and again, we'd never really engaged before this cruise."

"That seems strange," said Bud. I agreed—it did.

"I expect it does. But, you see, we had very different schedules on the ship, which kept us apart for most of the time. He had regular hours in the Games Room, but Malia and I have our responsibilities too. The other thing is, with his stateroom being up on Deck 3, rather than down on Decks 2 or 1 with the rest of us, he never used the crew facilities, though I know he could have done, so I assume he ate in the guest areas. He never came to a crew party, didn't mix with anyone—at least that I know of. He might have done, but I don't know about it."

"I guess your days and nights are busy on the ship?" asked Bud.

Kai seemed happy to talk. "We work as we are needed. Malia and I have our schedule from the cruise director. At this time it is Gordon. I believe he is a Canadian, like you. Do you know him? I do not mean merely because he is from Canada, of course," he grinned. "I know it is a large country, so much bigger than my own, small nation. I mean because he is such an active cruise director."

"We've seen him about," I replied.

"He's in charge of all the entertainment on board, so Malia and I report to him, and Tommy would have done as well. We're so busy running from place to place and, at least for Malia and me, trying to fit in costume changes and food, when we can. When we're not in front of the guests, we often retreat to our room to rest up. Sometimes I get a few hours when I can wander, and that's what happened this morning. I bumped into the Croppers when they were leaving the gym and they insisted that I join them in the Games Room. It's impossible for me to say no to the Croppers. They are valued guests. That's the only reason I was there when Tommy died." *An interesting point to make.*

"I know this might sound odd, but could you tell us something about poi?" I asked. I suspected Kai would know more about poi than most people on the ship.

Kai chuckled. "Now that I do know about," he said. "I love poi. In fact, like a lot of Hawaiian children, it was the first thing I ever ate, and I just kept going. My *Tutu*, my grandmother, used to make it," he explained. "The best two-finger sweet poi in the world. Nothing like it."

I half-raised my hand and said, "I know a little about poi, but I have to admit that I've probably only tasted the sort of stuff reserved for tourists. I hope it's not insulting to tell you that I found it pretty revolting. Someone told me that Tommy was some sort of poi connoisseur, so I am guessing he ate a different type. Could you explain to us what it tastes like, when it's the good stuff, what its texture would be, and so on? It's fascinating." *And I can better work out what sort of poison it might have hidden.*

"Sure," said Kai happily. "Poi 101 coming up. It's made from taro root, so it's really like a mashed potato in that respect. Because the taro has a different starch structure, it ends up with a unique consistency. Basically the root is boiled, then mashed. Most poi these days is made commercially and bought at the supermarket, though some people, the older ones especially, still make their own. The location where the taro is grown has an impact; the soil and climate can make some difference to the taste of the root you start with. The heat at which you boil it, and the length of time you boil it, can also make a difference. There's one company that specializes in boiling the root at a much higher temperature than the others—hotter than anyone could do on their own. Then they vacuum-pack it, and you can buy it chilled or frozen. People say it's sweeter that way, but it's not the flavor I like, personally. It's also a little more purple, which, again, I don't care for. Once you've boiled the root, then you adjust the water. Again, some say the water affects the flavor, but I guess my palate isn't up to telling the difference. You've probably had 'tourist' poi that's been thinned a great deal, to make it go further for the luaus. Most of the tourists just leave it on their plate in any case, but they expect it to be served. Two-finger poi is thick. You only need two fingers to pick it up, because it's still got its gelatinous qualities. Three-finger poi is thinner. Most of the stuff you tourists see? Four- or five-finger poi—or something for which you need a spoon."

Even as he was talking about the texture of poi I could feel my tummy turn. I suspected it was a cultural thing, and that I'd be just fine with it if I'd grown up with it—like Marmite.

"How long does it keep fresh?" I asked.

"Well, that's another thing," replied Kai. "You can eat it when it's really fresh, or when it's five days old. The older it is, the more sour it gets. Some say that sweet poi, in other words fresh poi, is just for babies, and that you might as well serve it with sugar and milk. A lot of the older folk won't consider eating it until it's at least a day old, and maybe not until it's two days old. I tried five-day-old poi once, and it's not for me."

"Do you know what Tommy preferred or ate?" I sounded as hopeful as I was.

"Why do you ask?"

I hesitated. "Well . . . my interest is piqued."

"Now that you bring it up, I do recall that I once asked Tommy why he carried poi with him everywhere," said Kai. "He did, you know, in a little baggy he had just for the purpose. It seemed like madness to me, and I've been brought up on the stuff. He said it reminded him of the woman he'd loved but had lost, which I thought was a strange and sad thing to say. He didn't tell me about the woman, just the poi. He rattled off a list of places where he bought it as we cruised, and it seems he'd lay in as much as he could, to last him as long as possible. The places he mentioned were all places I imagine he could buy small-batch poi, probably two-finger sweet. You seem unusually interested in poi," he remarked. "Why is that?"

I gushed, "Oh, you know, I want to have something to tell them back home."

Once again, Kai nodded gracefully. The people in the cinema began to leave and he excused himself to get ready for his presentation. We exchanged "Alohas," and Bud and I left.

Kai's insight had helped me understand a little about Tommy and his poi, but it led to yet another issue: the lack of poi in Tommy's room told me he'd had his entire "stock" with him in the Games Room, or else someone had entered his room and removed any that he'd stored there.

Security HQ—Deck 1, Amidships

IMMEDIATELY AFTER WE LEFT KAI, Bud and I found a house telephone and called Ezra, who told us he'd like to see us in his office. We still had a couple of hours before dinner, so we headed off right away. By the time we made our way through the discreet doorway of the security office, I was flagging. Apparently, relaxing for a couple of weeks with your new husband isn't the best training for conducting a series of interviews with murder suspects. I'd enjoyed spending so much time outside in the warmth of the Hawaiian air, with the unique scent that seemed to infuse it, that now I was starting to feel totally cooped up.

Ezra's office environment wasn't going to help, either. It was small, windowless, stuffed with all manner of high-visibility vests and bits of equipment, and had no cupboard space to speak of. Ezra was inserted behind his desk, which was almost entirely covered with neat piles of papers and a large, old-fashioned computer. Bud and I perched on two chairs, one of which had been dragged from another room. I recalled how Bud and I had often huddled in too-small spaces when we'd worked together on cases back in British Columbia.

"Just let me read this stuff a moment, will you?" said Ezra as we settled ourselves. We waited patiently. Well, I waited patiently, but Bud fidgeted. It reminded me that when I'd consulted for him on cases back in Canada, I was the one who'd learned how to wait for him; he'd been the one leading the investigations and always set the pace of the proceedings. This was new—and old—territory for Bud. I suspected his frustration stemmed from being accustomed to being the boss for so many years; he'd forgotten what it was like to have to wait to be brought up to speed.

As he read what was on his screen, Ezra's face clouded, cleared, and clouded again. After taking in the information, he spoke up.

"Well, here goes," he began, regarding us solemnly. "HPD got into Tommy's apartment. He has no living relatives and no roommates. He was unmarried and lived alone. They found a strange collection at his home. Hundreds, possibly thousands, of pieces of personal effects, all stolen, but with everything intact, just placed in transparent pockets in ring binders. The officer said that each wallet or purse was there, and everything had been removed and placed carefully in a binder. Most of the drivers' licenses were displayed on his walls. It's puzzling."

"You mean he stole people's wallets, emptied everything out, and kept it all in files or on display?" asked Bud in bewilderment.

Ezra nodded. "They found a lot credit cards, but no cash. They've run a few cursory checks and have been able to match some of the items with reports of thefts on the island. There's nothing to indicate that he used any of the credit cards, but there's no sign of the cash reported as missing. If he spent it, it wasn't on his home or his lifestyle, they said. He lived in a low-rent area, and had very few personal possessions. I understand that he might spend the cash he stole, but keeping all the other stuff? Displaying it? Cait—do you have any ideas why that might be? It's like his safe here, on the ship. I'm hoping this might be something you, a psychologist, would understand."

"I've never encountered anything exactly like it," I answered thoughtfully, "but give me some time to mull it over. Did HPD send you any photographs?"

"They did. Why don't you two stick your heads around here to see?"

Bud and I crowded behind Ezra and peered over his shoulder at his computer. The series of photographs on Ezra's screen began with establishing shots, showing the street location and the outside of a pretty run-down low-rise apartment building; Tommy had lived in a neighborhood devoid of the palm or plumeria trees that lined so many of Honolulu's streets. The photographs showed us a walk-up block with little charm, built in an area with even less appeal. Next we saw the front door to Tommy's dwelling; a metal swing-out gate was fitted in front of the door to the apartment, and suggested security issues. Wide-angle shots of a series of rooms followed, and I wasn't surprised to see a neatly appointed home, without a great deal of furniture or many overtly personal possessions. A few framed portraits were arranged on a windowsill, the sun streaming in behind them. One showed a rotund little boy in an over-large top hat, and a cloak with a splashy red lining; another featured a slim, youthful version of Tommy in military camouflage; another showed a peekaboo-view from what might have been a lookout point on one of the Islands.

Finally, Ezra reached a host of official photographs all taken in what I suspected had been designed to be a second bedroom. He scrolled through them quickly. Occasionally Bud let out low whistles, or else sucked in his breath.

I was fascinated by what I saw: hundreds of little plastic wallets had been pinned to all four walls of the room, and each contained a driver's license. Most were Hawaiian, but some were from other US states, and even other parts of the world. The arrangement was neat, with row upon row of evenly pinned photographs staring at us. What was most notable to me was the fact that all the photographs were of essentially the same two types of person. Two walls featured photographs of women with blond hair, dark eyes, and a generally fresh-looking face, but of a variety of ages; the other two walls showed photographs of men who all looked similar to Tommy Trussler himself, but, again, at a variety of ages.

Ezra looked nonplussed; Bud made some strange humming noises. Tommy Trussler—war hero and pickpocket—had just become even more interesting.

"I've never seen anything like it," said Ezra quietly. "Nor, it seems, has anyone in the HPD. Their memo to me gives no explanation for Tommy's selections. Indeed, other than telling me the man had no cash in his apartment, and only had about a hundred dollars in a checking account, they were able to tell me very little, though, as we can all imagine, they are now mounting a more thorough investigation. The person he listed as his emergency contact on the paperwork we had from him, both here on the ship and with the agents who booked him on our behalf, lives in the same complex, but claims to have only had a nodding acquaintance with Tommy. In fact, the woman in question wasn't even sure of Tommy's name, has no knowledge about him, and, apparently, has no intention of taking any actions now that he's dead. Trussler has no police record on the Islands, nor anywhere else in the US. Not even a ticket—for anything. The only mention the HPD can find of him locally is that his name appeared in a story in the *Honolulu Star-Advertiser* about two years ago, where he was thanked by a local charity for making a large donation. They're going to check it out with the guy who runs the charity."

"What does the charity do?" I asked.

Happy that we'd seen all we needed, Bud and I returned to our seats as Ezra scrolled through notes on the screen. "They support families of US veterans," said Ezra eventually.

It made sense.

"Any pattern of assaults on the type of woman in the photographs?" asked Bud curtly. Ezra smiled. "The HPD thought of that too," he replied. "No apparent correlation. It doesn't seem that any of these women were attacked in order to gain access to their ID; neither were the men. As far as HPD records are concerned, these licenses were reported as stolen from persons going about their business, or lost, rather than forcibly removed from victims of violent crimes."

Bud sighed. "So Tommy Trussler was a thief, but not a violent one."

Ezra nodded. "Yes. The HPD reports back up our knowledge that he was a pickpocket, but don't suggest he would break into and enter homes or hotel rooms, or carry out assaults."

"Not his profile," I muttered.

"Have you reached any concrete conclusions about our victim yet—something that might point us toward his killer?" asked Ezra directly.

I sighed. "Not really." I sounded as glum as I felt. "The collection of IDs at his home suggests an obsession with a specific type of woman. Without knowing more about Tommy's background, I'm racking my brain for any clue as to why that would be the case. Certainly, pickpocketing is a very personal crime—the thief has to get intimately close to the person they are stealing from, inserting their hand or hands into the clothing, or at least the possessions, of the victim. The thefts, therefore, might indicate an oblique sexual intent on Tommy's part. But, again, not knowing more about the man, I cannot say this with certainty. Tell me, does HPD know nothing more about his background? Did you get anything more about him from the agency used by the Stellar Cruise Line to find and retain him?"

Ezra shook his head. "The agency really dropped the ball with Tommy. In fact, I wouldn't be surprised to find that their hiring of him leads to them losing their contract. It's unforgivable that they would send us someone who's been stealing from guests. The business relationship between their head office in Miami and ours depends on their ability to thoroughly perform all standard checks on those they propose as suitable for us to have onboard."

"You said that Tommy had no police record," said Bud. "If he's never been detained or investigated as a pickpocket, how would any agency know? All I can say is that he must have been an excellent thief, because it was clearly not a newfound path for him. He seems to have been getting away with it for a long time."

"How do you know that?" asked Ezra.

"The sheer quantity of stolen licenses," replied Bud amiably.

"And they go back many years," I added.

Ezra guffawed. "You barely looked at the photos." He sounded dismissive.

"It's another thing Cait's good at—seeing something for a brief time, but being able to make sense of it," Bud said quietly. "She's good at spotting patterns."

"Anyone can see he was interested in blonds," said Ezra, now sounding more defensive.

"Look again at the photos on the licenses," I replied. "I happen to know that Hawai'i changed its driver's license design in 2010—I read about it when I was plowing through some old magazines that a colleague at the university brought back from holiday; he wanted to drool over the real estate adverts for dream homes he'd seen when he visited Hawai'i a handful of years ago. A good number of the licenses Tommy had on his walls are the old design, and the expiry dates go back several years before they were changed. The women in the photographs are young to middle aged, but they all look to be over twenty-five years of age, which means they'd be eligible for permits that last eight years. I'd guess he's been taking these for more than a decade. Another interesting fact is that the photographs have been arranged in age order, roughly speaking."

"What do you mean in age order?" asked Ezra, fiddling with his computer's mouse. "Look at the photos and their arrangement," I said. "Imagine that he's been collecting them for years, and that he began by pinning them roughly at eye level; you can see he started with younger photos, worked from left to right, then made a row below, then another, and then finally began to pin them above eye level. He's arranged the photos of the men and the women the same way. Very well organized. It tells me something critical—oh, and, hang on, got it—I think that Kai Pukui just furnished us with an explanation."

Ezra looked a little crestfallen, then shot me an accusing glance. I could tell I'd dented his personal and professional pride—after all, he'd seen what I'd seen, but hadn't been able to put it together in the way I had.

"What's that? What did Kai tell you that he hasn't told me?" he snapped.

"Kai told us that Tommy mentioned a woman he'd loved but had lost. I think he was . . . not searching for her, exactly, in the normal sense, but gathering photographs of how she might have looked as time passed. And he did the same for himself."

Ezra looked puzzled.

Bud said, "You mean he projected onto women who looked something like his lost love, and men who looked something like himself. These photographs are him playing 'Happy Families' with DMV photos."

I nodded.

"Why?" Bud and Ezra asked in unison.

"I think she died," I replied. "In fact, I'm pretty sure she must have. He started gathering photos of the way she would have looked if she'd lived. It's the only explanation I can think of. If she'd left him—*he* can't have left *her* or he wouldn't have told Kai he'd 'lost' her—then he might have gone so far as stalking her. That's the sort of obsession we're seeing here. He wasn't able to break from her at all. But he wasn't stalking a living person. If we can work out from the photos the time frame when he began his 'collection,' we might be able to pinpoint when she died, which could help—or not."

"Very enigmatic," scoffed Ezra.

I felt Bud bristle. Luckily a knock at Ezra's door prevented any further comment. Officer Ocampo stuck her head into the room at Ezra's bidding.

"Afrim is here to see you, sir," she announced.

"Two minutes," replied Ezra. He turned his attention from the computer to a file on his desk. "The server, Afrim," he said seriously. "I don't know him personally, but I have his record here. If Tommy ingested poison, it might well be that Afrim Ardit, our twenty-seven-year-old server from Albania, gave it to him. I see he's been with the company for three years and is a highly regarded employee. There's nothing on his record of any note, except commendations. However,

Albania has a bleak recent history. People of Afrim's age have grown up in an environment that can force a person to make dubious choices. You two can sit in on this interview. It will save time."

"What reason will you give Afrim for our presence?" asked Bud.

"I don't need to give him a reason. He works for the company, and he has to do as he's told," replied Ezra. It was obvious that his attitude toward staff differed greatly from the one he had toward guests.

There was a timid knock on the door.

"Come," said Ezra, loudly.

Afrim Ardit's big, dark eyes peered out of his worried, pale face as he stuck his head around the door.

"Don't stand out there, come and sit . . . stand in here," said Ezra, realizing there were no empty seats, nor room for another.

Afrim shuffled in, looked at Bud and myself with a terrified curiosity, and hovered in the corner of the room behind our chairs; we turned to face him, though indirectly. He held his hands in front of him, clenching and unclenching his fingers, as if trying to ensure good circulation. I could hear him breathing heavily. A cornered creature—literally and figuratively. My heart went out to him. Having gained some insight into the way that gossip and rumor crackled around the ship, I suspected that Afrim had been the center of attention, and accusation, since the morning's incident. I wondered where he'd been all that time.

"I have been waiting to come to talk to you, sir," he said quietly, "but I can wait a little longer, outside if you like, while you finish with these good people."

"They will remain while I ask you questions," was Ezra's terse response. Afrim looked too frightened to be surprised; he knew that his job, and maybe even his career at sea, was on the line.

Ezra began by asking Afrim what he had seen Tommy Trussler consume that morning. Afrim replied in a manner that told me he'd thought of little else since we'd all been ejected from the Games

Room. He recited a list he'd thought about, memorized, and was ready to repeat. It wasn't very illuminating, and contained less detail than Bud's list.

"You're sure of all this?" snapped Ezra.

The poor man almost jumped. "I think so, sir," he replied weakly. "Today was only my second day serving in the Games Room. It's a big step up from my previous duties in the coffee shop, where I was backup to the baristas. But my star, you see, sir, I got my star last week, so they gave me the new duties . . ." He trailed off, and seemed uneasy.

"Who used to serve in there, before you took over?" asked Ezra.

"Winston, sir, Winston Williams. He did it for a few weeks, in the mornings, before his shift at the Sundowner Bar in the afternoons, or else being on the shore crew—you know, he would serve the cool drinks and the iced towels at the quayside for guests waiting for the tender boats."

"Where's he been moved to, and why?" asked Ezra.

Afrim looked at the floor. "He's opened up the Pool Bar for the past couple of mornings. I don't know why he was moved, sir."

Ezra picked up a pencil and began to tap its end on his desk. "I'll have to ask the bar manager," he said, "though I am sure you could tell me if you wanted to. Afrim, it will look better if you are open with me."

"I heard something about a disagreement," muttered Afrim. "They had a big row in the Games Room before any of the guests arrived a few days ago. We were in port, so it was quiet. No one else knew about it. I overheard Winston saying that it must have been Mister Tommy who reported him. They moved me in and Winston out yesterday morning." He swallowed hard, and resumed the inspection of his toes.

Ezra looked hard at Afrim, then barked "Go!" Afrim reacted with a start and, keeping his eyes on the ground, scurried out of the room as quickly as he could.

"My instincts tell me he's terrified of being suspected rather than found out," suggested Bud. "There's a noticeable difference. Seen it a thousand times. Right, Cait?" He looked to me for agreement.

"Does Winston Williams say 'jingle bells' a lot and wear a Santa hat?" I asked.

Ezra looked puzzled. "I have no idea. Why?"

I looked at Bud. "Sundowner Bar Winston?"

"*Our* Winston?" said Bud.

"We like the Sundowner Bar," I explained. "It's a great place to hide from the poolside hordes and find some peace and quiet. Winston is the barman who 'adopted' us on embarkation day, and has attended to us every time we've used the bar since then."

"Do you think he's a suspect?" asked Ezra. "We've either run out of them or have too many."

I thought about Ezra's question and his follow-up comment.

"No, we haven't run out of suspects, Ezra, as you well know. We have the Croppers and the Knicelys in possession of possible poisons, and I noticed that Frannie Lang's bathroom contains a host of over-the-counter pharmaceuticals that could prove lethal if ingested in large enough quantities. Kai Pukui told us that, back on the Islands, his family runs a business that makes products from castor oil, and the castor bean is also a lethal item."

Ezra looked aghast. "When were you planning on telling me about the Lang woman and the Pukuis?"

"This has been my first chance," I said as calmly as I could, given that I was feeling very much under fire—albeit the "friendly" type.

"Right," said Ezra, sounding deflated. "You're telling me that everyone in that room had access to a means to kill Tommy, and that everyone had an opportunity to put poison in his poi, which we seem to have settled on as the most likely means of ingestion. You've also told me no one would have had the chance to remove the pot containing the poisoned poi in the general melee that occurred when the pod of dolphins passed. Is all of this is correct so far?"

I nodded.

"We just don't know enough about the victim yet, nor our suspects, to be able to narrow our field of inquiry in terms of possible motives." I was thinking as I spoke, so I knew I sounded vague.

Ezra's tone was impatient. "What do you propose we do about that?" he asked. "What did you do when you worked with Bud that's different from what we've done so far? You can't visit the victim's home to search through whatever personal items he had there—if there were any. And it's clear that no one on the ship knew the man well—in fact, no one knew the real man at all. Bud? What do you suggest?" I understood, and shared, his frustration.

Bud used his most calming voice. "You know what, Ezra? Cait's worked cases like this before. I know how she works. While we've agreed to operate under your direction for this case, I suggest you allow Cait and myself to continue to find less formal opportunities to talk to those people, so she can draw them out in ways that might bring motives to light. She's very good at that. That's my professional opinion."

"It's highly irregular," muttered Ezra.

"Irregular or not, it's working so far," said Bud. "We three can be an effective team, and Cait and I can contribute so much more—if only you'd let us. Or we could go back to relaxing on deck and enjoying our honeymoon."

Ezra's micro-expressions told me this wasn't an option he favored. He dropped his head in what I judged to be a sign of resignation. "I am sorry. I value your input." His jawline firmed as he stood and looked at his watch. "I'm going to check with Rachel to see if she's been able to run any helpful tests on the items taken from Tommy's stateroom, and from the buffet."

Ezra unnecessarily reorganized a few items on his desk, then, having regained his composure added, "You are correct, Bud, we can be a good team, but every team needs a leader and I must be that. I need to be advised of any and all information you gather, and you must understand the fact that I am giving you an extraordinary amount of latitude in this instance. The safety of everyone on this ship is my responsibility. It is now also yours. You may follow your own investigative path, so long as it does not endanger anyone's life, or the reputation of the company. You can run with it. But security. Discretion. Am I clear?" Ezra's military bearing had fully returned, though his eyes told me he was still struggling with having to accept help from guests he would have preferred to not need.

Bud and I agreed. I was delighted he'd agreed to let us get on with investigating in our own way. *Forget procedures! Now I can get going.*

Sundowner Bar—Deck 15, Aft

"I NEED SOME AIR," I whispered as we took our leave of Ezra.

Bud nodded. "Me too. It's been a bizarre day, and we've spent most of it inside. I'm desperate to feel the wind on my face again." He looked at his watch. "It's gone half past six. What do you think? Back to the room, or a quick once 'round the top deck?"

"How about a drink at the Sundowner Bar?" I countered. "Winston should be there."

Bud nodded his agreement. "You're right. Two birds, one stone," he said, and we headed for the elevators.

The Sundowner Bar was busy—and well named. Guests lingered there at the end of the day sipping drinks, because it gave an uninterrupted view of the ocean and, at the right time, the setting sun. It was blustery, and every passenger was aware we were sailing northwest toward Vancouver and cooler climes than any of us had been used to for nearly two weeks. Some folks were already dressed for the formal dinner; women attempted to look elegant as they held down their hairdos in the stiff breeze; men who rarely wore neckties tried to look nonchalant in bow ties and cummerbunds. The sight of those who'd recently left the poolside next to those in full evening dress was strange—an experience unique to cruiseships, I suspected.

"Jingle bells, jingle bells!" called Winston as he saw us approach. "Come hither, I have just the spot for you." His grin was cheery beneath his Santa hat, which, possibly because it was formal night, had the addition of a blinking star on its bobble. "It's Christmas every day here!" he continued, ushering us to a table and pulling out a chair. "What'll it be? The daytime medication, or the nighttime usual?"

"The daytime medication, please, Winston." Bud and I chorused.

He Christmas-carolled his way to the bar, returning no more than three minutes later with a glass of cold beer for Bud and a cider for me.

"Ch-chin, ch-chin," he said with a smile, placing the drinks in front of us. On our first visit to the bar I'd heard him say the same thing to any guest with a British accent; he'd picked up on my Welsh lilt right away, claiming Welsh blood in his own ancestry.

On this occasion, I took the immediate opportunity to engage Winston in conversation. I didn't even take more than a tiny sip of my drink, whereas Bud gulped down almost half of his.

"Been busy today, Winston?" I began.

"It comes in waves," replied the barman. "All in a day's work at sea, you know." While he smiled down at us, enjoying his own pun, I noted his eyes scanning the rest of the guests. He was attentive and professionally entertaining at the same time. I reckoned he was about forty, and he'd told me on a previous occasion that he'd worked for the Stellar Line for eight years. I also knew he was from Jamaica and had a wife and three children there, with his first grandchild on the way. Due any time, he'd said.

"Did you hear about the incident?" I asked quietly.

Winston bent down as if to wipe something from the table. "You mean this morning?"

I nodded.

He nodded, but said nothing. *Discretion?*

"We were there," I added. "In the Games Room, when the poor man died."

Winston stood upright. Glancing about, he kept his voice low. "Terrible sad, Missus Cait. Terrible sad."

When Bud and I had told him, on our first evening aboard, that we were on our belated honeymoon, he'd begun to call me Missus Cait. I liked it, and it had stuck.

"Did you know him?" I asked. I'd decided that "fussy confidante" was the right approach, and Winston seemed to accept it.

He tilted his head. "Not so much. You know he's been coming on these ships for years? But not a drinker, only ever water, so I didn't see much of him. Kept himself to himself."

"Didn't I see you two together when we were sailing close to the lava flow from Mount Kīlauea the other night?" I knew I had, but I wanted to see how Winston would react.

He rallied. "Knew a lot about it all, he did," was his thoughtful reply. "I think he knew a lot of t'ings 'bout a lot of t'ings," he added, allowing his Jamaican lilt to shine through his more formal addressing-the-guests voice.

"It was a wonderful sight, the lava flowing into the sea in the darkness that way," I gushed. "You're lucky to work at this bar at times like that. I don't suppose it ever gets old."

Winston looked wistful. "You right. Never gets old. Same every time we come here. But different too, you know? Sometimes we get real close to the lava, like the other night. But it is always beautiful."

"Are you happy here?" I dared.

Winston gave me an odd look. It must have been an unusual question for a guest to ask a server. His expression told me he was weighing his response. When it came, it surprised me.

"Happy is as happy does, Missus Cait. Some people is sad no matter how much they got, or how fine dey life. Some people is happy with not'ing. My mother told me that a smile can make you happy, and a frown can make you sad, so it's best to smile at the world, and it might just smile back at you. So that's what I do, Missus Cait. I smile, and it makes other people happy, and that makes me happy. See? Happy is as happy does. My mother was right."

Moving back to the bar humming "Rudolph the Red Nosed Reindeer," Winston Williams waved at a couple who'd decided it was time to make the move to change out of their damp pool clothes and get ready for dinner. Bud and I polished off our drinks and decided to do the same.

Despite the untimely death of Tommy Trussler, I was determined to make an effort to look my best for the evening ahead of us. I reasoned that all our suspects were likely to be milling about the bars before dinner in any case, especially the Croppers, who we'd half-arranged to meet for a pre-dinner cocktail.

Back in our stateroom, I hit the shower and makeup bag as quickly as I could; I formulated opening gambits as I applied mascara, and grappled with my uncooperative hair using a very large can of hairspray.

Crystal Bar, Deck 6

I EVENTUALLY MANAGED TO SQUEEZE into my bouncy-fabric, dark blue formal gown, which I was convinced must have shrunk in the closet—*all that sea air and humidity, I expect.* I felt pretty good about my appearance as Bud escorted me toward the uber-fancy Crystal Bar on Deck 6. We'd left it early the night before, choosing to wander the open deck before retiring, enjoying the stars and the sounds of the ship in the night. But in a long gown, and with Bud so nicely turned out in his good navy suit, I thought it best to avoid the open decks until my hairdo had managed to make it through dinner.

The bar was set to one side of the atrium, which overlooked the grand foyer three floors below. As we approached, I spotted two empty stools right next to Laurie and Derek Cropper. I pulled at Bud's hand, which was deliciously wrapped around my own, just to make sure we could claim the prime spot. I sidled up to Laurie Cropper as rapidly as I could, given my heels. She looked resplendent in a scarlet fitted gown with heavily sequinned matching jacket.

"I like the sparkly jacket," I said, mounting the high stool with as much elegance as possible for a short person. Bud gave me a final boost, and I wriggled into position.

"Thank you," said Laurie. "Gee, Bud, you wash up good." She winked at Bud, and I saw him swell with pride.

"So do you, Derek," I added.

He glowed, then Laurie said, "Lookin' good there, ain't he? That diet he's been on is working at last, right, honey?"

Derek patted his midsection and smiled weakly. "Sure is," he said, and winked at me.

Stepping away from his own stool, Derek stood beside Bud and the men shook hands as heartily as old friends who hadn't seen each other in an age. "We're just slipping in a cocktail before we join the captain's other guests in the private alcove." He waved an arm toward a curtained area set at the very far end of the seating area that surrounded the bar. Looking at his hideously large, expensive watch, he added, "Got twenty minutes before the guy turns up. Gonna join us for one?"

I thought we already had, but I realized that Derek meant that he'd like to order drinks for us, as signified by his next comment, directed toward me: "And what will it be for the little lady?"

I knew he meant to be polite, but few things grate on me more than being referred to in such a way. It never seemed to happen to me before I was married to Bud. I wondered if it was something all wives had to contend with. If it was, I could have done with an instruction manual among my wedding gifts.

As I grappled with these emotions, I answered automatically, "Silver Smoke Symphony, please." My choice drew a discreet cough from Bud; it was the drink I'd discovered the night before—to say it was strong was a bit of an understatement.

"Very adventurous," said Laurie, with a wicked glint in her eye. "I'll have one of those too, Derek," she added. "I've seen them. They look spectacular—do they taste good?"

She'd posed a question I'd have asked before ordering, but I replied evenly, "If you like gin, they are very pleasant."

Laurie winked. "Gin and I are good ol' friends, so I'm sure it'll be lovely."

"Same for you?" asked Derek of Bud. His tone was uncertain.

Bud shook his head. "Tried one last night. Not really my thing," he replied with a wan smile. "I'll take a Crown Royal, rocks, thanks." Bud's tastes don't extend to the exotic.

"And the usual for me, Simon," called Derek to the barman who was already tossing and twirling bottles and shakers in a theatrical manner.

Moments later, a round of "Cheers!" was exchanged as we all sipped our chosen beverages. I peered at Laurie through the haze of vapor that poured from the specialty swizzle sticks in our drinks. Before she'd even tasted it she looked delighted. "Look, glitter!" she pointed at the swirl of silver glitter in the glass, then sipped. "Oh Derek, it's fabulous! A real find. Cait, how clever and brave of you to try this."

It seemed that my choice of drink had led to Laurie Cropper and I becoming immediate best friends. While Bud and Derek stood behind us, chatting in low tones, Laurie and I turned on our stools to face each other. I leaned in and began to pump her for anything more I could find out about Tommy Trussler—without her knowing I was doing anything of the sort, of course.

"I know you said you went to Pearl Harbor when you were staying on O'ahu, but what about the other Islands, Laurie? What did you do then?"

"Oh honey, we've been *everywhere,* and have seen *everything.* My Derek has made such wonderful arrangements for us, and I've enjoyed every moment, truly I have. Now, I might forget the order because I can get a little muddled, but I know we started that first day in Maui. We got off in Lahaina and a lovely gentleman drove us right around the Island. Did you get a chance to do that?"

I nodded and tried to stop the vapor from my drink going up my nose.

"It was so beautiful, though I have to say I'm glad we did it in a closed car with air conditioning. Then, that evening we had dinner at a nice restaurant in one of those big old apartment hotels out at Kaanapali Beach. They have a lot of places for sale out that way, and it was a good chance to see one. Of course, I wanted to see it all in daylight, too, so the next day we went back there—but that was after we got back from Molokai."

My surprise must have shown.

"Yes," continued Laurie, "that was a lovely little treat from my honey. We got on a helicopter that morning and flew all over Maui. Oh my dear, if you ever get the chance, you should do it. The mountains, and the valleys, and the waterfalls—it's like something someone made up and put there just so human beings would be awestruck. The mountains? They're like someone carved them with a knife. Don't even look real. Like nothing I ever saw before. Not even on *Hawaii Five-O* on the TV. Well, maybe on that show; they do love their beauty shots, don't they? But it's so much bigger when you're there. Then we flew over to Molokai. You know how fabulous the sea looks from the ship?"

I nodded.

"Well, that's nothin'. Oh honey, the colors are mind-bogglin'. Eventually we landed near the cutest little beach, and some folks from a hotel there brought us a champagne picnic."

I couldn't help but sigh. It sounded idyllic.

"Oh my, how I laughed at Derek getting' in and out of the hammocks they had hanging between the trees," She carried on happily. "He's such a joker, my man. We weren't there too long. It was hot. But unspoiled, you know? I've liked all we've seen on the other Islands, but it's nice to have the chance to see what it must have been like before all of us turned up. You know, just the folks who belong there, and nature. Anyway, after that we went back to Kaanapali to see it in the daytime. And you'll never guess who I saw walking along the beach together!"

"I don't know," I said hopefully. "Do tell."

Laurie leaned in closer. "That poor dead man, Tommy, and that Canadian woman, Frannie Lang. Walking and talking they were. Very close, if you know what I mean."

I didn't, so I thought I'd better check. "Do you mean they were close like lovers might be?"

Laurie poked at the straw that was pouring vapor into her face and sipped her drink. "No, not really." She sounded disappointed.

Bud and I had walked along that same beach, and I knew that the roaring of the surf and the strength of the wind forced us to shout at each other to be heard, even when we were just a few inches apart. That could have accounted for the closeness of Frannie and Tommy.

"Did you see Tommy anywhere else on your travels?" I ventured.

Again Laurie sipped and thought. "The day we were at Kona—that was the next day, right? Well, the day we were there, we took another helicopter tour, right over all the lava fields, and way up over the volcano itself. I have to say it was amazing, but I think I preferred seeing the lava flow into the sea that night. It was better in the dark—more dramatic, glowing red. During the day it was mainly steam, and—oh my, dear me—the smell? Just awful, like the worst cheese that's gone off, with a dead rat wrapped around it. I was kinda glad to get away from it, but, once it got into the helicopter, it didn't go away. Lingered like the smell of a skunk. But, yeah, the Island was lovely. When we landed, we saw Tommy then. We went along to the Hulihe'e Palace in Kailua-Kona. Did you see it?"

"Yes—Bud and I enjoyed it there."

"Well, there was a hula performance just when we arrived, and Tommy was there, standing under a huge banyan tree. He seemed to be alone, but when we were leaving to walk back to the lines to get the tender boat back to the ship, I saw him talking to Nigel Knicely. Now there's a guy. 'Knicely with a K' all the time. Who talks like that?"

"Apparently Nigel does," I replied, inwardly agreeing with Laurie's disdain for the man's pretentiousness. "Was Janet, Nigel's wife, there?" I asked, trying to sound casual. *I must take some time to recollect what I saw when we visited the place*, I thought.

Laurie sucked at her straw again, then realized she had almost finished her drink. "I didn't see her, but it'd be easy to miss her. It's like that woman walks around in camouflage all the time, don't you think? I get it that some folks like to pack carefully for a vacation, but do you think she owns anything that's got any color at all? Looks like cookie dough all the time, she does. And not even the sort with chips, or fruit, or anything interesting in it."

Laurie's candor made me smile. Sometimes it's nice to be in the company of someone who'll say out loud what you only dare to think—and for me, that's unusual.

"You certainly made the most of your chances to get about," I said, hoping to learn more.

"We sure did. Derek planned it all so we would. Spent a lot of time organizing this trip. Not like him. He usually leaves it all up to me—and the travel agent, of course. I'm good at business, but I think it's best to hire someone who really knows what they're doing, if you need a job done well. Like the guy we've got running the place back home now. Good man. Derek's pretty keen on him taking it all off our hands, or so he says. Cannot let go, my husband."

We seemed to be straying from the topic I wanted to tackle— namely, any sightings of, or opinions about, Tommy Trussler. "You said something interesting about Tommy earlier today," I said. "What had he done to make you think he was untrustworthy?" *Best to be blunt.*

Laurie placed her all-but-empty glass on the bar and gave her answer some thought. *A test of our newly forged friendship?*

"Sometimes a guy gives a woman a come-on—a bit of a flirtatious nod and a wink. Know what I mean?"

It never seemed to happen to me, but I said, "Sure," as though it did.

"Well, first time we ran into him, he did that. I didn't mind. It's quite nice at my age, whoever does it. But then at the luau at our hotel? He was kinda looking at me funny. It stopped on the ship. Eventually. We'd see him at the gym, and he'd stopped doing it by then. But there was always something there. Even when we were playing cards. A sly, sideways look. And something in his eyes that said he knew something I didn't. And I guess he did." She sighed deeply. "Any more than that, well, I guess I shouldn't say. I've talked it over with Derek and he agrees. Better not to say. Hope you're okay with that, honey. Don't mean nothin' by it."

Rats! "Well, I suppose poor Tommy's estate will take some sorting out," I said. "You and Derek seemed to think he was alone in the world. I wonder what happens in a case like that."

"Lawyers'll get it all, I guess," said Laurie, shutting me down. Her mind was elsewhere. Looking around the bar, she added, "Given the amount of vapor the dry ice in these things gives off, I might get away with it, but Derek prefers if I go out to the smoking area to use this," she confided. She waggled the end of her fancy electronic cigarette at me from the open clasp of her evening purse. "Want to come?"

I could have hit her! At that precise moment, I'd have given at least one limb to be able to smoke a cigarette, but I'd worked so hard at giving up, I knew I'd be letting myself—and Bud—down if I caved in. But I was on a roll; she was telling me all sorts of little snippets about the dead man without even realizing it, so I agreed.

"That would be super," I said, "but let's tell the men we're off to the ladies.'"

She giggled. "Okay, but Derek will guess. Come on. Leave that there—or, better still, just knock it back." She cast an eye at my glass and I followed her second suggestion.

Neither Laurie nor I found it easy to dismount from our stools, so our husbands helped, and we went on our way. Seemingly experienced at finding her way from the Crystal Bar to the nearest smoking area, Laurie took my arm and steered me. I felt as though we were two schoolgirls rushing off to a secret rendezvous. It was quite fun.

The rather underwhelming smoking area set up just outside a door to the open deck was already being used by a dozen formally attired men and women, all of whom bore the same look of guilt and wicked enjoyment. *I used to be one of you*, I thought, and felt a rush of equal parts of pride and longing as I saw people inhale and exhale deeply in the night air.

"Do you smoke?" asked Laurie as she pulled her vaping implement from her purse.

I shook my head. "Used to," was all I could muster.

"Me too," smiled Laurie, "but now I do this instead." She sucked on the metal end of a glass tube with pink liquid inside, and exhaled a stream of white vapor. "I used to do this just to get me through the times when I couldn't get the real thing—you know, sneaking into the washrooms in restaurants and such where they don't know you're vaping. But I got sick of the smell of smoke on my clothes, so now I just do this. Wanna try?" She held the sucking end toward me, and rubbed it with a paper tissue from her purse. "I ain't got anything nasty, honest," she smiled.

I felt as though I was being tempted by some ancient evil. I even visualized myself with a little angel on one shoulder and a little devil on the other, like Tom the cat in the old *Tom and Jerry* cartoons. I'm pretty strong-willed when I need to be, and I was almost sure that one puff wouldn't be the start of a slippery slope, so I gave it a go. I regretted it immediately. Cherry flavor hit my taste buds, and I blew out the vapor as quickly as I could.

My expression must have spoken volumes, because Laurie said, "Don't like cherries?"

I shook my head. "Not that sort of cherry flavor, though I can nibble on one or two of the real thing now and again."

"They do lots of other flavors, honey," she added helpfully, relieving me of the device. "I guess you could try one of them. I hear the apple is very pleasant, and they do pineapple, orange, the lot. Or there's always the stuff that has no flavor at all."

I shook my head. I felt as though I'd dodged a bullet, though the nicotine rush was quite something—much more potent than the gum I'd been chewing for months.

As she wiped the mouthpiece, then sucked a couple more times herself, I said, "That's liquid nicotine in the tube, isn't it?"

Laurie nodded.

"I suppose you had to bring a lot of it with you for this trip. Is it easy to get hold of?" I asked.

Laurie slipped the tube back into her purse. "Sure thing," she said, leading me away from the smoking area. "Back home, there are stores most everywhere that sell it, though I made sure to bring a whole box of the little bottles with me. I didn't know if the habit had made its way to Hawai'i yet, and I didn't want to run out. Like I said, you should try it. It's so easy, and much more satisfying than that horrible old gum. That stuff? It made me look like a cow, chewing the cud—and it gave me gas."

But the gum's not lethal, unlike the bottle of liquid you have there, was what I wanted to say, but I didn't. Derek had obviously known exactly where we'd gone, and, when he and Bud arrived a moment later, he made it clear it was time for him and Laurie to join the rest of the select few who would dine with the ship's master that night. Laurie tucked away her vaping device, and we all left the smokers to their nefarious ways.

"See you for a nightcap?" called Laurie as she trotted toward the bar.

"Absolutely," I called back.

When they'd gone, Bud said to me, "We've still got half an hour before dinner—want to fill me in on what you and Laurie got up to?" He raised an eyebrow toward the sign that said, SMOKING AREA, looking almost angry.

"Well, I didn't smoke, I can tell you that much," I began, "but I can also tell you from what she said to me at the bar that Laurie seemed to think there was something going on between Frannie Lang and Tommy—something that was more than a tutor-pupil relationship. She said she'd seen them together on Maui. Frannie Lang was quite clear she'd met Tommy in Hilo—days after we'd left Maui. Was Laurie mistaken, or was Frannie Lang lying?"

Bud looked tired. "Everybody lies, and everyone has secrets," he said. "As for Frannie and Tommy? I can't see it."

"What's wrong?" I asked. Bud was far from his normal self. *What's happened?*

"I promised I wouldn't say anything," he replied, looking guilty. I could see turmoil in his eyes.

"As your wife, you promised you'd always tell me everything—well, everything you're legally allowed to, anyway."

Bud raked his hand through his hair. *You're stressed, Bud.* My mind was in a whirl. What could have got him into such a state?

Finally, Bud took both my hands in his, drew me toward a quiet corner, and looked me straight in the eyes. "You must promise not to say a word to anyone. And I'm specifically including Laurie in that 'anyone,' right?"

"Right . . ." I replied slowly. *What's the matter, Bud?* I wanted to scream.

"Promise?"

I nodded. "Just tell me. I promise."

"It's Derek. He's got cancer. Pancreatic. Stage four. He hasn't told his wife. No one."

I was almost speechless. "But he told *you*? Why? Why would you tell a complete stranger if he hasn't told his wife?"

Bud looked at me as though pleading to be understood. "He said I gave him a funny look or two earlier on today, when we were in their suite. Said he thought I'd guessed that something was seriously wrong with him, and that he needed to tell me the truth so I wouldn't say anything in front of his wife."

We were both silent for a moment or two.

"I'm so sorry, my darling," I said, hugging Bud to my side. I felt the weight of the news dragging him down. "He's passed a terrible responsibility to you. I think it's unfair of him. How dare he?" I was angry with Derek Cropper, and felt sad for him too. I was sad for Bud. And for Laurie. "Why on earth hasn't he told Laurie? Did you ask him? Did he say?"

Bud sighed and pulled away from me gently. "Cait, we were standing at a bar, and a man I hardly know told me he's dying, and that it's a secret. How do you think I reacted? Of course I asked him all the obvious questions, and he gave me all the obvious answers. He doesn't want her to worry. He doesn't want the treatment they've offered because it'll destroy his quality of life—what little he has left of it. They can't operate, so it would be chemo, radiation . . . you know the sort of thing. He says he feels fine, except that drinking makes his gut ache—but he does it anyway because he always has, and he enjoys it. He made it clear to me he plans on going out with a bang, and he wants Laurie to have a good time until he drops."

The vastness of Derek Cropper's decisions overwhelmed me.

"You'd tell me, wouldn't you?" I asked quietly. "You know . . . if . . ."

Bud smiled sadly at me. "I don't know," he said simply. "Would you tell me?"

I gave the matter some thought. "I see what you mean," I replied. "Not that straightforward, is it?"

I held Bud's hand as tight as I could without hurting him, then said, "Right, I'm having another drink before dinner. Coming?"

Bud looked at his watch. "They'll be letting us in in ten minutes, and I bet the bar's slammed." He sounded utterly deflated.

"You know how well I can wriggle my way to a bar and get the drinks in," I said, smiling with false bravado. "Come on, let's get a quick one and wander to the table a few minutes late."

Bud agreed, and we headed off. As I led the way, Bud said, rather more cheerily, "Get anything else useful from Laurie?"

I looked around and drew close to Bud's ear. "You'll have to wait until we're alone, but yes, she seems to have formed some strong opinions about Tommy, and I don't think they were all formed when Derek was around."

"What do you mean?" asked Bud, looking perplexed.

"I'll tell you when we can speak in private," was all I could manage as I pushed into the melee surrounding the Crystal Bar. Once there, I waved at Simon the happy barman.

Starlight Restaurant, Deck 6

BUD AND I HAD REQUESTED a table for two for the entire cruise. We'd been allocated a delightful one at the edge of the balcony on the upper of the two dining decks, where we had a good view of the entire dining room. My aversion to heights meant I had to sit with my back toward the balcony rail, so I looked across the upper deck rather than out over the lower one.

Seated at the table nearest our own were two women who appeared to be in their forties. As our time on the ship progressed, they became nodding, then smiling, companions. Diane, a delightful woman, was from Boston; she sported perfectly matched outfits for every meal, and never wore the same ensemble twice. As she and her companion left their table, they'd pass by ours, and Diane would routinely make some sort of witty comment as they breezed past. She was like a ray of sunshine—always laughing and joking with her much quieter companion.

On this occasion, she looked stunning—dazzling, even—in silver sequins and black velvet. She waved as we arrived and we waved back, safe in the knowledge we wouldn't have to engage in conversation; however, Diane surprised me by leaving her seat and rushing to our table.

Grasping her napkin, she bent toward Bud. "My, don't you two lovebirds look fabulous tonight!" she said. "Don't panic—I'm not going to interrupt your honeymoon dinner, but I heard you were in the Games Room when that guy died this morning. Was it his heart, or did his girlfriend kill him with an icepick?"

I must have looked horrified, because Diane laughed at my expression.

"It was very sudden, but we don't know what happened. Suffice to say, neither of us observed any icepicks." Bud was forcing jocularity, and it didn't work.

Diane pulled a face. "That's the Canadian take on it, eh?"

We all laughed, and she left.

"How does she know what happened, or that we were there? And where did the idea of an icepick come from?" whispered Bud behind his menu.

Peering across at Diane and her friend, I smiled and replied, "She's a natural communicator. She'd know everything that's going on, and a lot that isn't, I suspect."

"Well, let's not encourage her," said Bud. With that, we both gave our attention to what was in store for us for dinner.

The service and the food were spectacular. I had a small portion of grilled polenta topped with warm, crushed baby tomatoes and pearls of bocconcini cheese, draped with strands of emerald basil, and drizzled with warm, scented olive and basil oil; it looked and tasted fabulous. The big deal on the menu that night was lobster, but I've never cared for it, so I settled for succulent tournedos Rossini with a light madeira sauce and some tasty, beautifully presented vegetables, prepared with a Provençal flair.

Bud and I hardly spoke. My thoughts were on the Tommy Trussler case, but Bud didn't seem to be engaged with anything internal or external. It was as though he was daydreaming.

I noticed that the senior maître d' was making the rounds from table to table, and I reached across and tapped Bud on the arm just before he arrived at ours. Martin, who hailed from the Czech Republic, was dark, dapper, and always smiling. He had a way of putting everyone at ease, and ran his dining room as though we guests were the instruments and his staff the musicians, with the score provided by the kitchens.

"I hope everything is to your satisfaction this evening?" he asked, as he must have done on thousands of previous occasions. To his credit, he made the question sound fresh and genuine.

Despite the smile on his lips I could tell that Bud just wasn't with it, so I blustered on about how marvelous everything was, but that we'd probably pass on dessert and get a breath of air before dinner.

"Not tonight, please, no," said Martin. "Tonight we have our last-ever parade with the baked Alaska puddings, which will be alight. It is magnificent, but, having done this for many years, we are now told it is no longer safe to walk about with open flames. So tonight, this is it—the grand finale. You should stay. Cruising is changing all the time, but you are fortunate to be here to witness a great tradition. The quartet will play, the cruise director will host, and the captain will speak. Then we parade, sing 'Auld Lang Syne' together, and wave our napkins in the air. It will be fun."

A gale of laughter floated up from the main floor of the restaurant below us. I couldn't help myself—I turned toward the sound and saw that it was the party whooping it up at the captain's table. Derek and Laurie Cropper, to be exact. It appeared that Derek had just performed some sort of trick, which had him standing behind the master of the ship with a bottle of water in one hand and a large napkin in the other. The entire table was giving him a round of applause, and Laurie was on her feet leading the response. From where I was positioned, I could read the captain's body language, which told me he was taken aback by the proceedings, and feeling distinctly uncomfortable. I wondered how much more the Croppers had managed to drink after they'd left us; the sommelier down on the main floor seemed to be carrying several bottles of wine as he danced his way from glass to glass.

Just before he left, Martin leaned in toward us. "Ezra says he'd like to see you after the parade, in his office," he whispered. Affixing a smile on his face, he glided to a table across the walkway.

"If you're finished, I think we should go now," said Bud, half his meal still on his plate.

"Oh! You didn't like the Dover sole?"

He looked at his meal as if noticing it for the first time, "Not hungry. Buy you a drink at the Sundowner Bar?"

"Of course," I said, searching his face. I took the napkin from my lap, put it to the left of my plate, and stood to leave.

It took us ten minutes to get there, without so much as a word passing between us. When we arrived, we sat completely alone, save the relief barman. Winston was on his dinner break; soft Hawaiian music floated from the sound system; I hoped for some solace.

Bud got up restlessly and stood at the rail, looking out at our wake. It foamed in the moonlight then disappeared into the vastness of the black ocean.

"We're nothing, are we, Cait?" he said.

I left my seat and drink and stood beside him. "We are what we are," I replied quietly.

Smiling warmly, he said, "You know I love you, right?"

I silently stroked the back of his hand and murmured "Yes indeed, Husband."

"Good, because I do. And when I say we're nothing, I don't mean us. We're quite something, you and me. I mean it in the general sense. You put your finger on it earlier today: we see the world as *we* are, not how *it* is. I've spent my entire adult life upholding the rule of law. Making sure the good guys get help, and the bad guys get their just desserts. I've tried to be fair, to act decently. But life's not fair, is it? Despite all I've seen, including the body of my first wife lying on a beach, shot to death because some stupid scumbag thought she was me, I've never faced what Derek Cropper has made me face tonight. I've lost my wife to murder. I've lost colleagues to violent deaths and accidental ones. I've seen suspects and perpetrators killed. I've even helped rush a few wounded ones to hospital myself, because they might have done something terrible, but they didn't deserve to die. I've been forced to take a life on two occasions. I've seen and experienced a great deal that many haven't. But this? I suppose I've been fortunate, until now, that I haven't had too many people close to me who I know are dying, while there's not a single thing I can do to help. No one can. And the thing is, there's no one to blame. No criminal. No idiot with a shotgun or a pistol. No meth-head with a knife. Just cells—tiny little things that are supposed to keep you alive until they decide to kill you. I cannot imagine how you must feel if that's the person you see in the mirror, knowing you can't help yourself." Bud turned, picked up his drink, and downed it in one gulp.

"So, you *wouldn't* tell me, if you knew that was happening inside your body," I said. It wasn't a question.

"No. I wouldn't want you to feel what I'm feeling now. And this for a man I barely know."

"But I'd know, Bud. I'd see it in your eyes. We haven't been together very long, but I understand you well enough to know that I'd *know*. At least I'd suspect."

Bud shrugged. "Losing a life, under any circumstances, makes me angry. Murder more than anything. But at least with that there's a chance for justice. For Derek Cropper? And his wife? And all the people like them? No justice at all."

I sighed. My heart hurt. I'd never seen Bud like this before. As I pondered why he had been hit so hard by Derek Cropper's news, I felt an uneasiness creep into my soul.

"Look, Bud, I know you said you wouldn't tell me if you were sick—really sick—but, please, look at me. *Show* me you're okay."

I pulled him around and stared into the pale blue eyes I love so much. *Relief.* Bud's sadness wasn't for himself. He was fine. He wasn't hiding anything about his own health from me. *He couldn't.*

I decided it was time to tackle his mood head on. "Bud, I love you, and I'm terribly sorry that Derek's news has affected you like this, but we have a case to solve where justice *can* be delivered. Tommy Trussler didn't have time to put his affairs in order, to take one last, mad trip, and risk a fortune in the casino while drinking the best champagne. He had his life taken from him in an instant, and we have a chance to find out who did that, and why. So—are we on this case, or what?"

"Jingle bells, jingle bells, Mister and Missus!" called Winston Williams as he emerged from a door let into the side of the bar. "What you two doing out here when all the fun is back in the dinin' room? Fiery Baked Alaska tonight. Last time, too, they say. You missing somet'in' there, you know."

Bud shook his head just like Marty our black Lab does when he's been out in the rain. Winston chuckled, and I knew that my Bud was coming back to me.

"One for the ditch?" suggested Winston.

"How long before all the kerfuffle is over in the dining room?" asked Bud.

Winston looked at his watch. "'Bout half an hour, I'd say, then they all rush out, grab a drink at the bars, and run into the theatre for the show," he said sagely.

"Right then, two of our after-dinner usuals, please, Winston," said Bud, handing the barman his card.

"You can put that away, Mister Bud. I got your number by now. I bring your medication to you where you sit, you relax. You know, like they say on them islands back there over the sea, 'Hang loose,' or, like they say on mine, 'Don't worry, be happy!'"

Bud and I moved to a little table overlooking the sea. Two people on a ship in the middle of an ocean. Around us, blackness. Like a void. Tiny, insignificant beings, battling a newfound sense of mortality and determined to find a killer.

After Winston delivered a Bombay and tonic for me and a Crown on the rocks for Bud, Bud sipped, rallied, and opened with, "Right then, tell me what you learned about Tommy from Laurie. I'm all ears."

"Your ears aren't that big," I mugged.

We seemed to have weathered a storm, and I spoke quickly and quietly. "Laurie mentioned she'd seen Frannie and Tommy together, something that Frannie 'forgot' to tell us about. I don't think Laurie would have made up such a specific instance."

"Go on," encouraged Bud.

I drew closer, "She said she saw Frannie and Tommy walking together along Kaanapali Beach. Now, I know that the Knicelys said they met Tommy when he was on the same tour of Maui as them, but we were moored off Lahaina for two days, so I suppose Tommy might only have taken part in the organized tour on one of those days, leaving him free to explore the Island alone on the other. But we visited Maui before we visited the Big Island, and Frannie Lang was quite clear, insistent even, about meeting Tommy for the first time there, in Hilo. So, if Laurie is right, then Frannie lied about when she first met him."

"Laurie might have been confused, or mistaken about the identity of either Tommy or Frannie," said Bud.

I gave him a withering look. "For a retired cop, you're surprisingly quick to give a suspect the benefit of the doubt. She also told me she saw Tommy and Nigel together in Kona—though that was in the line-up to get the tender boats, so they might have bumped into each other by chance, I suppose. I'll give Nigel the benefit of the doubt before you do, shall I?"

Bud poked his tongue in my general direction, which was the sight that greeted Janet and Nigel Knicely as they rounded the corner of the rear deck and found us in our "secret spot." She was dressed in a pale gold gown that was as close to beige as evening wear could get, and Nigel wore a new-looking dinner jacket with a lurid bow tie. The cummerbund—which I was positive he was wearing in the correct manner—wasn't on view, hidden beneath his buttoned, double-breasted jacket.

"Look who it is," exclaimed Janet, quite loudly for her. I was oddly glad to see the Knicelys. *I have some questions for you.*

"Why not join us?" I said quickly. Bud rolled his eyes. "Hey, Winston, we'd like to buy our friends a drink," I called.

Janet Knicely gushed as she hurried toward me. I got the distinct impression that she and her husband weren't invited to join many groups or gatherings. Not twice, at least.

With the four of us finally settled, a mai tai in front of Janet and a beer for Nigel, I opened with an innocent enough question: "Did you discover the mai tai in Hawai'i, Janet?"

The mousey woman grinned toward me, eyes closed as she sipped. "Indeed I did. Aren't they lovely? So sweet and delicious. It's like having your afters in a glass."

"Dessert, Janet. Cait's not English anymore; she's an American now," said Nigel.

I didn't know which incorrect assertion by Nigel to react to first. Before I managed to open my mouth, I saw Bud stiffen.

"I never was English," I began. "Always Welsh. Through and through. And I'm now a Canadian, not an American. And I know that afters, and pudding, and dessert, all mean the same thing, as does anyone who's traveled, or watched television, or read a book." I didn't say more, because I knew I might not stop.

Nigel gave me a strange look and simply said, "It says a lot about the relationship between the English and the Welsh that it used to be legal for an Englishman to shoot a Welshman in the back and get away with it."

I heard Bud take a deep breath. He buried his face in his drink.

I bit.

"I think you might have a few of your facts wrong there," I replied as calmly as I could. "I believe you're referring to the often misquoted claim that it's legal to shoot a Welshman with a longbow on Sunday in the Cathedral Close in Hereford, or inside the city walls of Chester after midnight. I suspect this erroneous idea is connected with a rumored city ordinance, reputedly drawn up in 1403 in Chester, but never proven to exist. Granted, with the Glyndŵr Rising raging in the area from 1400 to 1415, it might have made sense to draw up such an ordinance, but it's unbelievable that anyone with an ounce of education, or manners, would cling to such a concept almost six hundred years after the last Welsh War of Independence. Unless, for some strange reason, they think it's funny."

I was seething. I'd had my fill of the day—enough to let it show. I never lose my temper. Well, almost never. Not unless it's for a good cause, anyway.

"Nigel didn't mean anything by it, did you, Nigel?" Janet said. "No, of course he didn't. He's just having you on. Right, Nigel?"

No, he's not.

Nigel's face was a mask of disdain. I wasn't sure if it was for me, every living Welsh person, or his wife. I supposed it could be all three.

Bud countered with, "Cait was just telling me the rumor is that Frannie Lang and poor Tommy Trussler were having a bit of an onboard romance. Anything to it, do you think?"

The zag, introduced when the entire conversation could have zigged, was pure Bud.

Janet drew close to Bud and me, seeming to completely forget the insults her husband had just hurled my way, and whispered, "I think you might be right. I saw them going at it hammer and tongs up at the front of the ship the other morning."

Ah—you do have your eyes open sometimes.

I wondered what Janet meant by "going at it," so I thought it best to ask. Ignoring Nigel completely, I said quietly, "Do tell—what were they up to, exactly?"

Nigel tutted loudly as Janet replied, "You know. Arguing. In public. Very impolite."

With my just having vented at her husband, I wondered what constituted an "argument" for Janet Knicely. Again, I decided to be direct. "How do you mean? Were they shouting at each other?"

Janet placed her drink on the plastic tub-table just as the under-lighting changed from blue to red. "Oh, did I do that?" she asked excitedly.

You have the attention span of a guppy, was what I wanted to say; instead I said, "So they were fighting?"

Janet looked at me—with her eyes open for once—a red glow now suffusing her bland complexion. "Yes, shouting. They looked angry."

"Did you hear what they were saying?" I tried for a conspiratorial air, but probably only managed to sound nosey.

Janet looked disappointed. "Not really. I think she said something about him being on fire. Though that doesn't make any sense, does it?" I was pretty sure that Janet hadn't heard any such thing, but she didn't want to admit to a total lack of knowledge.

"She told him he was a liar and a cheat," said Nigel vehemently, rather surprising both Bud and myself. Janet also looked taken aback.

"You weren't there, Nigel," she said. "I was walking the deck on my own at the time, and you'd gone to the Internet café."

Nigel's aggressive air left him and he simply said, "Really?" in a non-committal—and unconvincing—way.

"When was this, then?" I pressed.

Janet looked at Nigel as though he was about to bite her head off. "It was the last morning of the ashore days. The morning we were in Hilo, early. I know it was, because I wanted a walk before we sat on a bus all day to go to Hawai'i Volcanoes National Park, to see that Kīlauea volcano. I was very excited about it, especially after seeing all the lava flowing into the sea the night before. You said you had to go to check emails for work, Nigel, and I went for a walk. I know I did."

"Yes, dear," was Nigel's distracted response.

"And you were at the front of the ship?" I asked.

Janet nodded. "Up near those netball courts they have."

"Basketball," corrected Nigel. "It's basketball, not netball. I keep telling you."

Janet shrugged off her husband's put-down and smiled, with her eyes closed again. *Very telling.* "It's all the same, really," she observed, fiddling with her earrings.

"They're pretty," I said.

Janet smiled coyly. "Nigel gave them to me, for our recommitment, you know."

I peered at the small diamond droppers as they glittered in the moonlight, and reflected the red glow of the table lighting.

"Did you get them on the Islands?" I asked Nigel.

"In Maui," said Janet. "We'd said we wouldn't get anything for each other, but then I saw these, and Nigel decided to sneak away from me in Lahaina and get them as a surprise. He gave them to me for our first formal dinner, the first day we were moored off Maui. Isn't he lovely? Diamonds, for little me!"

"They certainly have a pretty setting," I remarked. *Exactly like the two pairs Tommy had in his safe.*

Bud looked puzzled when I followed up with, "I'm dreading trying to pack tomorrow. We bought so many gifts I don't know what we'll do." Actually, we hadn't. "Did you buy lots for your boys and their wives?" I asked innocently.

Nigel sipped his beer as Janet said, "Not too much. Some little beach things for the wives, a couple of hats for the boys, and I did get a string of pearls for each of the wives as well, but only at the ABC Store. They were so cheap, I couldn't believe it. And they're real too."

"Good value," I agreed, "and women always like jewelry."

"Pearls will always be classy," said Nigel, his tone smug and knowing.

"Not as classy as diamonds," said Janet.

"Pearls cost enough," said Nigel.

"Yes, dear," said Janet, and sipped her mai tai.

A Wind from The Islands

I'D DECIDED TO MAKE SOME headway with my gin and tonic when I smelled a familiar perfume. Just behind us stood Kai and Malia Pukui. The gown hugging Malia's slim figure had an intricate floral pattern. We'd seen any number of Hawaiian prints during the past couple of weeks, and some of them had been hideous. The effect seemed to be increased a thousand-fold when entire families wore clothing made from the same fabric, which one woman had told me she did so she could spot her husband when he wandered off. Malia's dress was was subtle, and even suggested an earlier age, before the proliferation of commercialized prints at places like Hilo Hattie's.

Malia's dark, bare arms glowed in the moonlight, one linked through her husband's dinner-jacketed arm. He'd teamed his classic dinner suit with a gleaming white dress shirt that had a hibiscus pattern in the weave itself; subtle, yet culturally appropriate. His wing collar and black tie were delightfully formal, and Kai's graceful appearance put Nigel Knicely's over-the-top outfit to shame.

"Aloha," said Kai and Malia simultaneously. Both Bud and I "Aloha'd" back, but Janet and Nigel both replied with "Good evening," despite the fact that it was about half past ten.

"I see you are enjoying a mai tai," said Kai, smiling at Janet. "This is a drink you discovered on our Islands, I guess. Many people do."

"You were very clever to invent it," said Janet, as though Kai himself was responsible.

Smiling, Kai replied, "But it is not a drink from Hawai'i at all. Like the ukulele and sweet bread, which came to us from Portugal, these things are now seen as Hawaiian. But the mai tai? Some say it was first made at Trader Vic's, others say it was by a man called Don the Beachcomber. Either way, it came from the mainland, California, where *tiki* bars were popular. However, I believe that many bartenders on our Islands are happy that it made its way across the sea."

"Sweet gloop," said Nigel offensively.

Janet giggled. "I think it's lovely," she said. "Will you join us?"

I noticed the smile on Malia's face become rigid. She was just about to speak when her husband said, "Of course."

"Jingle bells, jingle bells! Got quite de party goin' here, Missus Cait, Mister Bud," said Winston as he arrived at our table. Pulling chairs from other areas, the six of us soon sat facing each other.

Bud opened with, "Wonderful shirt you have there, Kai. I'm quite envious. I don't get many chances to dress up. I guess you get to do it a lot on these cruises."

Kai nodded. "It is always a pleasure to see all the ladies looking so beautiful in their gowns, and the men in their smart suits, on a perfect night like this," he replied slowly.

I jumped in with, "Malia, is that dress vintage? Or is it just a retro print?"

The woman who had entranced us with her graceful dance moves for many days gave us a bright smile, warm with genuine pride. "It belonged to my *Makuahine*, my mother, many years ago."

"I'm sure she looked just as beautiful in it as you do now," said Bud, smiling. "Is Hawaiian society given to wearing formal clothes much anymore? We mainly saw people in casual dress." Bud was trying really hard—he usually had no interest in what folks wore.

"Not these days," said Malia, sounding a little disappointed. "When my parents were in their prime, they often dressed formally. My *Makuakāne*, my father, was the harbor master in O'ahu. A very responsible job. He was a respected man."

I'd noticed that, whenever they were addressing guests, both Malia and Kai used the odd Hawaiian word, then explained it. I liked it. The Aloha Spirit—alive, well, and kicking at the Sundowner Bar.

"Is he dead now, dear?" asked Janet, having polished off her drink.

Again I saw Malia Pukui stiffen. She looked down at her lap and said softly, "He is."

"Aw, shame," said Janet.

Nigel threw her a withering glance, stood abruptly, and said, "Time for the show, Janet. It'll start before long, and you know I like to be front and center."

I bet you do.

We were all taken aback at his tone—all except Janet, who wobbled to her feet and walked away with her husband, looking a little unsteady.

"Maybe not her first mai tai of the evening," observed Bud as the couple departed.

Neither Kai nor Malia commented. They both just smiled. I noted they were both drinking sparkling water.

"Have you enjoyed your day today, despite its start?" asked Kai calmly.

I was about to say "Yes," then realized I should temper my enthusiasm for being on the hunt for a killer. "It's been . . . different," I said.

Malia nodded sagely. "That is good, because death being close to you often is not good; if it happens frequently, evil spirits can tread a path to you more easily."

It occurred to me that, although she'd caught my eye all those days ago during the embarkation process—and despite seeing her since then as she showed guests traditional Hawaiian dance moves and lei-making—I knew nothing of the woman herself. Indeed, I knew little of Kai as well. I decided to try to find out all I could about them. "I hear from Kai that your family is involved in the production of cosmetics back on the Islands," I began.

Malia nodded once. "We are. We are very fortunate that we are able to grow everything we need to produce some of the best things for the skin. Macadamia nuts, Kukui nuts, castor beans, cocoa butter, and so many fragrances from pineapples, apricots, plumeria, pikake, and so forth. Everything we make is natural, and truly of Hawai'i."

I enjoyed hearing the Pukuis pronounce the name of their home in the authentic manner, with the "w" sounding as a "v," and each distinct "i" at the end of the name. I'd tried it myself, but felt I'd come off as a bit pretentious, so I'd chosen to stick to the more familiar pronunciation.

"You both have lustrous skin, and always smell so good. Do you use your own products?"

"Of course," said Malia. "It is only a small company, and we need to promote what we do whenever we can, so we are our own advertisers. We are hoping to sign a big contract soon with a group of hotels on the Islands—not just for their properties there, but maybe around the world. Their guests like our little bars of soap, and we might have the chance to supply them for all their rooms. It would be a challenge, but it could change life for the better for our entire family."

"You live in an astoundingly lush and beautiful part of the world," said Bud. "It must be tough to work every day when you could be enjoying the countryside or surfing. Is it a stupid question to ask if you both surf?"

"It is not stupid," said Kai, smiling. "Not everyone who lives on our Islands surfs. Not everyone can, and not everyone wants to. But," he winked, "most can, and most want to. It's in our blood. I expect you visited the large, bronze statue of Duke Kahanamoku on Waikiki?"

"We did," said Bud. "We spent some time grazing on *pupus*, or 'appies' as we would call them, at Duke's Bar at the Outrigger Hotel on the evening of the day we embarked. They have a fair bit of historical stuff about the man there. He really changed Hawai'i, didn't he?"

"He was a man of royal blood, with a mission to share surfing with the world, and he allowed Hawai'i to have the tourist appeal it has today. My *Kupuna*, which is what I called my grandfather, knew him well," said Kai. "He was a good and kind man. Though driven, and of course very athletic, he was gentle, my grandfather said. A legend to be proud of."

"Well, it's a wonderful place," said Bud. "So bright. Everything is vivid. Those rows of colorful surfboards all chained up along the beach? We saw little kids collecting them and running into the surf. Looked like they were right out of their schoolrooms."

"They might have been," said Kai. He smiled, but I caught a flicker of sadness in his expression.

"Cait and I were amazed by the size of some of the plants you have outdoors, which we can only coax along as houseplants." Bud grinned at me. "Well, my wife isn't known for her horticultural skills, so I know our expectations are pretty low to begin with. But even so—some of those hibiscus flowers were as big as my head."

You're doing well, Bud.

"It is our climate," said Kai. "The climes at sea level and just above, I mean. Most visitors think of all the Hawaiian Islands as being the same as each other, and purely tropical. As you may know, this is not true."

"Your presentation a couple of days ago was fascinating," replied Bud, "and we learned a lot about how you have all types of climates, from tundra to desert, on the Big Island. You are a good speaker, Kai. It was very enjoyable. I just wish more passengers had attended."

Kai and Malia smiled. "The Aloha Spirit is not to be forced upon anyone," said Kai. "People come to play in the fiftieth state of the USA, and do not always wish to learn about how it differs from, or can complement, the others. We are grateful that they visit, and we welcome them with open arms and open hearts. You know, in some ways, it has allowed many of our old ways to begin to flourish again, because some of the people who visit us really do want to learn about the time before Captain Cook, and how we lived our lives then."

"I expect you benefit from the new popularity in eco-tourism too," I added. "I know we're finding that a great deal along the coast of British Columbia."

"Indeed," replied Malia. "We have such wonderful natural features for people to explore and enjoy. Of course, it's always a difficult balance to strike, but we are trying to do the right things, for the right reasons."

"You mentioned in your presentation the other day that you were involved with the Polynesian Cultural Center out near the Brigham Young University. Bud and I didn't have a chance to go. I understand it's very popular. How were you involved?"

Malia deferred to Kai, who replied, "It was one of those times when I had to decide whether to be involved and try to ensure that what was depicted was as close to realistic as a tourist attraction would allow, or to stand outside it and protest that it was oversimplifying our complex cultures. I decided to get involved, and I'm glad I did. It's not a Polynesian Disneyland—it does a fair job and, of course, it employs a lot of our people. As I said, the side effects have been interesting."

"Dare I say that Canadians often view the Hawaiian Islands very differently than do most Americans?" said Bud.

"You may say what you wish," said Malia enigmatically, "you are a guest. We find it best to avoid the topics of religion and politics upon the ships. We focus on historical cultural information, the bounty of our natural setting, and the traditions and crafts of our nation."

I found Malia's use of the word "nation" to be telling.

Deciding to revert back to my initial line of thought, I changed the subject again. "As Bud said, Kai, your knowledge of your indigenous and imported flora and fauna is impressive, as you showed in your presentation. It's fascinating that so much research is now focusing on ancient remedies using your native plants. But you'd know all about plants, given your business. You must need to be careful with some of the ingredients you use, like when you're dealing with the castor bean, for example. I know it's deadly. Is it difficult to handle?" I wanted to sound as innocent as possible, so I added, "As Bud said, I'm pretty useless when it comes to plants."

Kai smiled deferentially. "The castor plant grows much like a weed on our Islands, and rapidly too. Its 'beans' are really its seeds, and they simply fall, quite naturally, from the plants everywhere they grow. Because we harvest them we are careful but, as you say, pets, livestock, and sometimes—poor little things—even children die from ingesting them. They get mashed into the general detritus on the ground and eaten, or picked up and mistaken for a treat by small children who are happy to put almost anything into their mouths. It is a terrible tragedy."

Kai's tone was black; something set alarm bells ringing in my head.

"Do you have children?" I ventured.

Malia swallowed, and I sensed a dreadful sadness. She shook her head just once.

I suspected that Bud hadn't noticed what I'd seen, but he had picked up on what I was thinking about in terms of the poisonous properties of castor beans, so jumped in with, "Tommy's death was a tragedy too. Did you know Tommy, Malia?"

Considering her answer for a moment, the woman eventually replied, "I thought I knew him a little, but I did not know him well." She seemed satisfied with her answer.

"And you said you didn't know him really well, either, didn't you, Kai," said Bud.

Kai tilted his head in agreement.

I decided it was time to jump in. "So why did you say, 'Mahalo' when he died, Kai? I overheard you in the Games Room. 'Thank you' seems to be a strange thing to say when someone loses their life."

Kai Pukui's black eyes glittered. His wife grabbed his arm; she looked terrified, as though seeing a horror reveal itself in front of her eyes.

The couple exchanged a significant look, then Kai leaned toward Bud and myself and said quietly, "Because he killed our son."

Deep Waters

I WAS STUNNED. AS SOON as he'd spoken, Kai took his wife's hand in his and stroked her arm. Malia picked up a napkin from the table and wiped away a tear. Her flawless skin, her spare makeup, her beautiful figure all seemed to diminish. She was a grieving mother, doing her best not to give in to sobbing. She bit her lip, looked skyward, and breathed heavily, trying to rein in her emotions.

"Tell them," she managed to blurt out.

My heart went out to this couple, and I focused on Kai as he spoke, hesitantly at first, then with more confidence, anger even.

"It was eight years ago. Eight years and three months. Kanani, our son—it means 'beautiful'—was just seven years old. We attended the birthday party of one of his classmates, and they had an entertainer performing magic tricks for the children. It was all good fun until the magician produced a rabbit. It was white, with very large feet, I recall. Somehow it got away from the magician and began to hop among the children, who were all seated on the grass. It was a beautiful day," Kai paused and smiled, "though every day is beautiful in Hawai'i. It was early in the year, February, and the sun was bright. It hadn't rained that day. The children all thought the hopping rabbit was great fun. They sprang up, squealing, trying to catch the creature, but it escaped them all. All except our Kanani, who was very fast. He would have become a great athlete, I am sure. He managed to catch one of the rabbit's paws, which the rabbit didn't like. It bit him. He let it go, and it ran off toward the road. Our beautiful son ran after it, and was hit by a car. Of course we ran to his side, but there was nothing anyone could do. We held him as his *uhane*, his soul, left his *kino*, his little body, for the last time." Kai bowed his head as he finished speaking, then looked into his wife's tearful eyes.

Looking directly at me, Malia added, "I saw our son's *uhane* flutter over our heads before it departed. It was bright, like a white bird with a light in its heart. He was an innocent."

I felt the Pukuis' sadness in the pit of my stomach. "Tommy was driving the car?" I asked gently.

Kai looked at me as though waking from a dream. "No. Tommy was the magician. If it hadn't been for the rabbit escaping, our son would never have run into the road. He should have been more responsible with his rabbit." *White-hot anger. Struggling for control.*

Rather than challenge their logic, I said, "It must have been difficult for you both to work with Tommy over the years, feeling as you did about him."

"We didn't know it was him until eight days ago," said Malia. Her voice was bleak. Dead.

"How did you find out?"

"The eleventh annual Waikiki SPAM Jam," announced Kai.

Bud and I exchanged a puzzled glance. "We were there," I said. "It was held the day we boarded the ship, when we were berthed at the Aloha Tower. Bud and I wandered the entire street of vendors in Waikiki, and ate as we went. I didn't see you there."

"It was very busy, and we didn't stay for long," said Kai sadly. "It's not the sort of thing we would usually attend, but we had promised a friend who was visiting from the mainland that we would accompany him there. It's really for the tourists." He nodded gently. "My apologies," he added.

"Please, don't apologize," said Bud. "Cait and I were tourists. Still are. And you're right, the idea of dozens of food stalls using SPAM in different ways must be something that would appeal to visitors from around the world. How was Tommy involved?"

Kai sat back in his chair, and Malia patted him on his arm. She spoke softly and quickly. "There was a large truck parked at each end of the area set aside for the festival. Did you see them?"

"Yes," I said. "There was a rota of young, and I suspect local, bands—of varying degrees of competence—at one end, and a sort of circus stand for the children at the other, with a bouncy castle," I said.

Malia looked at her hands in her lap. "Tommy was dressed as a clown on that circus stand. He was entertaining the children with magic tricks. No rabbits."

"I saw the clown," I said aloud, and I scrunched up my eyes to recall the scene. "Of course! His hands. The clown had Tommy's hands. Long fingers, dexterous." Looking at Kai and Malia, I said, "But how did you recognize him with the wig and all that makeup?"

"We didn't. He approached us and said 'Hi.' He was entertained by our expressions at the time—he thought it was because he'd given a nice surprise to two people he knew from the cruise ship, but who didn't initially recognize him. What he didn't know was that seeing him like that, doing magic tricks and using patter we'd heard before, we both knew, right away, that he was the one who killed our son."

I was still puzzled. "So was Tommy wearing clown makeup the first time you encountered him—with the rabbit? You didn't see his face that time?" It was the only explanation I could think of for the couple not having recognized a man who was, for all intents and purposes, a co-worker, and had been for weeks at a time for several years.

Kai sighed heavily. "No, he wasn't wearing clown makeup the first time we met him because he was acting more as a magician in those days, but he *was* about 200 pounds heavier at the time. You saw him here, now. He was a slim man, and he has been like that ever since we met him on the cruises. The magician whose carelessness led to our son's death was very fat, very tanned, and very loud. He was called the Magic Muddle Man, and no one ever made him answer for what he did. He just vanished. We tried to track him down, but our friends who hired him only had his telephone number. The cops weren't interested in him at all. Everyone blamed the driver. Just the driver.

We didn't. He couldn't have stopped. Our poor boy ran in front of his car in an instant. And we watched it all happen." I felt the weight of their guilt as Kai spoke.

The four of us sat silently for a few moments while I ran scenarios through my mind. I had no doubt that both Kai and Malia Pukui had a very good reason to want Tommy Trussler dead, and that Kai would have had a chance to poison Tommy's poi. Things weren't looking good for the Pukuis, and that wasn't just because they'd lost their son in such a tragic way.

Unfortunately, that was the point at which Don Ho's "Tiny Bubbles" came over the sound system. I'd enjoyed hearing it the first dozen or so times, but it was beginning to get on my nerves, and its jollity was so out of place. There might have been a golden moon in the sky and a silver sea all around us, but I cursed inwardly at bubbles of any dimension. I wondered how to get away from the Pukuis and back to Ezra—because I had some important questions for him.

"Are we out of our medication?" called Winston, breaking the spell.

I took my chance. "Bud, we should get going," I said. Bud made it clear to Winston that we were leaving and stood. I followed suit. "I'm so terribly sorry about the loss of your son," I said to the Pukuis before we left.

"So are we," said Kai. "He is still with us, though. We have not lost him. *Ohana* never leaves you. We still believe in the ancient teachings that spirit is in all things, so our son is with us always."

Kai and Malia bowed their heads toward each other as Bud and I departed and made our way across the deck. I hoped that the couple was able to find solace in their belief system, and promised myself I'd find out more about it, along with any concepts of retribution it might hold.

"Frannie Lang lost a sister. The Pukuis lost a son. Derek Cropper is dying. Tommy has been murdered. We are surrounded by death and despair," said Bud. He sounded bleak.

I sighed. My mind was racing. I paused in my stride, took one look at Bud, and said, "Bud, come on. You cannot let this get you down. You're acting in a most un-Bud-like way. Please explain to me what's going on in your head. I'm getting concerned about you."

We were alone on the deck, and it might have looked to anyone who could have seen us that we were sharing a romantic interlude.

"I'm very much in love with you," said Bud. "But I loved Jan, too, as you know. And she was taken from me. I cannot face that happening to me again. I want you to be safe. To live forever. I want to wrap you in cotton wool and keep you at home, beside me, with Marty at our feet. Wherever we go we see death. And here? Today? That's all we seem to be encountering." He looked bewildered. "When I was on the job, I faced danger all the time. I must be getting old and soft, because now . . . I don't know. I thought that working a proper case would make me feel like I used to. But I don't. I'm not the same man I was back then."

I gave Bud's words the consideration they deserved, then said, "You're right. You're not. Experience changes us all, Bud. Sometimes it hits us like a wall, so vast we cannot fail to acknowledge it. Other times it seeps through the cracks in our daily lives until we accommodate it, almost without noticing. But it changes us all. It's how we grow and become the people we are today. I love the Bud you are now. And I believe you love the Cait I am now. But we've both been forged in many fires, and that won't stop. We will continue to be changed by the lives we lead, and by the experiences we have. And that's a good thing, Bud. A healthy thing—as long as we accept it, and see it, and acknowledge it. Some people don't understand what's happening to them when experiences upend their lives. We must, or we could grow apart."

"Never," said Bud. "I won't let that happen."

"So let's be sure we share everything we can, so we can grow together," I said.

Bud tilted his head. "You mean, let's get on with catching this killer, don't you?"

I kissed him gently and pulled on his arm. "Come on, I need Ezra to use his procedures to help us now, rather than us just helping him."

As we made our way to the elevator, heading for Ezra's office, I mused how useful it was to have the head of security at one's disposal.

The Murder Wall

UPON ENTERING THE SECURITY DEPARTMENT'S area we were told there'd be a delay before we could see Ezra, so Bud and I waited as patiently as possible. A couple of minutes after our arrival, we heard Ezra's office door being unlocked behind us, then he stuck his head into the outer office and called us in.

The sight that met my eyes was unexpected. The tiny office had been rearranged to free up one wall, on which Ezra had arranged blown-up photographs of every person who'd been in the Games Room that morning. The photographs were mounted on larger sheets of paper, and notes appeared under the names of the people shown there. Tommy Trussler was at the center, and everyone else appeared around him. I read the notes, and it was clear that Ezra had listed connections, possible sources of poison, and, in one case, a motive.

"You have Afrim Ardit pegged as a possible killer for hire?" said Bud.

"Yes," said Ezra forcefully. "It might be the case."

I could see that Ezra was beginning to show signs of strain. He and his people had put a lot of energy into gathering and organizing the facts—however, I suspected he was beginning to realize just how very different detection was from investigation. Gathering facts is one thing; interpreting them, and making the pieces of the puzzle fit together, is quite another.

"We've come here to ask for your help," I said with what I hoped was a winsome smile.

Gesturing that we should sit, Ezra stood in front of his wall and puffed out his chest. "But of course," he replied loftily. "What can I do for you?"

"I have a list of requests that will need all your expertise," I began.

"I need you to find out if the Honolulu Police Department can trace Tommy Trussler as Buster the Clown, a children's entertainer."

Ezra's surprised expression led me to explain our encounter with the Pukuis. Eventually he nodded. "And this name comes from?"

"I saw it painted on a board on the truck where he was performing at the SPAM Jam Festival. I also need you to find out if the jewelry store in Maui named on the receipt and the bag we found in Tommy's stateroom containing two pairs of diamond earrings, has any security footage of the person who bought those earrings."

Ezra scribbled, lifted his head, and said, "Because?"

I decided to play it safe. "Because I think I know who bought them. I believe it was Nigel Knicely, but I'd like it confirmed. It was the first day we were moored off Maui, and there was a time stamp on the receipt, which should help. And I believe he'd have paid cash. I don't think he'd want the purchase to show up on any credit card statements. And that's something else; can you please trace any other Knicely residences in the UK?"

Ezra looked alarmed.

"This couple lives near Bristol, and I expect you have their address in your records. I'm interested in people of the same name living in Kent, possibly near Sandwich, and also near Birmingham." I paused. "And check into Nigel Knicely's employment record too. The pharmaceutical company Nigel Knicely works for," I spelled out the name for him, "has its head office in Sandwich, its sales head office in Bristol, and a training center in Birmingham. I know because it's a big company, and they are written about a great deal in journals I read."

Bud looked bemused as I rattled on—I'd given him lists like this when we'd been working together on cases back at home in BC. "And we need to know about the exact nature of Tommy Trussler's battle injuries, and where and when he was treated after Desert Storm."

Ezra nodded.

"We also need to find out about a road traffic accident involving

Frannie Lang's sister. I can't tell you enough about it for that to be a reasonable request right now, so I'll have to do some more digging. I don't even know her maiden name, so there's nothing to go on there."

"Lang *is* her maiden name," said Ezra. "She reverted to it after her divorce."

"And just how do you know that?" I asked.

"Her ticket was booked under her married name, Mawhinney, which caused problems when she presented herself at the port for embarkation with a passport that said Lang. One of my officers was called and it was all explained satisfactorily. So I should look for information about a woman called Lang who died . . . where? When?"

I shook my head. "Not necessarily Lang. She might have been married, though Frannie mentioned a boyfriend. Honolulu was the location, she said, but it could have been on any road on O'ahu. I don't have a time frame, though I am going to suggest it was around 1992 to 1995."

"Has Rachel come up with anything on any of her tests yet?" Bud asked.

Ezra sighed. "All I can tell you is that nothing you gathered from the Games Room contains any illegal drug. She's run a whole range of NIK tests. Nothing." Both Bud and I were familiar with the brand of field narcotics testing kits he'd mentioned, so Ezra didn't have to explain more.

"So, can you get all this information?" I asked.

Ezra looked at the list he'd made, then his watch. "I suspect it's too late for me to be able to get anything from the Maui store, or the HPD, until the morning, though I will try the HPD right away. The UK? The timing is good, but I'm not sure if the head of security on a cruise ship in the Pacific Ocean is going to be able to get what you need." He sounded disappointed and frustrated.

"I might be able to call in a few favors from some old contacts," said Bud.

It was a delicate moment.

"I would appreciate that," replied Ezra. *Good.*

"Can I leave the both of you to it while I try to track down Frannie Lang?" I asked, knowing the response I'd get.

Bud was on his feet, and the two law enforcement professionals were ready to go. *Hello there, Commander Anderson.*

"Sure," they said in unison.

I stood and smiled. "Well then, I'll be on my way," I said. "Though I'm not sure where to start."

"Come with me," said Ezra. He led me out of his office through the reception area and into a room full of video monitors, each of which displayed the views from four security cameras.

"I had no idea there were so many cameras on the ship," I said.

"We keep a good eye on things," he said. Then, to the operative he said, "Frannie Lang, location."

"Starz Theater, sir," said the young man without looking away from his monitors. "Went in on Deck 5, portside. Been watching her, as requested."

"Are you watching us all?" I asked.

Ezra didn't answer; instead he looked at his watch. "The show will let out in ten minutes, or thereabouts. You might be able to intercept her as she leaves. Most people use the exit nearest their seat."

"Thanks. And one more thing: How long do you keep records of what these cameras capture?"

"Why?" asked Ezra.

"I believe that Frannie Lang and Tommy Trussler had some sort of encounter on the top deck, near the basketball courts, on the morning we were docked in Hilo. It would have been early, before disembarkation time. I also believe that Nigel Knicely was in the vicinity. I can see you have a couple of cameras in that area; could you check, please?"

Ezra nodded. "I can make that a priority."

"Thanks," I said. "Now I'd better run to the theater to catch Frannie, if I can."

"Good luck," called Ezra.

As I left, I was delighted that the men were taking charge of the data gathering, freeing me to dig for information in my own way. Moving quickly, I got to the theater in time to hear the cruise director making his announcements about the disembarkation process we'd soon undertake; he also described the packages everyone would find in their staterooms, which would contain instructions on what to do with our luggage the next night.

I lounged on a comfy seat, listening to him talk as people began to drift out of the auditorium. I felt as though the spirit of Don Ho himself was stalking me on the ship, because his blessed song was playing in the background yet again, this time an instrumental version performed by the string quartet in the grand foyer below me. *Honestly! Can't they give it a rest?*

To distract myself from the all-too-haunting melody, I decided to give some thought to my first encounter with Frannie, back before we'd set sail from Honolulu.

Humuhumunukunukuapua'a

AFTER WE'D EMBARKED THE *Stellar Sol*, we'd taken the Pukuis' advice and had headed for the Sundowner Bar. I'd been surprised by how quickly time had passed that afternoon, and we'd been lucky enough to find our bags outside our stateroom by 3:00 PM. I'd taken the chance to change my clothes and, after we'd unpacked and put everything away in its designated spot, we decided to head into Honolulu for an early dinner and a delightful evening, this time at Duke's on the beach. We'd arrived back at the ship around ten o'clock, continued with our exploration of the beautiful vessel we were calling home, then spent our first night afloat—albeit with the ship in port.

The next morning, after a hearty breakfast, we met Frannie Lang. We'd decided to walk as far as the *Falls of Clyde*, the only surviving iron-hulled four-masted full-rigged ship, and the only surviving sail-driven oil tanker in the world. It was only a short way from the pier where our own ship was berthed.

Looking up at the rusty hull of the ship that had once done its part to change the world, I noticed a little machine that dispensed fish food. Curiosity drew me to it, and that's where I first set eyes on the woman who introduced herself to me as Frannie Lang.

Our initial conversation had been about how tricky it was to get the money into, and the food out of, the little machine. Eventually we both managed it, right before we were joined by Bud. More introductions followed, and Frannie seemed to be genuinely delighted to meet two more Canadians who'd be sharing her journey.

Her enthusiasm bubbled as she said, "I met a whole multi-generation family from Vancouver at the breakfast buffet. I wish I could have had my boys with me, but they work so much, they couldn't possibly get the time off. But I'm happy to talk to complete strangers. It's surprising how pleasant people are."

We hardly noticed the commotion in the shallows while we stood on a little road-bridge, chatting about Canada and dropping tiny pieces of food over the rail into the waters below. A splash drew our attention, and we were all amazed to see the host of fish that had been drawn to the tasty tidbits. From minute to massive, the creatures were every shape and color imaginable. Gobbling, splashing, fighting each other for the food, they were delightful and utterly fascinating.

"Do you think any of them is a hummer fish?" asked Frannie.

"A hummer fish?" said Bud.

"You know—it's a really long word." Frannie sounded a little embarrassed.

"You mean the *humuhumunukunukuapua'a*?" I asked.

Frannie's face lit up with glee. "That's it! Can you say it again, more slowly?"

"Hoo-moo hoo-moo noo-koo noo-koo a poo a a," I repeated.

Frannie and Bud said it with me, eliciting giggles from the Canadian woman whose spare frame, lank blond hair, and dark, soulful eyes were almost the antithesis of my own shape and coloring.

Small talk about the *Falls of Clyde* followed, though Frannie didn't seem to be terribly interested, or to share my enthusiasm for the role the ship had played in nautical history. She seemed much more interested in talking about the fish and Hawaiian culture. I'd done a fair amount of reading about the history, culture, and mythologies of the people who inhabited the islands, so I was able to satiate her desire for knowledge. She seemed to be especially interested in the ways in which the Hawaiians thought of life after death, which puzzled me at the time. She seemed to be trying to make sense of some deep emotion. We parted company with her seeming eager to visit the Polynesian Cultural Center, which I felt a little guilty about, because Bud and I had already decided that the only cultural activity we were going to partake of that day was to attend SPAM Jam festival in Honolulu that evening. *Not exactly Polynesian.*

Recollecting that day, I felt I'd met a woman who was well balanced and happy to be on vacation alone, though there was an air of sadness about her. On the day before we first met her, Frannie must have been out looking for the spot where her sister died. That might have explained her interest in a mythology that speaks of spirits being able to re-enter dead bodies if they can be called back from the underworld.

But now, all these days later? There was something else there— more than just sadness because her sister had died some time ago. The Frannie Lang who'd spoken so angrily about her ex-husband—and lied about where and when she'd met Tommy Trussler—was not quite the same person that Bud and I had met and fed fish with. I wondered what had happened to change her.

Starz Theater Bar, Deck 5, Forward

"HI, CAIT. WAITING FOR BUD?"

I must have looked startled, because Frannie Lang laughed aloud as she added, "Sorry, didn't mean to make you jump."

I stood up from the comfy chair I'd been lounging in, and felt cross with myself that I'd become so lost in reverie that I could have missed my quarry. "It's okay," I replied, a little flustered. "I was just distracted. Listening to the string quartet," I added by way of a non-explanation.

"I hate that song," smirked Frannie. "Now."

"Me too. Overkill, right?"

"Most definitely."

"Fancy a drink?" I said recklessly.

"Oh—you're not waiting for Bud?" Frannie asked. She sounded puzzled.

Quick, Cait, think!

"He's gone back to our room to try to find some indigestion stuff. I couldn't fit anything into this little thing," I held up my tiny evening purse, "and couldn't remember where I'd left them. I think I overindulged a bit too much tonight at dinner." I smiled and patted my tummy.

Looking at my midsection, the slim Frannie gave me a pitying look. "You'd think you'd be used to it," she said.

Thank you very much! I'm just a bit bigger than average—not a stick insect like some I could mention. I kept my thoughts to myself and laughed politely instead. "Don't worry, he'll find us. So, can I get you something before we're killed in the rush from the theater?"

I realized as I spoke that I could have chosen a more appropriate turn of phrase, but Frannie didn't seem to notice.

"Good idea," she replied. "Where do you fancy? There are so many bars on this ship, it's hard to choose."

"How about the Starz Theater Bar, just here, around the corner? There's a good pianist there and some lovely armchairs, and I bet most of the folks coming out of the performance will just keep going until they find another spot."

"All right, then," she replied. We began to walk, just as the house lights came up in the theater and the crowds began to congregate behind us.

Finally settled with a couple of drinks, I listened as Frannie talked about how she'd enjoyed the trip. She mentioned Kaanapali Beach, where Laurie had told me she'd seen her with Tommy; she mentioned walking the deck in the early mornings, where Janet had told me she'd seen her with Tommy; she even mentioned nibbling her way around the SPAM Jam festival, where I knew Tommy had been—but she didn't mention Tommy at all. To be fair to the woman, not even I had recognized Tommy in his clown getup at the SPAM event, so I decided to let that one slide; still, I knew she was lying—it was written all over her. I'm excellent at reading people's body language and expressions, and Frannie Lang was a woman trying to lie her way out of a tumultuous situation. What was most interesting was not that she was lying about when she'd encountered Tommy Trussler for the first time on our trip, but why she would do that. Was it because she wanted me to focus on them being together in Hilo?

Frannie Lang's face told me I'd hit her with a bolt out of the blue when I asked, "When did your sister die, Frannie?" I'd expected her to be shocked, so I followed up with, "As I told you, my parents died in a car accident. It was more than ten years ago, but it seems as bad as if it were yesterday—especially if something happens to make me think of them, or of the circumstances of the crash." I felt pretty bad using the loss of my parents as a device to winkle information out of a suspect. It wasn't the first time I'd needed to play the "empathy" card, and it probably wouldn't be the last.

Frannie's expression softened as she saw in me the fellow grieving family member I was portraying myself to be. "It was 1995, in May. But you're right, it seems like just yesterday."

I noticed her touching the locket at her throat again, and decided to go for it. "Your sister's always close to you?"

Frannie drew her fingers from the piece on her neck and looked guilty. "Do you think that's weird? My husband said it was. Said I couldn't let go of her. He always used to hurl that one at me whenever we had an argument. Like it was a bad thing. Back in the day, he didn't mention it. He said he liked the locket. I guess a lot changed as the years passed."

"Except your feelings for your sister," I said gently. "You were close?"

"Very. Two peas in a pod, they said."

"You were twins?"

Frannie nodded. When Frannie had first told me about her sister she'd referred to her as her "kid sister," and I'd assumed a real difference in age. "Far apart?" I asked.

"Ten minutes," she said, almost proudly. "But it's a big difference when you're little." She smiled warmly. I wondered what visions of youthful joint birthday celebrations might be playing on her internal home-movie screen.

"I have a younger sister," I said, again trying to empathize with Frannie, "but she and I are years apart. I was a bit too old to want to play with her when we were growing up. It must have been lovely to have a true companion."

"Fay was the light of my life," said Frannie. "I'm not sure I'll ever get over her death."

"You said it was on O'ahu, I believe."

"Yes. Dangerous roads, not like back home."

Personally, I was happier on roads that wound and climbed rather than those covered in snow for half the year, but I supposed it all depended what you were used to.

"Was she driving?"

Frannie shook her head. "Her boyfriend was, but he survived." She took a deep breath. "No seatbelt. He told us in a letter he sent to Mom and Dad that she refused to wear one because it would have creased her dress. How dumb is that? I never thought of Fay as dumb, or particularly worried about how she looked, but maybe she'd changed."

"So you and she hadn't been in contact for some time before she died?"

Frannie's micro-expressions told me she was having an internal dialogue, trying to make a decision. Finally, she squared her shoulders, and had clearly made up her mind so she jumped in, feet first. "Fay and I both became nurses, but she ended up working surgical, whereas I stuck with general. She was very good. I preferred dealing with patients who were conscious; she preferred them out cold. At least, that's what she said. More technical than me, you see. She married a guy from New York. A doctor, of course. They met when he was visiting the hospital where she worked in Toronto for some sort of training thing. She was very young. It was before I got married. It didn't last. She followed him as he moved up the pecking order in different hospitals, and finally got her Green Card. So, by the time they split, she was an American, living near Virginia. Met a guy there, this boyfriend, and they went to Hawai'i on vacation after they'd been together a fair time. We were in touch, you know, but I hadn't seen her in a while."

"So you never met the boyfriend?"

"I never did," she said. Then, surprising me, she seemed to change tack. "Were you married to anyone else before Bud?"

"No—Bud's the only man I'll ever marry."

"Lucky you. Trust me when I tell you that divorce can change a person. It did me." I noted a spark of anger in her eyes as she spoke. "So maybe she'd changed a bit, after hers. There weren't any children, but there's no such thing as a non-messy divorce. When I went through it, it was like being ripped apart." She gave me a piercing look as she added, "It's terrible to realize you've been a fool. That you've given your life to someone, only to have them throw it back in your face as though you've done a bad thing." She paused and composed herself slightly. "But Fay wasn't like me in some respects. She was always . . . more forgiving. I don't think she'd have changed deep down in that way, so maybe she was able to 'move on,' as they say. She always loved a laugh and a joke. Like I said, she was the light of my life." She looked into the distance. "Maybe she was the only real light *in* my life."

"It must have been tough for you, when she died."

"Yes. It was bad enough she was gone—but for it to happen so far away was devastating. Mom and Dad made all the arrangements to get Fay back home. The boyfriend didn't attend the funeral. In hospital in Hawai'i. Pretty banged up, I heard."

"And what was his name?"

Frannie looked confused. "B . . . no, K . . . no, Michael. That was it—Michael, um, Craft."

Odd.

"Did you try to get in touch with him on this visit, or did he return to the Virginia area?" I was curious.

"Why would I do that?" snapped Frannie, immediately angry. "Why would I want to meet him face-to-face?"

I could think of a several excellent reasons, but—for once—I managed to press my internal "edit" button because I didn't want to show my hand. I contented myself with, "So, Fay Lang died in Hawai'i, and you had a chance to visit the spot."

"No, Fay Banks died in Hawai'i," replied Frannie. "She kept her ex-husband's name. Big mistake. Stuck with it forever, now, because we had to use her legal name on her headstone." Frannie gazed into the middle distance, and back across the years. "Funny things, names," she added.

"They certainly are."

"I can't get my mouth around most of the Hawaiian place names at all," she said, almost sounding bright. "But they look pretty on the signs. Very exotic."

"Hey, there you are," called Laurie Cropper, as she tottered out of the ladies' restroom. "Derek and I thought we were meeting you and Bud for a drink after the show. We're back at the same spot as before. Why don't you come along too?" Laurie's naturally hospitable nature showed in her warm smile, but Frannie was immediately on her feet, fussing with her lightweight shawl.

"Oh no, it's very late, and it's been a long and emotional day. I'm off." With that, she strode out of the bar area and toward the elevators. I had little choice but to accompany Laurie—which wasn't a bad thing.

Bar Hopping

DEREK'S WELCOMING HUG FELT ODD; being greeted by a dying man made me feel uncomfortable. I knew I'd have to work hard to disguise my emotions, so I began by adopting an overenthusiastic, slightly tipsy persona.

"I'm not sure I should have another," I announced, giggling, as I extricated myself from Derek's embrace.

"Too late," he said, "I saw you two gals sashaying over, and put Simon to work immediately. Ah, there it is—your favorite." *I don't have a single sashaying bone in my body.*

I balanced the brimful martini glass very carefully, and wondered how I was going to manage to drink another large dose of pure alcohol—albeit with vapor and sparkles.

"Whadda ya Welsh guys say?" slurred Derek.

"*Iechyd da,*" I replied.

"I didn't get that," said Laurie.

"Yeah-chi-da," I repeated loudly.

The Croppers giggled as they tried to make the guttural noise required by the greeting. "That's a hoot," said Laurie.

"A hoot an' a half," added Derek, winking.

I said, "'Get it down your neck,' will do in a pinch," which garnered more laughter.

"Go on then," said Derek, tipping up the base of my glass, which was poised on my bottom lip. Within seconds, the entire drink was swilling about inside me, rather than the crystal vessel in which it had been served. I noticed, with dread, that I'd also drunk all the glitter, which I suspected could lead to interesting consequences.

"Good girl," said Derek, relinquishing his own glass, and giving me a round of applause. "That husband should be proud of you. Where is he, by the way? Thought you guys were inseparable."

"He offered to pop back to the room for something I needed," I lied.

"You gals," said Derek, unsteady on his feet, "just like my little lady. Always something you need to go back to the room for. Laurie's forever leaving me at the tables to do something in our room, then she never comes back." He squinted at his wristwatch. "Hey, speaking of tables, time for a bit of a flutter, I think. You coming?"

Derek's gaze was so unfocused that I wasn't sure who he was talking to—me or Laurie.

"If you're off to the casino, I'll go and give Bud a call. Ask him to join us there," I said, spotting a way to escape and connect with Bud at Ezra's office.

"Sure," said Derek. Laurie smiled impishly and steered him toward the elevators.

"Come on, honey, let's not risk the stairs," I heard her say as they wobbled away.

I grabbed the nearest house telephone and dialed Ezra's number. When he answered, I asked for Bud, whose voice sounded crisp, alert, and businesslike, especially when compared with Derek's.

"Hi, are you done yet?" I asked.

"Nope. And you need to come here—Ezra and I have managed to dig up a lot you need to know. Can you come back to his office now?"

I sighed. "I'll find the Croppers in the casino and tell them we can't join them after all, then I'll come right down, okay?"

The casino was heaving. I wondered if it was the dinner jackets, or the long gowns, but either way, the place had an unexpectedly manic edge to it. Noisy, busy, waiters holding trays of drinks above their heads, people shouting at the craps table as though their lives depended on it, the flashing lights, the constant ringing of slot-machine bells—it was a little overwhelming. I realized, almost too late, that the drink I'd swallowed whole had gone straight to my head. I felt quite faint, and had to be given a stool beside a poker table to rest on.

I put my head into my hands for a moment, and tried to recover my composure. Someone bumped into my back, and I heard a man's voice say, "They say he turned blue, then collapsed. I heard he was holding aces and eights. Dead man's hand." *The good old rumor mill in overdrive.*

I turned and saw two men's backs move away from me. They greeted Laurie Cropper, who was standing beside Derek at the casino bar. Looking toward the men, she saw me and waved. I needed to ask her who the men were, so I pulled myself together and weaved my way through the throng.

I finally made it to the bar, but this time I was more firm about declining a drink.

"Who were those chaps?" I asked Laurie, waving toward the backs that had departed. I felt I should elaborate. "One of them was quite dishy," I lied. *Who knew? At least their backs looked fine.*

Laurie looked toward the men in question. "Just nodding acquaintances from the gym," she replied, a little too casually. *You're hiding something—but from me, or Derek?*

I was just about to tell the Croppers that I was going to join Bud "back at our cabin," when a young man who looked to be in his thirties jostled Laurie's arm, causing her to almost spill her drink.

Spinning to apologize, the man's expression changed when he saw Laurie. "Hey, Laurie! Gee, I'm sorry. It's kinda full here tonight. Didn't mean to spill your drink."

Laurie smiled. "It's quite alright, my dear, I didn't waste a drop."

The young man leaned in close to Laurie's ear; they were both close enough to me to catch their low tones: "So, I guess it's a non-starter at your place tonight?"

"Of course," she murmured.

An affair?

The man smiled pleasantly, winked, and rejoined his group.

"Busy in here tonight," I said.

Laurie looked around. "I guess," she replied calmly. "I'm not usually here this late. I like to get my beauty sleep. But tonight? Well, I think Derek might need a little help to get back to our place."

Derek swooped upon us, having heard his wife's words. "Don't need no help, but you're welcome to stay," he all but shouted. "Join me for my last hurrah, why don't you?"

His words carried a meaning for me I knew they didn't for his wife.

"Of course I'll stay, honey. Now, you're not going to play, tonight, are you? Not in this state?"

Derek grinned. "I'm perfectly fine, honey mine. Just you watch me take 'em for everything they've got. Coming, Cait? And where's my buddy Bud?" Derek burst out laughing at his own joke. "Ha! My buddy Bud! Did you hear that, honey? My buddy Bud."

Laurie put down her almost-untouched drink and stuffed her evening purse right up under her armpit. "Come along now, Derek Cropper, I'm taking you home."

"I really must join Bud," I said, as I slipped away, leaving the Croppers to work out who was going to win the battle of the wills.

Passing the tables, I noticed just how many chips were in play. They looked jolly, almost like children's toys, with their vivid hues and the *Stellar* logo printed in the center. I wondered how many thousands of dollars they represented.

Backs against the Murder Wall

I COULD FEEL MYSELF BEGINNING to tire as I made my way, yet again, toward Ezra's offices. It was almost one in the morning and I wondered when I was going to get to bed. I was cursing the heels I'd chosen to wear, and internally cursing Derek Cropper even more for making me knock back that drink.

I was ushered to Ezra's door by one of his minions, who took the chance to whisper in his boss's ear. The response Ezra gave him was clearly the one he'd been hoping for because he grinned, nodded, called to two colleagues, and left the place before Ezra had even locked his office door behind me.

"Those chaps seemed happy to leave," I said. "Long day?"

"Yes, and tomorrow will be too. They begin at 6:00 AM sharp, guarding the sales, and then they'll be on late shift overseeing the baggage collection."

I understood the need for there to be security oversight where guests' bags were concerned, but had no idea what Ezra meant about sales. As I settled myself in front of the redecorated Murder Wall, and accepted a glass of fizzy water with great relief, I asked, "What sales?"

Ezra shrugged. "At 10:00 AM tomorrow, the stores on Deck 5 have their blow-out sale. It's always a feeding frenzy."

"And your staff will be guarding the stock? I must say, I'm surprised. Surely you don't get much shoplifting onboard?"

Ezra's look spoke volumes. "You have no idea," he said with a heavy sigh.

Sipping my fizzy water and looking around the room, I spotted a couple of discarded pizza boxes on the floor in the corner of the tiny office.

"Rachel came to give me this," said Ezra, holding up a sheaf of papers. "She thought I might be hungry, so she brought something from the pizza kitchen on Deck 14 for us to share while she talked me through her findings."

I didn't have to wonder why an email and a phone call weren't sufficient.

"And what are those findings?" I asked.

Ezra looked frustrated. "I suppose we should be pleased that she hasn't been able to detect anything unexpected in any of the foodstuffs from the Games Room. She wasn't able to perform any tests for all of the potions, pills, and potential carriers of poison on the items taken from Tommy's room—like his toothbrush or razor. But that wasn't her priority; her responsibility is the living souls on this ship, so that's where she spent her time."

"Coffee grounds on the victim's hands?" I asked.

Ezra shook his head.

"Hmm, I thought not. And I assume the white substance on the carpet in the Games Room was salt?"

Bud tutted, and Ezra nodded.

"Thank Rachel for all that work," I said. "So we're all much more comfortable with the conclusion, if ever there was any doubt, that this wasn't an accidental killing of Tommy by a person happy to poison something anyone could have ingested."

"I am relieved to agree," said Ezra. It was clear to me that this was a worry that had continued to plague him until Rachel's reports had arrived.

"The approach we've been taking has been appropriate—that of trying to discern who set out to kill one man, that man being Tommy Trussler, so let's get to it," I said. "I've been reading your updated Murder Wall as I've been sitting here."

Bud cleared his throat. "As you can see, we've been busy, and productive," he said proudly, waving at the notes on the wall.

The mounted photographs were now accompanied by fresh information, which I continued to read through.

"I see from your updated notes that Tommy's military record shows he was shot in the abdomen—am I right?" At Ezra's nod, I continued. "That explains the 'appendectomy' scar." I noticed a puzzled glance from Bud, but went on. "Let's move on to Nigel Knicely. You have identified him as the man who bought three pairs of diamond earrings in Maui, yes?"

"I managed to get hold of the store manager, who checked, and he emailed me a video file," said Ezra. "We have a positive ID of Nigel buying the earrings. He was alone and paid cash."

"Good," I said. "That supports my theory. And what about seeing him on camera on the ship, close to an encounter between Frannie Lang and Tommy Trussler?"

"Again, yes," said Ezra brightly. He swigged coffee as he passed me a pile of stills from a digital recording. I wondered how many gallons of caffeine he'd drunk that day. He seemed pretty wired.

I looked at the series of photographs of a man who was identifiably Nigel Knicely, standing close to the front of the ship, in a position where it was likely he'd have been able to overhear a conversation between two people who were equally identifiable as Frannie and Tommy. At that spot on the ship you had to shout to be heard, and I knew how sound could travel on the stiff breezes—sometimes being better heard at a distance than by someone right next to you.

"We know several things," I said. "Frannie was lying about not seeing more of Tommy than she let on, and Janet told the truth about seeing them together. And while he divulged the truth about overhearing Frannie and Tommy arguing—because that's what it looks like to me in these photos—Nigel Knicely lied to his wife about his whereabouts at that time. Did you manage to find any shots with Janet in them?"

Ezra shook his head.

"Ah well, you can't always have everything you want," I noted. "What about Nigel's employment record?"

"It's odd," replied Bud. "If we believe what she said to us, he's told his wife that he retired from the pharmaceutical company he worked for, and they hired him back to run training programs. But they didn't."

"When did they fire him?" I asked.

Bud sighed and rolled his eyes. "You just want us here to dig up the facts that back up your theories, don't you?" he said indulgently. "They got rid of him about four years ago, long before he'd have retired. I pulled a few strings to get another piece of information you might like."

I smiled. "What did they think he'd stolen?" I knew that was where Bud was going.

Ezra watched us as though at a tennis match, his head turning, watching each point play out.

"Very good," said Bud, as though congratulating a puppy who'd just learned how to sit on command. "The company he worked for is most famous for the pills it makes to address the problem of erectile dysfunction. They suspect, though they cannot prove, that he somehow spirited away a couple of million dollars' worth of the stuff."

I was surprised, and almost impressed. "That much? I suppose shipments went missing over a long period of time?"

Bud nodded. "They investigated him for a couple of years, but couldn't get him for anything specific. Seems a couple of the accounts he handled turned out to be nonexistent, though he swore he didn't know, and no one was able to trace the missing product. The British cops haven't given up, though."

"Good," I replied. "And I can see from the wall that you located two more addresses with Knicelys at them, as I suspected. Did you get names? Particulars? Photos?"

Bud and Ezra exchanged a glance. "With the help of various UK agencies, we discovered several Knicely households in the UK, but whittled them down to these three," said Bud. "Nigel's known address outside Bristol, where he lives with Janet, his wife. There's another home just outside Birmingham, and another just outside Sandwich in Kent. These are the only ones that match your criteria. We were very lucky it was an uncommon name. Oddly, all the men have the first initial, N, but no real details other than householder names yet, and no photos either."

"As I suspected. They are all Nigel."

"But no," said Ezra, jumping in. "One is our Nigel, one is Norman, and one is Nate. We know that much. And that they're family homes, not apartments."

"Okay," I replied, "we know Janet is fifty, and I'm going to suggest that one other Mrs. Knicely is in her early forties, and one is in her late thirties. They'll probably have a couple of kids each. Nice homes, not fancy. Housewives watch the kids and run the home, husband out at work. Travels a lot."

Both men looked puzzled. "Why do you say all this?" asked Ezra.

"Look, I will bet you anything that, if you get the drivers' licenses of the three male householders, they will all look exactly like Nigel Knicely, because they *are* Nigel Knicely. The man's a bigamist, with three families on the go, none knowing about the others. Furthermore, I suggest you get back to your police contacts in the UK and tell them to try to find another address where a single male householder with the initials NK has lived since just before the time the pills started to go missing—you know, the time the company thinks he started to steal from them. I would suggest somewhere around Cambridge. That would give him a location to stash his stolen goods at the top right-hand corner of the grid where he lives his life. Janet, bottom left near the sales office, another wife bottom right, near the company HQ, another family top left, near the training center, and his secret place top right."

Ezra fidgeted. "I don't know the UK very well," he said, "but why would anyone live their life the way you described? It's most peculiar."

"I'll use myself and my life to illustrate what I mean," I answered. "Most of us live and work in one small part of the world. I used to have my route to and from work, a shopping area I used habitually, regular places for entertainment, eating out, takeaway, activities, and so forth. In other words, we all know and feel comfortable in our own 'neck of the woods,' however we might define that for ourselves. As I said, I know I always have. Now, with Bud and I having bought a new home in a more rural area, I am feeling a certain discomfort at having to rebuild my own geographic life framework. It was a cop from Vancouver, Dr. Kim Rossmo, who developed the process of geographic profiling, and it's now widely accepted. Indeed, it's a process I often use when building a full profile of a victim. I can see a pattern in Nigel Knicely's life, largely dictated by the three corporate hubs of the organization he used to work for, and allowing him to keep three families apart. This triangle would comprise his general 'comfort zone,' so he'd likely move outside it to secrete something he wanted kept apart from the life he had with his families. Possibly unconsciously, he's most likely to have chosen the 'fourth corner' of the rough square I have described. I would suggest, therefore, that if he wanted to keep the pills hidden, and at a safe distance from his three other lives, the area around Cambridge would be his general choice. It's also a big enough place that he could use various means to hide his distribution methods. I lived in Cambridge for some years. I happen to know it's not only an ancient seat of learning, and a very attractive tourist center, but also a pretty popular base for companies wanting to distribute products across the UK, and even to continental Europe."

"You got three wives from three pairs of earrings?" asked Bud, bemused.

"No, not just three pairs of earrings. I got it from multiple cues; his peacock style, his desire to be the center of attention, his utter disdain for his wife, his love of the romance of a wedding. These all speak of a man with narcissistic tendencies. But there's more in his case: he has deep rooted misogynistic traits and also some control issues. His desire for the 'perfect life' might well lead him to not just fantasize about being irreplaceable—to his family as well as his employer—but might lead him to act out such fantasies. My next question is about—"

"But wait," said Ezra, jumping from his seat. "If it is as you say, then we have Nigel Knicely with multiple wives, multiple homes, a criminal background, and a possible source of illegal income—to keep his three families going—from stolen pills. However, we don't have a reason for him to kill Tommy Trussler. I'm pleased we might be able to help the British police find stolen goods, and even prosecute this man, but what about *my* case?" He sounded quite cross.

I sat forward in my terribly uncomfortable chair. "Nigel lied to his wife about where he was, when we know he was very close to Tommy on the morning we were in Hilo. Why was he where he was? I believe he was due to meet Tommy, because Tommy had stolen the earrings he'd bought for his two other wives. Nigel couldn't report them as stolen, because he couldn't explain two extra pairs of diamond earrings to Janet. Tommy obviously knew from whom he'd stolen them. What would you think if you found a man had bought three pairs of earrings, and his wife was wearing one pair to our first formal dinner? Tommy wasn't a stupid man—obsessed, yes, but not stupid—he might have talked to Nigel about the other diamonds. We know Tommy and Nigel had a run-in in the Games Room, after Tommy made a remark about Nigel knowing how to look after his wife. Frannie Lang told us about it, and I believe, on that occasion, Frannie was telling the truth. I suggest to you that Tommy was goading Nigel about the earrings, and about how his wife only had one of three pairs. I wouldn't put a spot of blackmail past Tommy. I can't be sure, of course, but it fits. I'd like to put that to Nigel, to see how he reacts."

Ezra held up his hand. "I have conceded much during this case, but I cannot have you accusing guests of murder, or of anything else, Cait. I only have the right to detain, not charge." He paused for a moment as he considered what he'd just said. "If we get to that point," he added. "Nigel Knicely has a possible motive, he had the opportunity, but did he have the means?"

"The poisoned beads from his wife's bracelet," I replied. "You wrote that on the Murder Wall yourself."

"But they belonged to his wife, and how would he, or either of them, get to the poison in the center of the bead, as you described?"

"I've been giving that some thought," I replied, "and I think I've worked it out. As we all know, both he and Janet wear spectacles. Everyone I know who wears prescription spectacles carries a repair kit with them containing tiny little screwdrivers, and so forth. With a great deal of care, he could have extracted enough of the center of a couple of the beads to effectively poison Tommy's pot of poi. It would have been a daring plan, but I read him as possessing sufficient self-belief that he would have thought he could get away with it."

Ezra didn't look happy. "So, it is Nigel?" he said.

"Not necessarily," I replied. "It might have been Derek Cropper."

"What?" chorused Bud and Ezra.

"To be certain of my theory, we'll need to question Michael, the butler in the Cropper's suite, but I believe that Laurie Cropper has been hosting illicit, private poker parties while Derek's been at the tables in the casino. I saw gambling chips in the Cropper's suite when we visited, Bud. I initially thought that Derek had brought them back from the casino, but I saw this evening that all the ones used there have the *Stellar* logo on them. The ones in the Cropper's suite were differently colored, and, I believe, will match the $100 denomination of chips that Tommy Trussler had in a set in his room. If Derek found the chips, he might have discovered what his wife was up to. You saw how delighted he was that he was $40,000 up, Bud. What if Laurie was losing? That might explain her comments about Tommy being untrustworthy, and Derek's about how she'd made him wise to the fact. A young man spoke to Laurie earlier on about 'tonight' being off.

I don't believe for one minute she's having an affair, and that seals it for me. And remember that huge roll of cash we found in Tommy's safe?" I raised an eyebrow toward Ezra and he nodded. "I reckon that's his winnings. The cash in the wallets provided his stake, and he's used his ability at sleight of hand to take a lot of money off folks who didn't know how good he was at cheating at cards."

"How do you know he was good at that?" asked Ezra, nonplussed.

"That one's easy. When I was watching him play gin rummy with Bud, he had a run of diamonds in his hand. The cards that Rachel ripped from his dead fingers didn't contain a single diamond. And I watched as he 'entertained' the Knicelys with his tricks. It all takes quite some doing. He was an experienced cardsharp. Something that ties in with his work as a magician, no doubt."

"But how would Derek Cropper have killed him?" asked Ezra. "Wait, yes, I see. His wife's liquid nicotine." He paused for thought. "We know about that already. He could have poured it into Tommy's poi quite easily. Would he do this because of money? He has a lot of money, and he makes a lot more every year," said Ezra. "He is a very successful businessman—everyone on the ship knows it."

"He's a very successful businessman who is dying," said Bud quietly.

Ezra stopped pacing about and sat down. "This is news to me," he said. "How do you know this?"

Bud sighed. "I've done a very dumb thing, Ezra: I allowed myself to be knocked sideways by emotion. I got personally involved with a suspect, and filed a piece of information under 'irrelevant,' when it was anything but."

"You have, but I think it's understandable, Husband." Turning my attention to Ezra I added, "Derek Cropper hasn't got long to live, and he shared that knowledge with Bud. Now, while it's true that he and his wife have spent their lives aiming to fill their 'Cropper Coffers,' his determination to set up Laurie as best he could for the life she'll have to live without him is clear. He's dying, yet he works until the last hours before they leave on vacation; he's gambling big to win big, which he has; he's giving Laurie one last fabulous vacation. She'll be alone when he's gone—they chose to have no children. If he found out she'd been taken advantage of, he would be very angry. Frannie Lang told us he was angry enough with Nigel, who made a comment about him not being considerate toward Laurie, to have a loud argument with him. I judge that to be unusual for a man of his polite nature. Laurie is his life, and he might not have killed Tommy Trussler because of the money—after all, he'd never get it back then—but he might have done it if he thought his wife had been cheated, slighted, and made a fool of. So, anger, an easily available poison, and, of course, the fact he has nothing to lose even if he is found out, might have allowed him to do this. Or, maybe Laurie did it, not thinking for one moment she'd be found out."

"So, it was Derek, or Laurie, Cropper?" said Ezra, sounding hesitant.

"Or Frannie Lang, or the Pukuis," I replied.

Ezra slapped his hand on his desk in exasperation. "What's this now?"

"Frannie Lang's sister, Fay Banks. I believe that Tommy Trussler was her boyfriend, and was driving the car in which she died," I said. "I'm basing this assessment on everything she told me tonight, though I have no proof, as yet. I can see from the wall that you have no more information about that incident."

"No, we do not," said Ezra. On his feet once again, he continued, "That's it. This is becoming quite ridiculous. How could Frannie Lang have killed him?"

"Over-the-counter meds. She used to be a nurse," said Bud.

"And the Pukuis?" said Ezra, sounding angry.

"He was mixed up in the death of their son, as I told you," said Bud. "And the Pukuis found out about Tommy before they got on the ship. Either one of them could have brought a preparation of deadly castor nuts, with the intention of killing him."

Ezra, utterly frustrated, raised his voice. "So, we've been at this all day, and we're back where we started—except now it's much worse. Originally I believed that no one on my ship could have had access to poison to kill this man. Now you tell me that everyone in the room did, *and* they all wanted him dead. Is this how all your cases work out, Bud? Every suspect remains a suspect? Is this all we are able to achieve by our investigations?"

Bud looked at Ezra with sympathy. "No. Things don't usually turn out this way," he said. "But, on this occasion, they have. Gathering facts can only go so far. Now we have to work to interpret those facts. We appear to have compelling circumstantial evidence against both Pukuis, though only Kai was in the room; both Croppers, though the husband was the only one with nothing to lose; and both Knicelys, though I can't really envisage the wife possessing enough emotion to kill someone."

"And what about Afrim, the server? He was there. He could have done it. It might not be any of the guests," said Ezra.

"I really don't think so," I said. "I believe our real problem is that any of the people in the Games Room this morning could point to the circumstantial evidence pertaining to the others, and raise reasonable doubts about their guilt in the mind of a jury. So the guilty would get off while the innocent would have their lives shredded. The courts and the press can destroy people—*especially* the press. Believe me, as someone who was essentially hounded out of a country by the tabloids, I wouldn't want anyone to experience that."

Ezra was completely worn out. He sagged as he said, "But detaining is all I can do. All I have the authority to do. What am I to tell the captain? That I must lock up several guests and a couple working on behalf of the cruise line?"

"No, I don't think you should do that," replied Bud. "I think you have to let Cait take one more step."

"And what would that be?" scoffed Ezra. "Prove to me there's just as much evidence against fifty other people on the ship?"

"No," I responded calmly. "I suggest you give me the chance to get the killer to confess."

Ezra shook his head. "And how do you plan to achieve this?"

"How about a gathering tomorrow morning—say eleven o'clock? People will be in bed now, so you'll need some time in the morning to alert people, or invite them politely, to get it organized. I suggest you propose a memorial gathering. Everyone who was there when Tommy Trussler died should attend, plus Rachel White, Bartholomew Goodman, Winston Williams, you, of course, and Officer Ocampo. Maybe the worst of the sales rush will be over by then."

"If the captain and I allow this to happen, you believe you can extract a confession from the guilty party?" said Ezra. I nodded. "Do you think your wife can do this?" he asked Bud.

Bud smiled warmly at me and said, "If Cait says she can, she can."

"Thank you, Bud," I said.

"I will speak to the captain and will telephone you in the morning. I suggest we all try to get some sleep, so go now, please." Ezra dismissed us with a curt nod of the head, unlocked his door so we could leave, and all but kicked us out.

I was done in, and I held onto Bud's arm as we made the final journey of the day to our stateroom.

When we got there, I pulled off my fancy frock, peeled myself out of my horrid "shapewear," and dropped everything onto the floor. I didn't even take off my makeup—I just fell into the bed and wriggled in the cool sheets. I imagined myself adrift on a sea of pillowy foam, being carried to a land where a suspect would walk up to me and beg forgiveness. Of course, I couldn't sleep at all, so as Bud snored, I lay there and sorted through all the data that he and Ezra had compiled. I assessed its value against my own discussions with, and judgments of, our pool of suspects.

I sat up, rubbed my eyes—*mistake*—then nestled into my pillows. I knew I had to try my wakeful dreaming technique. I was in our room, and Bud was beside me, so I was safe. I closed my eyes and stopped searching for sleep; instead I searched for the place where dreams and reality mix, where I can allow facts and circumstances, suspicions and realities, to mix and intermingle, then settle into patterns that make sense—for me, in any case. I told myself to let go—to trust the technique I knew had helped on so many former occasions, and to allow it to work. I hoped I wasn't too tired, and went with it . . .

All At Sea

I AM FLOATING. I AM not on a ship—I am floating in the air, which smells of pineapple, hibiscus, and plumeria. I can taste the air. It is sweet. I know I am floating down toward a lush landscape. It is beneath my feet, just a little below me now, and I prepare for the thump when I land. But there is none. I am cushioned by a bed of tropical plants; they grow around me as I lay in their embrace. They grow quickly, and I am soon struggling to be released.

I burst out of the foliage and run away to higher ground. As I run, the plants from which I have escaped rear up and shoot giant seeds at me. I know that if they touch me I will die. I run, but I do not move. I am running on an elliptical machine, and I am slaving up a steep incline. I smell sulfur. The earth is moving beneath my machine, and I can see the glow of what I know is lava ahead of me, pouring down the hillside on which I and my machine stand.

A clown in a hot air balloon appears above me and throws a rope so I can escape the lava flow. I grab the rope and begin to struggle up it, but it's very short. Then I am inside a bouncy castle, filled with squealing children, each wearing a hat that looks like a white rabbit, but the children have no color, nor blood in their veins. I know they are all dead, and their squeals are of horror, not amusement. I try to bounce my way out of the castle that's now massive, but there's no exit. Above me is the clown, leering at me, and cheering on the children, who begin to throw playing cards at me as missiles. They cut me when they make contact with my skin, but I do not bleed. Instead my broken skin weeps with fragrant lotions that become blooms of exotic flowers.

I am melting into nothing; then I am in the Games Room. I am alone, save the presence of Tommy Trussler. He is sitting in a giant pot of poi, eating his way out. He slurps and squelches. It makes me feel sick. I push over the pot so he can escape, but he chooses to remain inside it, laughing at me, even as it rolls across the floor, which is covered with a sandy beach of white powder.

"I can help you out," I call to him, but he is rolling into the distance of the now-massive room. It runs to the horizon, black and silver, red and gold. He is escaping me. I cannot run as fast as his pot is rolling, my footing is soft, and white sands are dragging me back.

Kai and Malia appear as if floating toward me from the horizon, both dressed in the traditional outfits from their stage performances. Each of them is carrying a surfboard under one arm, and a castor plant in their other hand. They are crying, and I know that their tears are the Pineapple Express, sending heavy rains to my home in British Columbia. I tell them to stop, that there is too much rain, but they cry even more. The water pours from their eyes, though they both smile at me. They are speaking to each other in a language I do not understand, and bubbles start to come from their mouths. "For you," says Malia when she reaches me, and she hands me the castor plant. It is very heavy. It pulls me down through the white sands until I am in a forest of surfboards, unable to escape.

"I can save you," says Tommy Trussler. He is bleeding from his legs, and his gut, and from his mouth. I don't want to take his bloodied hand, but I do. It is slippery with poi and blood. I cannot hold onto it. I am being crushed by the weight of surfboards, which crash onto me on crystal waves laced with silver glitter.

"No, me—come to me," says Laurie Cropper. She's standing on the solid ground that I know is just inches from me. "Don't tell Derek, but I have this for you." She passes a giant vaping stick to me. I grab the end, which she pulls, and I am now beside her. We are both smoking cigars that taste of apples, and Derek and Bud walk toward us with fire extinguishers.

"No naked flames," says Bud, covering me with white powder. "Gotta get rid of the evil weed," he says above the noise of the extinguisher.

"Of course," I say, and bathe in the powder, feeling it cleanse me as though I am in a shower.

As the powder clears, I see Nigel Knicely with a group of children. They all look exactly like him. Beside him is Frannie Lang. "My boys," she says, smiling and twirling her blond hair as though she's a small child. "It's our birthday. Do you want some cake?" she asks. Her voice sounds like a chorus. She passes me a pot of pills, which are all tiny cupcakes with sprinkles. "These are my sister's favorites," she says, pushing the pot of pills into my hand, which I notice has incredibly long fingers. I look at my other hand. It is encased in a diamond-encrusted glove. The glittering stones transform themselves into tiny playing cards, all in the suit of diamonds. As they do this I feel pain searing through my right leg, then my left.

"This will stop the bleeding," says Janet Knicely. She hands me a fat rope made of many strands of string, looped into a noose. She is wearing a bracelet made of massive red pearls, each with a clown face painted on them, and giant chandelier diamond earrings. "Nigel gave them to me. He loves me so much. I'm his bride. I'll always be his bride. He married me twice, that's how much he loves me."

I run from Janet. She frightens me. She is so sure of her husband. She loves him. That frightens me. I know now that it was Nigel Knicely who was the clown who was laughing at me. I know this with certainty. And I know why he is so angry with me: he hates me because I am with Bud. He hates Bud, so he hates me.

Ezra appears with a machine gun in his hands. It's made of pineapple, but I know it's a machine gun. He marches toward Nigel and demands that he release Rachel. Nigel dissolves, and Rachel appears. She is dressed in white and her skin is very white. She wears white latex gloves. Bartholomew Goodman runs from behind me, slamming the door of the dispensary, scattering slugs he's been holding in a pot as he passes by. "Got to get a cup of coffee," he shouts.

"Cait? Do you want a coffee?" It was Bud. "It's almost eight. I'm going to run to the library to get a quick cup."

I managed to *harrumph* a yes, then dragged myself from between the sheets to face myself in the bathroom. Raccoon eyes, rats' tail hair, bags under bags under my eyes. *Great! Happy honeymoon, Cait!*

Getting it Ship Shape

BY THE TIME BUD RETURNED with our coffee and a couple of bananas, I was at least clean, if not very tidy. Bundled up in the fleecy robe provided by the ship, I blew on the steaming mug, then gave in and put some cold water into it; it was far too hot for me, and I needed caffeine.

Bud was quiet. Already dressed for the day's events, he'd elected to wear long pants for the first time since we'd flown out of Vancouver. I suspected it was a wise choice. We were due to be in for a taxing morning, and a long day after that.

Rolling up his empty banana skin and wrapping it in a napkin, he said, "Did you do your wakeful dreaming thing? And did it work?"

"I tried," I said quietly, "but it became fully-asleep dreaming, so I can't be sure if it all made sense."

Bud's expression was less than happy when he asked the critical question. "Do you know who did it, Cait? Because, I have to be honest, I know everyone who could have done it, and I go along with whys and the hows, but I can't put my hand on my heart and say I know for sure."

"I think I do."

Bud was silent for a moment. "Not going to tell me, are you?" he said, thin lipped.

I shook my head.

"Think the captain will let us go through with this?"

I shrugged.

The phone startled me so much I spilled my coffee. "Can you get that?" I said, mopping at the sleeve of my robe, no longer snowy white.

I mopped and Bud listened. He grunted a few times, then hung up.

"Not gonna happen, Cait. Ezra says the captain says no way. We arrive in port in less than twenty-four hours. They are both convinced that no one else on the ship is in danger—thanks to our investigation—and they feel it's a step too far to constrain any of the suspects."

"You're kidding!"

Bud shook his head. "I wouldn't. Not about this." His expression was dour. "I think they are wrong, Cait. Whoever did it could easily escape justice because of the circumstantial evidence against the others. I don't like it. I faced this all the time on the force. This is wrong."

Bud pulled open the door, just as I opened my mouth. "I'm not taking this lying down, Cait. Leave it to me. I'll sort it. Get ready for battle, Wife. You *will* be performing later on. Maybe not when we had planned, but it will happen. I assure you of that."

I called after him, but he'd already gone. I'd seen Bud like this before, when we'd been after a perp who was just out of reach. Nothing had stopped him then, and I suspected nothing would stop him now. I didn't know where he'd gone, but having seen him in action before, I suspected he'd start at the top. I wondered how one went about collaring the master of the ship, when, other than at formal duty time, he was essentially invisible. But I knew that if anyone could manage it, Bud would.

I decided I'd better put in a bit of an effort on my appearance. Pulling together a navy two-piece that had a business casual flair, which I gauged to be the right note to strike, I applied a bit of makeup, pulled back my hair, then mused on my wakeful, and sleeping, dreams of the previous hours. Not knowing how long it would take Bud to return, or to get in touch with me, I decided it was best to stay in the room and begin to pack.

An hour flew past without me realizing it. There's a certain soothing feeling that comes from packing. It's so much easier when you're packing to go home, because you have to pack everything—no choices, no need to pack neatly; just get it all in knowing it'll all be washed in any case. The other strange joy was to handle clothing and recall where we'd been when I'd worn it.

The striped overshirt I'd worn to travel had done well on the flight, and then got soaked through when we arrived at Honolulu airport in the rain. I'd chosen it because Bud said it helped him spot me in a crowd.

I shoved Bud's swimming shorts into one of the pockets in the cover of the suitcase, and pushed my own swimsuits in to join them. Even though I knew they were dry, I didn't want them to touch other clothing. I knew it was a saltwater pool on the ship, much more natural than lots of chemicals, and in keeping with the Aloha Spirit but . . . *of course!* That explained the white powder. I felt better about that mental discovery, because it helped me decide who hadn't killed Tommy.

I carried on gathering items from around the cabin. A Christmas tree decoration of a surfing Santa, with "Mele Kalikamaka" painted on his longboard, a glass bauble for the same tree, filled with other little bubbles—in honor of the Don Ho song, which suddenly seemed less appealing. I tried to push it back into its protective box, but it didn't seem to want to fit, which was annoying—it had come out of there, so it had to go back in. I pulled out the tissue paper and repacked it more carefully, finally getting the box to close.

Of course—Tommy's poi pot! I'd seen the pot, clear-ish plastic with a blue lid, and stepped sides. Stepped sides! How could I not have worked that out? Good for packing, of course. He'd have figured that out for his travels.

I was almost finished when Bud returned. The closet still held a selection of clothing, our toiletries were still all in the bathroom, and I was feeling quite proud of myself—and of the things I'd worked out. But I could tell by the look on his face that I was about to feel even more proud of Bud.

"So?" I asked, wanting him to have the chance to tell me what he'd done.

"It's sorted. We'll all meet in what they call the Board Room at one this afternoon, just as you wanted, but with the additional presence of the captain himself."

I felt my eyebrows rise. "Really?"

"The only basis upon which he would allow it to happen," said Bud in his official voice.

"Very well then," I replied. I checked the time. "Ninety minutes until zero hour."

"Ready for it?" asked Bud.

"Almost," I replied.

Bud pulled me into his chest. "Cait, you need to be sure. You are sure, right?"

"I will be when the time comes. You, Ezra, and I all know who could have done it, and why, and how. I have to draw out the culprit; what I say in that room, and how people react to it, will still be a part of my process. It won't be easy for anyone. Lives will be changed forever."

"You mean Derek?"

I nodded. "Do you want to give him a fighting chance, Bud?"

My husband nibbled his lip. "It's only fair, don't you think? I would hope someone would do the same for me."

"But they wouldn't need to, would they, Bud?"

"Probably not," was all he said as he opened the door again. "He deserves this face-to-face, man-to-man."

Sometimes the price of justice is alarmingly high. Murder doesn't just affect the lives of those it touches directly; it infects those close to it—as does a natural death, of course. But the poison of murder can travel faster, and hurt more deeply. It is an experience that leaves everyone changed.

I considered our group and wondered how everyone would ultimately be affected by Tommy's murder. I couldn't be sure, but I had a terrible feeling it might damage the innocent more than the guilty. Yes, justice can come at a terrible cost, but secrets and lies cannot always remain hidden, and the bright light of a murder inquiry can cast a very long shadow.

The Gathering Storm

WAITING IN OUR STATEROOM, WE could see through our balcony doors that the sea was becoming an ever-darker gray; the whitecaps were more frequent, and there was rain on the horizon. The grim weather matched our mood. Eventually, the appointed time arrived, and, as Bud and I were ushered into the meeting room being used for the "memorial gathering," I could see it had been set up to resemble the arrangements of the morning before in the Games Room, with tables dotted about the place. People had taken seats as they saw appropriate, and I noted with interest that Winston, Afrim, Rachel, and Bartholomew had taken the table at what had become the "back" of the room—farthest from the designated "front," which was where Ezra sat, with an empty seat beside him, awaiting the arrival of Captain Andreas.

At another table sat the Knicelys and the Croppers. The Knicelys sat apart from each other, but Derek and Laurie held hands. Laurie's face was puffy from crying; it looked as though Derek had finally shared his news with his wife. Frannie Lang sat at a table with the Pukuis and, as Bud and I entered, they began to fuss about to grab an extra seat so we could join them. Ezra jumped up, did the job for her, and we settled ourselves as best we could.

It was notable that a table with no chair filled the same relative spot in the room where Tommy Trussler's little desk had been in the Games Room the previous morning—which seemed a lot longer than twenty-six hours ago.

Given how Ezra had spent that entire time, I was amazed at how fresh he looked. His crisp white shirt was pressed with creases so sharp they were almost a weaponization of his sleeves; his hair looked especially lustrous, and his eyes were bright. I wondered if he'd slept at all, or was still awash with coffee and energy drinks. I couldn't help but also notice the way he studiously avoided Rachel's curious glances. I sighed as I realized I was about to make their lives a little more miserable than they already undoubtedly were.

Officer Ocampo stood at the door and pulled it wide to allow for the late entrance of our final attendee, Captain Andreas. Ezra leapt to his feet, as did the ship's crew members. Captain Andreas removed his hat from its spot between his arm and his side and placed it on the table in front of Ezra. There couldn't have been a more obvious signal that he was in charge—if any had been needed.

Clearing his throat, the captain began. "Thank you all for being here," he said, nodding and smiling at the guests, "even if you had no choice in the matter." *Good start, Captain—put everyone at ease.*

"I do not have to tell you that we are here for a very sad reason. We are here to remember one of our own—a member of the *Stellar* family for many years: Tommy Trussler. Or, as he should be properly known," the captain referred to a notepad he'd pulled out of his pocket, "Sergeant Thomas Jefferson Trussler, of the 3rd Armored Division, United States Army." There were surprised looks from the Pukuis and the Knicelys, while the Croppers began to hiss and whisper to each other. "Tommy Trussler was the same rank, and served in the same battalion, as Elvis Presley—though Tommy served many decades later in Desert Storm, where he was awarded the Silver Star for heroic action under fire, and received the Purple Heart in recognition of the fact that he was wounded at this time. Our very own Tommy Trussler was a war hero."

I could see that Ezra had put his background on Tommy to good use, and the captain was allowing this 'get together' to shape up as an honest-to-goodness remembrance of our dead shipmate. *Go, Team Justice!*

"What feels especially bad to me, therefore, as the master of this ship, is that Tommy survived serving his country, only to lose his life here, now. It is a tragedy that has touched us all." He dropped his head and paused for effect; everyone in the room automatically bowed their head for a second or two as well.

The captain continued. "While it is true that Tommy had no living relatives, he will be missed by his family members here at the Stellar Cruise Line. But we must do more than miss him: we must recognize that he lived and worked with us here, and we must tackle the question of his death."

Puzzled looks from most people, a beat of hesitation in the breathing of a few.

"You see, ladies and gentlemen, I have not been able to tell you this until now, and I would ask you to be most discreet about how you share this information after this gathering, but Tommy Trussler's death was not a natural one."

The atmosphere in the room changes in a heartbeat.

"The moment I knew of the suspicious nature of his passing, I charged my trusted Head of Security Services, Officer Ezra Eisen, with going about his duties and responsibilities toward the remaining passengers and crew upon this vessel. Since then, he has been doing just that, in a most diligent manner. I invite Officer Eisen to take the floor and bring you up to speed with his inquiries."

Captain Andreas sat and Ezra stood, straightening his pants. He nodded his thanks to his superior, and lifted his head to face the group.

"We do not believe that Tommy Tussler took his own life, and it was not an accidental death. All evidence points to Tommy Trussler having been murdered, by a person, or persons, unknown." He let the idea hang in the air for a few seconds, then acknowledged Frannie Lang's half-raised hand.

She spoke quietly. "Are we all quite safe?"

Ezra nodded. "We believe that whoever killed Tommy Trussler intended to kill him, and only him. You are all perfectly safe. Please do not be concerned."

Seeing Derek also begin to raise a hand, Ezra said quickly, "I am sure you will all have many questions, but maybe if we tell you what we have discovered, the facts will address your worries. Our Senior Medical Officer, Dr. Rachel White, has conducted a detailed and thorough examination of the body, as well as any foodstuffs that were in the Games Room at the time of Tommy's death—"

"You mean he was poisoned? Good grief man, we could all be dead," said Nigel loudly, making his wife jump.

Rachel stood in response to Nigel, looking every inch the cool professional. She didn't refer to notes, but held her head high, and allowed the confidence in her voice to work in her favor. "Yes, I examined the body of Tommy Trussler, and without going into detail, I surmised that he had ingested a toxic substance moments before his death. We are most fortunate, on this ship, to have a nurse practitioner, Bartholomew Goodman, who has extensive training and experience in dealing with poisons. Using his expertise, we examined everything that anyone in the Games Room yesterday morning could have touched or consumed, and found no trace of any toxic substance. At all."

Rachel sat, and all eyes turned back to Ezra. As far as I could tell, everyone looked equally puzzled.

"So how—" was out of Nigel Knicely's mouth before he could stop himself. *You really aren't used to not being in control—not being the leader of the pack, are you?*

Ezra sighed, then continued. "Thank you, Dr. White, Nurse Goodman, for all your efforts in this matter." He was unable to disguise the warmth in his tone. "My trained security officers secured the crime scene, and have been gathering information, as well as liaising with the necessary authorities about this matter. Although they are not present at this time, since they have many other duties to attend to, I would like to officially thank them for their excellent efforts."

The formal stuff had to come first, I knew that, but I was anxious for Ezra to begin to make some real headway. I didn't have to wait any longer.

"But now I come to a most difficult and delicate matter, and I would request that you all," he looked directly at Nigel Knicely, "refrain from making any comments. I can assure you, you will all have a chance to speak."

Ezra turned his attention to Bud and me. "As some of you might know, Mr. Bud Anderson was a high-ranking law enforcement officer, prior to his retirement, and his wife, Professor Cait Morgan, is a well-known and respected criminal psychologist." There were shocked looks all around. "They kindly agreed to lend their expertise to my investigation."

The looks directed at us from around the room suggest we've just sprouted an extra head each.

"Now look here," said Nigel Knicely, "and don't try to shut me up," he sneered at Ezra, "you can't just question people without—some sort of proper warning, can you?" Ending up sounding a lot less sure of himself than when he'd started, he looked from Ezra to Captain Andreas.

The captain answered. "I am responsible for the life of every person on this ship, as well as for the ship itself. If I believe an inquiry needs to be made into discovering who might be responsible for killing one of my passengers or crew, an inquiry can take place. No charges have been made, merely inquiries." His manner, as well as his tone, seemed to stop Nigel in his tracks.

Nigel Knicely practiced his harrumphing technique again, then pouted.

"You all know Bud and Cait," said Ezra. "They are your fellow guests, on their honeymoon. They have been as keen as me to work out if anyone else has been under threat. That was their priority." *You lie quite well.* "By speaking to everyone concerned, and working alongside me and my staff, they have helped me reach the conclusion that no one else is at risk." He beamed. *Less convincing.*

As Bud and Ezra had discussed, Ezra had managed to say almost nothing while making everyone feel he would say no more. I had advised Bud that would be the best way to allow me an opportunity to draw out the culprit. *A false sense of security can be fatal.*

Ezra sat down. *Confused faces. Puzzled looks. Mouthed anxieties. All as expected. Good.*

It fell to Derek Cropper to break the tension. He stood and cleared his throat. "I can only speak on behalf of myself and my good lady-wife, but I guess everyone here feels the same, so I'll go ahead and say it anyway. It was a real shock seeing Tommy keel over like that yesterday, and I know we guessed it mighta been his heart. But to hear that someone killed him is mighty upsetting, though we appreciate the work you and your people have done, Captain Andreas, to establish that we are all safe here." He saluted the captain, who nodded back. "But look, someone's gotta say this. We were all in there together yesterday when Tommy died—" he paused and looked at the crew table, adding, "—well, almost all, and the doctor said he ate something that poisoned him just before he died. So how'd that work? What was it he ate? And how come it was something that none of us ate? I don't get it. I, for one, want to know what happened."

"And who did it," added Laurie, looking up at Derek with pride.

"And why," added Malia Pukui, looking right at me. *Sharp woman.*

Ezra looked toward Bud and myself. "With Bud's expert advice, I made a very comprehensive study of those who were present yesterday. You." I noticed a slight glint in his eyes. "Of course, I worked only with the information that is readily available in the public domain, and through the normal channels to which I have access." *A few uneasy shoulder movements around the room.* "I discussed my findings with Bud and Cait, and their insights and expertise helped me to understand one thing very clearly. In response to your very valid concerns, therefore, I have to tell you that my inquiries have proved that everyone who was in the Games Room yesterday morning had an opportunity to poison Tommy Trussler, and to conceal the fact that they had done so. I have also established that everyone there had access to a toxic substance that could have been used to kill him, *and* that everyone had a distinct motive to want the man dead."

The uproar is immediate. Good.

The Storm Breaks

EZRA HELD UP HIS HAND, requesting silence. "Please, everyone, I know it is a shock, but that is the truth."

"When I said I wanted to know who'd killed him, I didn't expect you to say it might have been me," said Derek.

Ezra nodded graciously, shooting Derek a quick glance of gratitude. "I realize that, Mr. Cropper, so I feel I should explain." Even Nigel settled himself down, with an expectant look on his face. "I interviewed everyone as a witness to what happened yesterday, and I had to carry out some background checks on everyone. My findings are not all my own." Finally Ezra looked at Bud and me and said, "I am inviting Bud and Cait to speak at this point and I am sure you will understand why."

Ezra sat, and I stood. "Thank you Officer Eisen. Captain," I nodded, and he did the same in return—*best to get his blessing before I begin*— "and fellow shipmates. I realize the fact that my husband and I have shared our observations and insights about all of you with Ezra will not make us popular. I have to say we both felt it our duty to help Ezra in his tasks, because we have a deeply felt desire to not only root out who killed a man, but also to help protect the innocent." *Puzzled looks. Good.*

"Let me explain," I said, trying not to use my professorial voice. "Ezra has indicated that more than one person here might, and I emphasize *might*, have killed Tommy Trussler. Everyone had the opportunity, the means, and the motive to do so. As you look around at the faces in this room, you may wonder what dark secrets someone else has that could have led them to become a killer. Well, my husband put his finger on it yesterday, when, during a quiet chat, he said 'Everyone lies, and everyone has secrets.' They do. We *all* do."

I didn't want to overplay my hand, but I needed everyone to feel the pressure. I pushed on, after giving the people in the room a moment for silent contemplation.

"I am about to share secrets, mine and yours. It will be very uncomfortable for all of us, but it must be done. All of us have already had a life-changing experience. Now we're all in for another one."

Behind me I heard a violent vibration, and we all looked at the captain, who slapped his little telephone to his ear. He said only one word: "Immediately." He stood, bent to speak quietly to Ezra, then said to us, "I must leave. I am required on the bridge. The senior officer in the room is Dr. White," he nodded at Rachel, "but for this process Officer Eisen leads." He left through the door hurriedly opened by Officer Ocampo, who then resumed her guard.

I tried to not lose my momentum. "I will begin by revealing something about myself that is not generally known. I was once arrested on suspicion of having murdered an ex-boyfriend of mine." At this revelation, the curious expressions of those in the room quickly changed to shock and wariness. "I was investigated and cleared, but the press reaction to my situation made my life unbearable. So you see, I understand that the innocent can be impacted by a sudden death, as well as the guilty. And it is my desire to ensure that does not happen. Believe me when I tell you it is a very unpleasant experience, with serious consequences that change a person's life forever. In Bud's case, he carries in his heart the sadness that his first wife was killed by a man who mistook her for him." Bud had known I'd be likely to do this, but it still hurt me to reveal him this way. *At least you're getting sympathetic looks, Bud.*

"And it's not just me and Bud—as I said, everyone has secrets. Take Officer Eisen and Dr. White, for example. To begin with Rachel: I have observed a gesture she makes with her thumb and forefinger, drawing them down her chin when she's thoughtful. To me this suggests her father had a beard and did the same. She's picked up this habit from him, over time. Despite the lack of facial hair."

Rachel blushed and shrugged. *Okay, here we go.*

"Also, Rachel and Ezra are a couple. She's about to go on leave, and they are struggling with what that will mean for their relationship. They even had a quarrel the other day. Ezra grabbed her arm, she pulled it from him, and gave herself a nasty bruise in the process. I believe it was when Ezra asked her to marry him, and tried to present her with a diamond engagement ring. That's right isn't it, Rachel? Ezra?"

They both flushed with embarrassment, especially as everyone looked at them and smiled. They each nodded, grudgingly.

"Now, neither Ezra nor Rachel told me about this directly," I added. "I saw what I saw, and worked out what it meant. It's what Bud and I have been doing." At this there was an increase in nervous fidgeting throughout the room.

"Secrets and lies," I continued. "They make good cover for a killer. Kai and Malia," their heads popped around to look at me, "you told me that Tommy Trussler killed your son."

I heard a few gasps, and the Pukuis nodded sadly. Malia studied the table in front of her. "When you discovered that Tommy was the children's entertainer whose escaping rabbit led to the accidental death of your son, you must have been very angry. Troubled and in turmoil. You had access to potentially lethal castor nut products, which you could easily have brought onto the ship from your family's toiletry-manufacturing business in O'ahu. Kai certainly had the chance to put a poisonous substance into Tommy's poi pot yesterday morning, then take the pot when we were all looking at the dolphins."

Every eye in the room was on Kai. Without flinching, he said, "I did not kill him, though I admit that Malia and I had made a decision that, when we returned home, we would report him to the authorities. I would not kill him. Nor anyone. My wife and I are peaceful people."

"Except that you were thankful that he was dead," I said. "You believed he was a bad man. You showed me this by surreptitiously sprinkling salt all around the Games Room before we left. You took the little packets from the buffet, ripped them open, sprinkled the salt to prevent his evil spirit from finding you, then stuffed the wrappers into your pocket."

Kai nodded. "Yes, but it was not to protect me—it was to prevent his evil spirit from returning to his body if someone tried to revive him. You saw me do this?" he asked, surprised.

I shook my head. "No, but I found the salt on the floor, and I know a little of the traditional Hawaiian customs that you and Malia hold dear."

"Mahalo," said Kai quietly.

Derek raised his hand, and I nodded. "You said that Kai could have poisoned Tommy's poi pot?" I nodded. "Is that how he was killed then? 'Cause that would explain why none of the rest of us was poisoned."

"We believe it was," I replied calmly. A few faces showed understanding.

Laurie followed her husband's example and raised her hand. I invited her to speak.

"I get that," she began thoughtfully, "but couldn't the poi have already been poisoned? You know, like days before, or something? Not by someone there yesterday morning at all?"

"Good point," I replied, trying to not sound patronizing, "and one that we addressed ourselves. The answer to that lies in the fact that, when the Games Room was cleared, there was no pot of poi to be found."

"I don't get it," said Derek.

"Well, you see," I said with import, "Only someone knowing that the pot contained the remnants of poisoned poi would bother to remove it. It was a risky business to pick it up, unnoticed, to remove it from the scene. The culprit must have been in the room, or someone who was protecting the culprit was there. Someone who knew that Tommy's poi had been poisoned."

I allowed the facts to sink in. They did. I could almost hear the pennies dropping.

"I repeat that I did not poison Tommy Trussler's poi," said Kai more forcefully.

I was compelled to reply, "You might not have done, but your wife could have at an earlier time, and with your knowledge. Then, you simply picked up the evidence and walked out with it."

I noticed both Kai and Malia's jaws clench, though neither said a word.

"Or what about you, Ezra and Rachel?" At this, there was a sharp intake of breath from Ezra. "Rachel has an entire dispensary from which she could remove any number of deadly pharmaceuticals, and deposit them in Tommy's poi at an earlier time. Then, either of you could have removed the pot from the crime scene. You were both there after the fact, and would have been able to count on that."

I knew I'd caught both of the officers off-guard. I wasn't surprised when Rachel White leapt to her feet and cried, "Neither Ezra nor I have any reason to do that."

"Tommy could have been a bit of a fly in the ointment of your relationship. I know that liaisons between officers are not disallowed by this cruise line, but they can be tricky. What if Tommy was goading one or both of you about how true the love of the other was?"

Rachel plopped back into her seat. "Rubbish," was all she had to say.

"Then there's you, Derek," I said quickly, "or you, Laurie."

"But how? Why?" said Laurie, before she thought better of it.

"Laurie, you and Derek have access to enough liquid nicotine, the stuff in your e-cigarettes, to kill everyone in this room, and there's the little matter of your secret gambling sessions in your suite. My money's on Tommy having taken you and your guests for quite a bit, being the cardsharp that he was."

Laurie and Derek looked completely nonplussed—first at me, then at each other.

"How did you know?" asked Laurie.

"Chips from a set owned by Tommy in your suite, and a bit too much emphasis, on your part, on how you were learning lessons about poker that you said were hard to take."

"We wouldn't kill a man because of that!" said Derek. "It's just money—and I, more than most, know there's no way a human life weighs well in the balance against a few measly dollars."

I tried to instill my tone with all the meaning it deserved when I replied, "You might if the love of your life—as well as folks who were her guests at the private games—had been duped, basically robbed, and you had nothing to lose." I knew no one else would have the slightest idea *why* Derek had nothing to lose, but I felt I'd leave him just one secret.

The Croppers fell silent.

"Of course, there's also Bartholomew," I said. Rachel glared at me, then turned to face her nurse, who looked horrified.

"What do you mean?" she said on the man's behalf.

"Two words: coffee grounds," I replied.

"Explain," said Rachel sharply.

"I think Bartholomew can do that better than I could," I said, wondering how far the doctor would go to defend her trusted aide.

"I don't know what you mean," said Bartholomew loudly. "I ain't got nothing to do with no coffee grounds."

"You and Bud found traces of coffee grounds in the carpet in the Games Room," I said. "That's correct, isn't it?" Bartholomew nodded reluctantly. "They couldn't have been there before the place was opened up, so they must have got there, somehow, afterward. Correct?"

"I suppose."

"How better for them to end up on the carpet just where the dead man was positioned than by being dropped there by the first professional on the scene—you. So why did you have coffee grounds about your person, Bartholomew? Could you be secreting illicit drugs in the place they are least likely to be found? In the locked dispensary, surrounded by coffee grounds, ready for them to leave the ship with you, undetected? Might a nurse practitioner be a good person to traffic drugs across the oceans, especially when he has access to such a great hiding place? You are the person who orders, then clears to board, any re-supply of medical supplies at each port. What a wonderful way to bring illegal drugs onto the ship—along with those legitimately required for the dispensary. And what if Tommy Trussler had suspected this? It's interesting, you know: I found a scribbled note in Tommy's room. He was using it as a bookmark, which is probably why you failed to discover it when you, oh so conveniently, got to search his room. On the back of the piece of paper, Tommy had scribbled a cryptic list: 'Benny 2K 10%, Cigar Man out, Queenie $$$, K—⅓=$?' That's what it said. I think that Queenie refers to Laurie Cropper. And I reckon you're Benny. 'Benny' Goodman. And '2K?' What about two kilos—of what, I'm not sure. Tommy was a man who could spot sleight of hand, because he was so good at it. He lived by his wits, and could likely see a guilty act a mile off. He's probably been keeping an eye on you for some time. Did he confront you about it? Demand money? A cut—maybe ten percent? Did you take some drugs from the dispensary, something that might not be missed because it's essentially harmless, unless taken in quantity, manage to slip the stuff into his poi at an earlier time, and wait until he got to what was, after all, his last pot? You knew he'd eat the stuff eventually, and, of course, you could easily make sure you were the first to respond to the Star code in the Games Room, and remove the empty pot."

Bartholomew stood up. "It's rubbish. Honest it is. I haven't got any drugs. And if there are any hidden in the dispensary, who's to say I put them there? It could be anyone."

"It could only be one of seven people on this ship," said Rachel. "What have you done, Bartholomew? Tell me! I relied on you to check and sign for all the supplies. You've been my right hand. I've been such a fool. I *trusted* you." She cursed under her breath.

"I'm not saying anything," said Bartholomew, folding his arms.

"That is your right," said Ezra. He nodded at Officer Ocampo; she pulled open the door, beckoning in two security officers who, unbeknownst to me, had been placed outside the room. As they entered, Ezra stood and said, "You two officers will accompany Nurse Bartholomew Goodman to the cells in our security offices. You will secure him there, then one of you will make your way to the dispensary in the medical facility, and bar anyone from entering it until I arrive. In case of an emergency, you are to accompany anyone who must enter, note what they remove, and report to me. Understood?"

Bartholomew shot a hateful glare toward Ezra as he was led away. "True love? It don't pay the bills, you know!" he said.

There was silence after the doors closed behind Bartholemew, and I allowed a couple of moments for the shock waves to subside.

Ezra looked at me with an intensity that told me he thought it all might be over.

"So, did Bartholomew do it?" said Derek, sounding surprised to hear his own voice.

"The medical bag Bartholomew had with him—he's the only one who could have removed the poi pot from the room," said Ezra. "Of course!"

I shook my head. "No. Bartholomew was the one person in my sight the whole time—he didn't go anywhere near Tommy's little desk where the pot stood. He didn't take the pot, but he didn't need to. I realized earlier today, when I was packing, that anyone could have taken it. You see, Tommy was a seasoned traveler—his was a collapsible pot. The stepped sides should have told me that. Bartholomew could have killed Tommy, and he might have wanted to, but he didn't need to. Someone else got rid of his blackmailer for him, which was lucky for him. Which brings me to our next suspect. That would be you, Afrim."

The man jumped. He looked terrified.

"I?" he managed to squeak.

"Yes, you—the invisible server, the man who had the most

opportunities to poison Tommy Trussler. What reason did you have to want the man dead?"

Afrim shook his head violently. "None. I had no reason. I did not know the man at all."

"Maybe not," I replied, "But Winston might have." It was the jolly bartender's turn to look alarmed.

"You and Tommy had an argument, didn't you, Winston? He reported you, and got you demoted. Right? His little note mentioned 'Cigar man out.' That would be you."

Winston's usually broad grin shrank to a tiny, hopeful smile. "I don't smoke cigars. Why you t'ink dat's me?"

"Because of the man you were named after," I replied evenly.

"Me Dad?" he looked puzzled.

"No, Winston Churchill. Churchill cigars," I said quietly.

Winston's face cleared. "Right, mon. Churchill." He grinned, then his face fell into a sullen look. "It's not such a bad demotion, just a small one. I still have my evening shifts at the best bar on the ship. Is madness to t'ink I kill a man for dis. How I kill him, anyways?"

"Like the Pukuis could have done—you put the poison in his poi. Maybe some over-the-counter medication you could easily get hold of. Then Afrim sneaked the pot out of the Games Room."

Winston and Afrim looked at each other, then me, with puzzlement. "But we ain't even good mates," said Winston, as if that explained everything.

"So *you* say," I replied, "but, if you don't mind me asking, what was it that you and Tommy rowed about in any case?"

Winston shifted uncomfortably in his seat. Pulling himself upright, he said, "I not sure I should say." He glanced at Ezra, then dropped his gaze.

"Out with it," said Ezra forcefully.

"It's okay, I can see it's making him squirm," I replied. "Besides, I'm pretty sure I know what it was."

Winston looked at me with an unblinking stare of disbelief.

"What did I tell you about it, Bud?" I said.

All eyes turned to Bud, most filled with real curiosity. Bud's voice was music to my ears. "You said that Winston and Tommy were likely arguing because when Winston was serving cold drinks on the pier at Kona, he had overheard a conversation between Tommy and a guest, where Tommy was either attempting to blackmail a guest, or make it clear that he had incriminating evidence that could be used against them."

Winston sucked his teeth loudly. "That's about right," he replied. "Tommy Trussler's not de man you all t'ink he was. Might'a been a war hero an' all, but he weren't a good man."

"Quite right," said Nigel, unwisely. "He might have won some medals, but the man was a horrid little sneak-thief." He looked over at Laurie and said, "I'm not surprised to find out he took your money at cards. The man was utterly dishonest."

I pounced. "How do you know he was a thief, Nigel?"

Rearranging his shoulders, Nigel replied quickly, "Well, you yourself said he stole money from Laurie through cheating at cards. That's theft." *Almost a good catch.*

"True," I replied, "and you're right. We found evidence in Tommy's stateroom that he was more than a cardsharp; he was, in fact, a pickpocket."

Amazement. Shock. Dismay. Judgment.

I waited a beat, then continued. "And he stole something from you, didn't he, Nigel?" I stopped the man from blustering by holding up my hand. "There's no point denying it: we have you on camera in the store in Maui buying three pairs of diamond earrings. I dare say a pair just like those that Janet wore at dinner last night will end up gracing the ears of a woman who lives near Birmingham, and another pair will be worn by a woman who lives just outside Sandwich, in Kent." *I can see you collapsing internally, Nigel. Terror will set in any moment.*

"Janet, look at me," I said firmly. Janet eventually turned her face toward me. She looked frightened. "You need to open your eyes, Janet. The man you are married to lives a life you know nothing about. He's likely to be taken into custody by the British police very shortly, for having stolen millions of dollars' worth of pills from his ex-employer. He was fired four years ago, he owns at least two other homes with families in them—his—and he's lied to you for pretty much your whole married life." I knew I was being tough on the woman, but I also knew, from experience, that when you've got a bad 'un, someone else has to save you from them.

Janet stared at me round-eyed. She didn't blink. Not once. I knew in that instant that she was allowing herself to believe, for the first time, that all the signs she'd seen and all the instincts she'd ignored over decades were, in fact, credible.

"But why?" she said quietly. I knew she was asking Nigel, as well as me, but I was also equally sure he wouldn't answer her.

"Because he's a sociopath with narcissistic tendencies who loves the thrill of living on the edge. He adores the attention he gets at events like weddings, so why not have a lot of them? He enjoys the company of a woman who knows her place, owes him everything, and becomes accustomed to doing his bidding, allowing him to live his exciting life." I could see that Nigel Knicely was, quite literally, getting hot under the collar; his neck was pulsating red, and he was seething with anger.

"Look at him now, Janet. Look at the man who calmly told you twenty-dollar pearls from the ABC Store were good enough for your daughters-in-law, but bought three pairs of diamond earrings, one for each of his wives. This isn't a man who is sorry for what he's done—he's angry that he's been found out! And *who* found him out? Tommy Trussler, who picked his pocket, and realized how very odd it was that a man would buy three pairs of earrings, and give only one set to his wife. Tommy Trussler, a cheat, a thief, and a chancer who confronted him about it in the line-up for the tender boats in Kona. Tommy Trussler, with whom he had a very public argument in the Games Room because he was being goaded, and with whom he had a rendezvous when he told you he was going to the Internet café. I reckon Tommy was blackmailing him. His scribbled note said 'K—⅓=$?' referring to you wearing one of three pairs of earrings. I think we can all guess that 'K' is Nigel. And by the way, Janet—your special red bracelet is made of highly toxic seeds. They are seeds he could easily—if carefully—have used to poison the poi he knew Tommy carried with him at all times."

Janet looked at me helplessly. "He married other women?" *An expected response—that's all she's heard.*

"I can explain everything," said Nigel, his voice shaking with anger.

"No, you can't," I said firmly. I turned to Frannie Lang, beside me and said, "And then there's you, Frannie."

The woman looked up at me with clear, dark eyes and said, "What about me?" *A challenge?*

"Your locket. Your dead sister. When I asked you the name of her boyfriend, the one she was with when she was killed on the road in O'ahu you spluttered B . . . K . . . Michael Craft."

"So?" she looked puzzled.

"It's odd, the way our minds work," I said. "I'm a psychologist, so trust me, I know. When I asked you his name, you realized you might give yourself away, so your brain did some fast word association. You stopped yourself from saying 'Buster,' your mind flew to 'Keaton,' then to 'Michael,' from which it was a short hop to 'Craft.' Buster. Buster the Clown. Buster Keaton. Michael Keaton. Michael's craft shops—they're all over Canada and the USA. The scrapbookers' Mecca. You knew your sister's boyfriend as 'Buster,' and 'Buster' was the name of Tommy Trussler's clown character—the one you saw at the SPAM festival in Waikiki. That was when you knew who he was. You told me your sister loved a joke and a laugh; who better to provide that for a nurse living near Virginia than a wounded soldier with a penchant for tricks?"

"I had no idea," said Frannie quietly. "He was a thief too?"

"Bud?" I said. He deserved to shine, and I needed a break.

"Upon entering Tommy Trussler's home in O'ahu, it was discovered that he had a large collection of drivers' licenses, all depicting the same sort of woman—blond, dark-eyed, very similar in looks to you, Frannie—and, to be fair, to Laurie and Janet too." All three women looked taken aback. "Tommy told Kai Pukui he'd lost the love of his life; we believe he honed his pickpocketing skills trying to 'get her back' in some way."

"He was obsessed by his loss of her," I added. "He'd been sober since the time of the accident, and he'd stayed on O'ahu to be closer to the memory of her, even though her body had been shipped back to the mainland. He suffered a serious leg injury in the car smash, and walked with a limp afterward. The lack of mobility he suffered led to him gaining a great deal of weight as time passed. He sustained himself by spending the cash from the wallets he stole, and as a large, jocular children's entertainer, albeit one who had a clumsy moment which ended in tragedy. After that he performed under a different name, continued his thefts, but lived a different lifestyle, which involved exercise. His corpse, as well as the Pukuis, told me he'd been heavy once and lost weight. The man you met, Frannie—the man you knew to be your dead sister's boyfriend—must have known who you were as soon as he saw you. He'd been searching for a face that looked like the one he'd lost so long ago; it must have been a shock to his system to see you. We know that you and he spent time together in Maui, and here on the ship, as well as at Hilo. You might have hated him enough to want to see him dead—I know you tackled the issue of managing your anger in counseling. With your predilection for over-the-counter pharmaceuticals—which I saw in your bathroom—and your nursing knowledge, I have no doubt you had enough toxins in your possession, and the knowledge of how to use them, to be able to kill him."

"Well, I didn't," said Frannie. "What would be the point? It wouldn't bring my sister back, would it?"

I sighed. "No, Frannie, it wouldn't."

Frannie looked at the table in front of her, then up at me. Her eyes were full of tears. "It didn't feel the way I thought it would," she said softly. *The room is so quiet.*

"You told me that before, when you spoke about visiting the site of the accident that killed your sister. There's nothing sweet about it, is there?"

Fat tears rolled down her cheeks. "No. Nothing. It's just cold, and empty. Like I've been since Fay went away. Half of me gone. Having my boys with me helped, but they grew up, and off they went to live their lives. Then Barry left me, and then there he was: Buster. Buster Trussler. That's what she called him in her letters to me. 'Funny name, funny guy,' she said. I'll always remember that. Made her laugh, she said. Especially after her boring doctor husband. She needed something different, she said. A new start."

Pulling a tissue from her purse, Frannie Lang composed herself. The mood in the room was somber, to say the least; everyone was aware they were watching a tragedy play out. *So much loss and grief in one room.*

"He was a dreadful man, wasn't he? So much worse than any one of us knew or suspected. Who would think a man brave enough to risk his life to save his comrades could be so awful?" she whispered.

"I believe that, for Tommy Trussler, it was his experiences in war, and then the loss of your sister Fay, that changed the way he saw risk taking. What most people would see as dangerous activities that would end badly if they were discovered—like stealing from individuals, cheating at cards, and so on—he likely didn't see as chancy at all. I don't believe he was living a life he *knew* to be wrong, but did it anyway—like some do." I looked at Nigel, who seemed to be mentally talking his way out of his situation. "No, he was living the only way he thought he could—getting by on his skills and his wits, and hunting for the woman whose death finally broke his connection with real judgment. As I suspect your recent losses have done to you."

Derek Cropper leapt up and shouted, "Y'all shut up!" startling everyone in the room—me included.

Having gained everyone's attention, Derek looked down at his wife, touched her gently on the shoulder and said, "Forgive me, honey." Laurie began to cry. He cast his gaze around the room, then looked directly at me. "You said earlier that you're putting us through this to protect the innocent. I guess that's because whoever killed Tommy could use what you've dug up about the rest of us to create reasonable doubt in the mind of a jury, right?"

I felt compelled to nod again. *Rats!*

Laurie's silent crying escalated to loud sobbing. Her husband continued. "Well, then, just so everyone knows they won't have to see their dirty laundry aired in public—except you, Nigel, and, let's be honest, man, you deserve it—then I will confess to killing Tommy Trussler."

"Don't say any more Derek," begged Laurie. "We can have a little time together yet, honey. Whatever time you have left, we can have it together."

Derek looked at his wife and tenderly stroked her hair. "My dear, dear honey child. You are the love of my life, and I want nothing more than to spend my last weeks, maybe months, being with you. But I can do something that makes a difference. I can save innocent people, and people who might have acted out of grief, or loss, or sadness. I can take this on my shoulders. It won't have to rest there for long. Ezra, all I ask is that you allow me this one last night with my wife, then I will surrender myself to the authorities when we dock. I won't make a fuss. It'll all be by the book."

Laurie grabbed his hand and began to wail. "Oh Derek. What am I gonna do without you? I can't go on—I *won't!*"

"Oh yes you will, my dear. I'm gonna be gone very soon, but you're still young and beautiful, and you're well provided for." He looked at Bud and added, "If this poor guy can lose his wife, and find himself a new life, as Bud and Cait have, then maybe you can do the same. But me going now, or in a little while, won't make a whole heap a'difference. I'm guessing the Canadian cops'll be gentle with an old guy who's dying."

"You're dying?" said Janet, amazed. Her expression suggested she hadn't really been taking in everything going on about her. *Not surprising.*

"Yes, ma'am," said Derek. "Inoperable cancer, and I don't want them doin' nothin' to me. Gonna go on my own terms."

"There's no such thing with cancer," said Frannie Lang bleakly. "It always gets you exactly the way it wants to." *Inexcusably cruel.*

Laurie gasped and sobbed, grabbing at her husband's hand. Ezra looked confused, to say the least. He remained in his seat, but was on full alert.

"Now hang on a minute, Derek," I said. "No one's accused you of anything here."

"I know it," said the man in his gentle drawl. He sounded completely calm, totally in control of himself and the situation. "Look here, if I put my hands up to it, none of these folks will have to have their lives ripped apart in court. I can save them from that."

"You'd be saving a killer from facing justice," I said. "That's not right. This is about justice, Derek, not sacrifice. You didn't kill Tommy, nor did Laurie. Why should either of you suffer because someone chose to take his life? You deserve to spend your last months on this earth together, not with you stuck in a cell somewhere."

Laurie grabbed at her husband's arm. "She's right, Derek Cropper. We have our own battles to fight. Don't waste time trying to fight someone else's. Besides, if someone in this room has killed once, what's to stop them from doing it again? You could be covering for someone who'll take it into their head that there's someone else walking God's good earth that they prefer didn't, and then you'd be responsible for another life, or lives, taken. Like Cait said, it's not right. I'm not just saying this for myself, honey—I'm saying it because it's true."

Derek took his seat beside his wife and they hugged. He looked completely deflated. "Maybe you're right," he said. "I thought I could, you know, protect people. Innocent people. I've never done anything for anyone my whole life. Just me. Us. I always put the business first. Looked for the angle, the profit. And now, at the end of it all? I thought—oh, I don't know what I thought. I guess maybe that I could be a bit of a hero, not just a guy with a pile of money in the bank, but no time left to spend it."

"You're my hero," said Laurie, sobbing.

"So, if they didn't do it, who did?" said Janet Knicely. She looked across the table at her husband. "Was it you?" Her tone was no longer that of a simpering acolyte. She was seething. I sensed claws hidden in her velvet paws.

Nigel looked genuinely shocked. "Me? What on earth . . . why would I . . . what would make you . . ." He had no way to finish any sentence. Everyone in the room clearly believed the man capable of anything, and that included his wife.

Looking directly at him, Janet said, "Is it true, what she said about you? Three families?"

Nigel didn't say a word.

"I'll take that as a yes, then. Did you marry either of your other wives twice, like you did with me?"

"No."

"Good." *Oh, for heaven's sake! Is she going to forgive him?* "Then, when I confront them with the fact that they aren't married to you at all, I'll be able to console them with the knowledge that I was the only one stupid enough to marry you twice. Renew our vows, indeed?

Renew them? They were never real, were they? You're a complete and utter . . . I hate you!"

Janet Knicely wasn't living up to her name at all. She was out of her seat, beating her husband around the head before anyone could stop her. Cursing and screaming, she had to be pulled off by the swift-footed Officer Ocampo, who managed to separate the couple. Settling Janet at the front table, away from her husband, who was crying like a little boy, Ezra moved to calm the situation as quickly as possible.

"Cait, wind it up, please. Now," he said.

I nodded. "There's no easy way to do this, because I'm not 'allowed' to accuse anyone of anything on this ship. I have no official role, nor does Bud. Ezra has the power to detain, but it's the Canadian authorities that'll do the charging. What I'd hoped was that the guilty party would feel enough compassion for everyone else here to confess their crime, and to understand the grief they would cause if they used the circumstantial evidence against their shipmates." *I hope this last gambit works.*

"Compassion?" said Frannie Lang. "What good does *compassion* do? Compassion won't bring back the Pukuis' dead son, or my dead sister. It won't make you feel less like a fool, Laurie, or you, Janet. That's what we are—a ship of fools. All thinking that when Tommy Trussler was dead, we'd be safe, happy again. We'd find ourselves the way we were, not the way we are. We'd find the light that had gone out in our lives."

Amazed faces all around, watching Frannie unravel.

"You feel no better, do you Frannie?" I whispered.

Frannie slammed the table with her fist. "No, I don't. And I should. I *should* feel better. He's gone. But I'm still alone. All alone. He made me be different. I didn't deserve to lose her. I needed her in my life to make me whole, and he took her away from me. I didn't know he was as terrible as it turns out he was, but he deserved to die just because of what he did to Fay. He was the one talking about *Sasana* in Hilo. He was the one all for everything having a payback. Fawning all over me he was, at first, kept telling me I was beautiful. It made my skin crawl. Then I told him who I was and he went all pathetic, like it wasn't his fault. Swore he hadn't been drinking the day she died. Swore he begged her to wear her seat belt. I didn't believe a word of it. *He* was the one to blame. She'd never have driven drunk. She would have worn her belt. She wasn't wild and reckless, like he said she was. It wasn't enough that he killed her, he even tried to kill my memories of her. He said they were going to get married that day. Can you imagine that? She'd have told me. I'm her sister. She wouldn't have done that without telling me. Driving to their wedding after a toast or two? It was ridiculous. All a fantasy. And then he hit me with the pity party—how terrible it had been for him without her. How he'd spent months in the hospital, could hardly walk after the accident. How he'd wallowed, allowed himself to get all out of shape. Terrible for *him*? What about me? Nothing was ever the same for me after she was gone. My husband used to go on and on about how I needed to let go of her, get over her being dead. 'Move on,' he'd say. *Move on?* He didn't get it. Never did. Why not? He knew how much she meant to me. He even got my mom and dad on his side, you know? They talked to me about counseling, so I gave in, but not even the counsellors helped. They didn't get it either. Too stupid. Not even the one I went to after the divorce. And my boys? They don't say anything, but I can see it in their eyes when I talk about her. They raise their glasses when I toast her at my birthday, but they don't mean it. Grown up? Huh. See how they feel when people begin to leave them."

Sympathetic looks flickered around the room, laced with apprehension. *They haven't seen this happen to a person before, like Bud and I have.*

"Did you grind up pills and drop them into his poi?" I asked.

Frannie nodded.

"And, as everyone was fussing about, you squashed his collapsible pot and popped it into your pocket, right?"

She nodded again.

"Did you throw it over the side of the ship?"

More silent nodding.

"Did it feel good at the time?"

Frannie's head shot up. Her eyes blazed. "Oh yes," she said with passion. "Seeing him convulse was a wonderful feeling. I just wish my husband had been sitting next to him, doing the same thing. And those stupid counselors they made me see. Useless, all of them. Terrible people. There are so many terrible people on this planet. Why do they all get to take up so much space? They suck the life out of us, and take away the ones we love. They shouldn't be allowed to get away with it."

Any sympathy in the room evaporated. Ezra stood. "Frannie Lang, I'm asking you to come with me to your stateroom, where you will be required to remain until we reach the Port of Vancouver, where I will deliver you to the proper authorities."

Silence fell upon the room.

"Sure," was all Frannie had to say. Looking up at Ezra, she added, "Do you think my boys will come to my trial? It would be nice to have some real time with them."

Ezra, shocked, said, "Maybe. I—I expect so."

There was no fuss. Ezra, Frannie, and Officer Ocampo left the room, and everyone sat looking dazed.

"Hell of a day at sea, sir," said Derek Cropper.

Laurie let out a wailing laugh and sobbed, "Oh Derek, honey." Looking at me through rolling tears, she said, "From our favorite movie, *Overboard*, that is." Beaming at her husband, she flung her arms in the air and said, "Arturo!"

Derek matched her actions, saying, "Caterina!" They hugged, sobbing on each other's shoulders.

Since Ezra had left, Rachel White stood, taking command of the room. "It's been a traumatic experience for everyone. I hope that the confidences exposed here today never leave this room. I urge you all to consider what you say about today very carefully. It would appear that we all do have secrets, and we all tell lies. Aside from those who have broken the law," she glared at Nigel, "I believe no good will come of those details being discussed, ever again. I suggest we clear the room, and get back to our duties—our lives—as best we can. Thank you Bud, Cait. Although we might not feel it, you've helped us weather a difficult situation in a gentler way than might have otherwise been the case."

I looked over at the cool blue eyes beneath copper bangs. "Thank you for understanding that sometimes every option is unpleasant, but a decision still has to be made. I believe my decision to lay bare every secret will now allow us to keep them between ourselves," I said.

"I dare say," replied Rachel curtly.

A Safe Berth

BUD AND I WEREN'T IN a hurry to disembark. We clung to the last moments on the ship as though we'd never get the chance to cruise again, even though the Stellar line had offered us a free trip to thank us for our contribution to the case. We'd caught a glimpse of a cowed Nigel and a blazing Janet as they'd walked along the glass-encased gangway. I was certain they were heading for what would be a very unhappy bus tour of Vancouver. We hadn't seen anyone else from the previous day's events, not even Winston.

Just as we were finishing our last cup of coffee, we were alarmed to hear our names announced over the loudspeaker requesting our appearance at the Guest Relations desk on Deck 3. Once there, we saw Ezra, who beckoned to us to join him and Rachel in a back office.

"I don't want to delay you," he said, "but I wanted to let you know that your guys," he nodded at Bud, "have taken Bartholomew Goodman into custody. We found his cache of drugs in the dispensary, packaged as acetaminophen, and surrounded with layers of coffee grounds—he must have repacked them at regular intervals. He still hasn't spoken, but he's done for, I'm sure of it. They also took Frannie Lang into custody. Even as I was transferring her, and they were reading her rights, she was telling them all about it. Couldn't shut her up. I think the innocent will be safe now, because of what you did. And I wanted to thank you. It was quite an experience, one I will value, and from which I have learned a great deal."

Bud and I smiled, acknowledging the man's gratitude.

"And there's one more thing," he said, smiling. "I don't know how you guessed, but you were right about me and Rachel. And we thought you might like to know . . ."

He paused, and Rachel lifted her left hand in front of us. She was wearing an engagement ring.

"Congratulations!" We all hugged, even Bud and Ezra. I beamed and said, "I hope you two are as happy as Bud and I are. Marriage can be a wonderful thing, even for a career woman who wasn't sure it would ever happen to her." I winked at Rachel. "I suspect that was a part of the reason for your hesitation, yes?"

Rachel nodded. "You're right, but how did you know? I mean, about the argument, the ring—well, everything?"

Bud hugged me proudly as I replied, "The way you looked at each other, or didn't. Your cryptic comment about 'access all areas.' The bruise on your arm—a straight line of a bruise, the sort you'd get if you hit your arm against a hand rail when you'd pulled away from someone. And the ring? Ezra, when we found those earrings in Tommy's cabin, remember? No man knows as much as you did about the four C's of assessing diamonds unless he's been shopping for a diamond engagement ring. You seem to be a good match, and I wish you well."

"Me too," said Bud. "He's a good man, Rachel."

"I know," she smiled. "Seeing the Croppers made me realize we never know how long we have, do we? So why wait? Isn't it better to try than wonder?"

"Always," I said. "Experience all you can, to learn, to grow. Sometimes there'll be disappointments, sometimes maybe sadness, but to never take a chance? To always be looking back? It's not healthy."

"You're right," said Bud. "So let's get going, Cait. We'll collect the car, pick up Marty from his holiday home with the Whites in Hatzic, and get home. I've missed it."

"Me too," I said. "Though home is where the heart is."

"Aloha, and mahalo," said Ezra.

"And aloha and mahalo to you too," I said, "and say hello to the Islands for us when you get back to them next week. Maybe we'll visit again one day. It's very beautiful there."

Bud nudged me. "How about we stay home for a while and get ourselves properly settled in before we go wandering again, eh?"

"Yes, Husband, I'd like that," I said. And I meant it.

Acknowledgments

THE HAWAI'IAN ISLANDS ARE SPECIAL to me: I've spent a fair amount of time on several of the Islands, my husband and I were married at a friend's home on O'ahu, and our honeymoon was spent on a cruise around the Islands and back to Vancouver, BC. (Fortunately for us, no corpses were involved!) It's impossible to thank everyone by name who's invited me to their home, shared their knowledge and love of the history and culture, and fed me their wonderful local foods over the years, but you all know who you are, so here's a group *Mahalo*.

It's a similar situation when it comes to cruise ships: I've worked out that, over the last decade, I've spent more than an entire year on various cruise ships! During that time, I've been shown nothing but the greatest kindness and generosity by all types and ranks of people who work on these modern floating palaces. I've taken some of my "insider" knowledge and put it to use in this book, but, while I've remained true to general practices on board ships for the timeframe within which this book is set, I know that rules, regulations, and working methods change often; any discrepancies between what I have written and what you might witness or be told, on any ship you might be lucky enough to sail upon, are my own choice, or fault. To all those I've met at sea (crew and guests): I hope our paths cross again one day, and thank you for sharing your time with me.

As always, my husband, mum, and sister have been tremendously supportive throughout the entire period I was working on this book; there were times I might have thrown in the towel without their kind words of encouragement, or without a friendly nuzzle from my ever-present writing companions, my chocolate Labradors, Gabby and Poppy. Thank you—I love you all.

Once again, I thank everyone who is a member of the TouchWood Editions family for their help, and all the people who, through their professionalism and interest, allowed this book to end up in your hands. I hope you enjoy your time with Cait and Bud, and I thank *you* for choosing to take this journey with them, and me.

Welsh Canadian mystery author CATHY ACE is the creator of the Cait Morgan Mysteries, which include *The Corpse with the Silver Tongue, The Corpse with the Golden Nose, The Corpse with the Emerald Thumb, The Corpse with the Platinum Hair*, and *The Corpse with the Sapphire Eyes*. Born, raised, and educated in Wales, Cathy enjoyed a successful career in marketing and training across Europe before immigrating to Vancouver, Canada, where she taught in MBA and undergraduate marketing programs at various universities. Her eclectic tastes in art, music, food, and drink have been developed during her decades of extensive travel, which she continues whenever possible. Now a full-time author, Cathy's short stories have appeared in multiple anthologies, as well as on BBC Radio 4. She and her husband are keen gardeners who enjoy being helped out around their acreage by their green-pawed Labradors. Cathy is also the author of the WISE Enquiries Agency Mysteries. Cathy's website can be found at cathyace.com.